T0267612

UNBECOMING

OMING

A NOVEL
& SELF-HELP GUIDE

SEEMA YASMIN

SIMON & SCHUSTER BFYR

New York London Toronto Sydney New Delhi

SIMON & SCHUSTER BFYR

An imprint of Simon & Schuster Children's Publishing Division
1230 Avenue of the Americas, New York, New York 10020

Simon & Schuster: Celebrating 100 Years of Publishing in 2024
For information about special discounts for bulk purchases, please contact Simon &
Schuster Special Sales at 1-866-506-1949 or business@simonandschuster.com.
The Simon & Schuster Speakers Bureau can bring authors to your live event. For
more information or to book an event, contact the Simon & Schuster Speakers
Bureau at 1-866-248-3049 or visit our website at www.simonspeakers.com.
Book design by Laura Eckes
The text for this book was set in Garamond Pro.
Manufactured in the United States of America
First Edition
10 9 8 7 6 5 4 3 2 1
CIP data for this book is available from the Library of Congress.
ISBN 9781665938440
ISBN 9781665938464 (ebook)

UNBECOMING

For my mother
& her mother

& for Kundiman
& the Third Dessert

Dear reader,

I began writing this book in the summer of 2019, a summer in which I closed my eyes and imagined a dystopian future in which abortions were banned across America and pregnant people and their doctors thrown into jail—or onto death row—for even thinking about ending a pregnancy.

Then 2022 happened. A leaked draft decision of the Supreme Court of the United States showed a majority of the Court's nine justices would vote to overturn *Roe v. Wade*, the landmark ruling that had legalized abortion in 1973.

On June 24, 2022, it became official. Five justices reversed *Roe v. Wade*. The constitutional right to abortion in America, a right upheld for nearly a half century, vanished. Just like that, the draft novel saved on my laptop was no longer speculative fiction. Laylah Khan's worst nightmare had become our collective reality.

Where do we go from here? I grew up in England, a country with one of the highest teen pregnancy rates in Europe. I live in America, a country with one of the highest teen pregnancy and teen abortion rates in the developed *world*. Around seventeen hundred teenagers become pregnant in the United States every day; one in four of those teens has an abortion. While the rest of the world is generally on track to make pregnancy and ending a pregnancy safer, things are moving backwards in the United States. Americans are more likely to die during or soon after pregnancy compared to pregnant people in many parts of the developed world. Black Americans are four times more likely to die during or soon after pregnancy compared to White Americans.

And Texas, well, Texas is a story unto itself. As well as being Laylah's home and my former home, Texas is the birthplace of *Roe v. Wade*. Jane Roe was a pregnant Texas woman, real name Norma McCorvey. (Jane was the name of Norma's childhood imaginary friend, and Roe rhymed with Doe, the last name given to a woman whose name is not known or is being kept secret.)

Norma had two kids. Both of them were cared for by other people. When Norma was pregnant a third time in 1970, she decided the best thing to do would be to terminate her pregnancy. After a doctor refused to perform an abortion because it was illegal, Norma saved up $200 (equivalent to $1,600 in 2024), took a bus to the other side of Dallas, and tried to get an abortion at a dentist's-office-turned-illegal-abortion-clinic. But the clinic had been shut down the previous week.

Norma's other option was to deliver the baby and put the child up for adoption. It was this path that led her to Sara Weddington and Linda Coffee, two young lawyers fresh out of law school who were introduced to Norma by her adoption attorney. Sara and Linda took Norma's case and went head-to-head against the abortion-hating district attorney of Dallas County, Henry Wade. They argued that Norma's right to abortion was protected by the Constitution of the United States. The trio won the case and *Roe v. Wade* legalized abortion all across America on January 22, 1973. It was a huge milestone for America, but it was too late for Norma. She had already had her baby.

That was more than fifty years ago. Today, Texas is the most dangerous place in America to be pregnant. When I was a health and science reporter at the *Dallas Morning News*, I learned that because Texas was such an outrageous outlier, pregnancy researchers would delete Texas from their national calculations because Texas skewed the overall picture of the pregnancy death rate and made the national numbers look even worse.

But this isn't a novel about numbers. This isn't a story about statistics. *Unbecoming* is the story of Laylah, an ambitious, highly organized, emotionally messy teenager who is fighting to live the life she has meticulously planned. Laylah wants control of her body and her future. But in the world she lives in—the world we live in—this means taking extraordinary measures and crashing up against the truest meanings of friendship, family, and faith.

A heads-up: There are sex scenes in this book (yep, hijaabi girls get horny). There are scenes in backstreet abortion clinics, where desperate people take desperate measures. There is conflict around different people's perspectives of "right" and "wrong"—I'll let you be the judge—and there are twists and turns, especially regarding Islam's perspective on abortion, which might surprise you.

One final thought: For every hour you spend reading this book, seventy American teens will become pregnant. That's seventy Laylahs hurrying to figure out what to do next. It's seventy Noors scrambling to help their best friends. It's seventy Joshua Jacksons panicking or plotting or weeping—or all three at the same time. It's all of us, really, because this is a story about a teenager, her best friend, her family, and their future. And whether you ever get pregnant or not, whether you think you care about pregnancy or not, this is a story about who gets to decide how you live your life.

I hope *you* always get to make that choice.

With faith and optimism,
Seema

*What would happen if one woman
told the truth about her life?*

The world would split open.

—MURIEL RUKEYSER

Medical Students Take a New Oath

By NOOR AWAD

DALLAS—Khadijah Moore knew exactly the words she would have to utter on her first day as a medical student. Still, the 22-year-old was so shocked that she stumbled and messed up her words on Monday morning. In a hall filled with 350 fellow students, Moore was ordered to raise her right hand and swear on the Bible that she would report anyone trying to end a pregnancy to the Dallas Police Department and the Texas Ministry of Family Preservation—even if her future patients would die without an abortion. Moore and her classmates at the Collegiate University of North Texas were participating in a white coat ceremony, a rite of passage that symbolizes their entry into the medical profession. They are the first generation of medical students to take the new oath. "They already sent us the text in a welcome packet so I knew what it would say, but it's a lot," Moore told the *Booker T. Washington High School Tribune.* "I looked at the old oath from last year and it was all about doing no harm, protecting your patients' secrets, and trying your hardest to help people. There was nothing in there about reporting pregnant patients to the government for tracking, or to the police so they could be taken to prison."

The graduate of Stanford University and Dallas's Eddie Bernice Johnson STEM Academy said she felt she had to take the new oath because there is no way of matriculating without it. "Everyone in my family is a doctor," said

Moore, who has dreamed of becoming a pediatrician since she was eight. "My mom and dad actually met at Collegiate Med in the nineties. They both can't believe how much being a doctor is changing." The new Texas law makes abortion a crime punishable by a life sentence. People trying to get an abortion and anyone trying to help them by offering assistance, which includes giving a ride or walking with a pregnant person to an underground clinic, risk imprisonment. This applies if an abortion is carried out at less than twenty weeks or is needed to save the patient's life. Doctors must also routinely test for pregnancy and report every pregnant patient to a state registry, or risk losing their medical license. The new law builds on the U.S. Supreme Court's 2022 ruling, which overturned *Roe v. Wade* and ended the right to legal abortion. This opened the door for states to pass their own antiabortion laws. The Texas legislature is currently debating a new bill, SB 601, which would make abortion, or aiding and abetting abortion, a crime punishable by death. That bill is expected to pass.

The Texas Teen's Guide to Safe Abortion

By
Noor Awad
&
Laylah Khan

Anonymous Armadillo
at 21:41

We really should keep our names off this. We're getting in too deep

Anonymous Seahorse
at 21:42

This guide is going to SAVE LIVES! You should be proud.

Anonymous Armadillo
at 21:44

Proud and NOT in prison, Noor! They'll say we are aiding and abetting. This doc is extreeeeemely illegal!

Anonymous Seahorse
at 21:45

Ugh fine. But delete our names in like 20 minutes, OK? I want to show it to someone first.

Anonymous Armadillo
at 21:46

Which someone is it now?
I thought we were saving LIVES! Not impressing your latest crush!!!

Anonymous Seahorse
at 22:21

You can delete the names now!! And cool it with the Bollywood drama, Laylah. If you were more worried about what we're going through RIGHT NOW and not obsessed with getting into med school four years early, we'd have finished writing this whole thing already.

Anonymous Armadillo
at 22:30

It's not four years early! That's...not how it works :/ Swear to me you won't tell ANYONE about this idc how hot they are

Anonymous Seahorse
at 22:32

Stop freaking out! What we're doing is radical and revolutionary. I'm telling you, Laylah. You don't get it. This guide is going to change the WORLD.

STEP 1

KEEP CALM & GET MEDS

LAYLAH

I CAN HEAR them whispering about me. The nurse and the doctor. They look at me and they think they know me.

What they see:

Brown face.
Lilac hijaab.
Pierced nose.

What they think:

Naïve.
Exotic.
Oppressed.

All they know are stereotypes pieced together from news headlines. Stories of ISIS brides and housewives, arranged marriages and girls controlled by other people. I am none of those things.

The nurse stares at me, her blond dreadlocks piled high on her small head like a bird's nest. I think of Asma, who repeats the Texan mantra "The taller the hair, the closer to God" any time she peels back her scarf at a girls-only mosque event to reveal a bouncy, back-combed blowout or a shiny updo that somehow survived the hijaab-covered commute to the Richardson Islamic Cultural Center without displacing a single strand of that perfect brown hair. Miraculous.

If Asma were here, she would sneer at this nurse and attack her nest of matted hair with a detangling spray and brush. Then she would sneer at me for landing myself in this haraamy mess. *How could anyone who calls me their role model do this to themselves? You're supposed to be a representative of the RICC's youth leadership program, Laylah. I was thinking of promoting you to head volunteer!* I imagine her chastising me as she lifts the oversized Fendi sunglasses off her nose to reveal liquid eyeliner winged at a precise forty-five-degree angle.

Jesus H. Christ. If Asma were here, my life really would be over. How will I ever look her in the face?

The nurse looks down at her iPad, the edges of her unblended blue eyeshadow on display. She swipes the screen, looks at me, and looks back at the iPad as if none of this makes sense, which it doesn't. The Laylah Life Plan (LLP) does not include lying in the back of a Tito's Tacos food truck converted into a mobile clinic at the far end of an old Walmart parking lot off the George Bush Turnpike with my izzat puddled on the floor around a box labeled meat-tenderizing powders, my shirt pulled up to my bra, and my jeans around my knees while two White women prepare to poke around my private parts.

"Feel your butt go numb on an ice-cold metal gurney" is nowhere to be found on pages two to fourteen of the LLP. Not between "Achievement #4: Write the most inclusive, straight-forward, and helpful guide for Texas teens on how to get a safe abortion since Texas made abortion beyond illegal" and "Achievement #11: Get into Brown University's Liberal Medical Education Program," which takes you straight from an undergraduate program into medical school. And absolutely nowhere before or after "Achievement #16: Get into a fellowship program to train in emergency obstetrics" does it say that I should squat in the corner of a food truck and try to angle my pitiful stream of pee into a plastic cup. "Sorry, we don't have a toilet fitted yet," the doctor had said a few minutes ago, turning her back while I closed my eyes and pictured waterfalls.

Everything happening right now is extremely *anti*–Laylah Life Plan.

The nurse flings a pink curtain across a rail and splits the tiny truck into halves. I'm stuck in the half with a cold, metal "bed." A silver ventilation hood teeters from the opposite wall as if it might come crashing to the floor at any minute. Beneath it, a mounted rack is jammed with a box of latex gloves where

I imagine there used to be bottles of red and green taco sauces.

The nurse and doctor stand on the other side of the pink curtain in the part of the truck they have tried to kit out like a medical office. The whole place smells less like iodine and bleach and more like chimichurri and carne asada. Bless their hearts.

Oh. My. God. They're whispering about me, *again*, as if I can't hear them! As if this cutesy curtain can block out the stupid shit they're getting wrong.

Voice 1: "Yes. She is seventeen, barely. Do you think she's really pregnant?" [I think that's the nurse.]

Voice 2: "Run the test again." [That must be the doctor. She pressed her icy fingers into my stomach two minutes ago, when I was writhing beneath a white paper sheet as thin as a dupatta. She smelled of dry shampoo and coffee. I focused on her blond highlights while she poked her icicle fingers into my groin. I gritted my teeth and squinted at the two-inch black roots ruining an otherwise decent haircut. She needs a touch-up ASAP. (Yes, I notice these things, even when my throat tastes like melted batteries and the ceiling is spinning in circles.)]

Nurse: "She wears that headscarf thing."

Doctor: "But she says she's pregnant."

Nurse: "Do you think she's married?"

Doctor: "I thought you said she was seventeen?"

Nurse: "She could be one of those child brides! I heard about them when I was serving in the Peace Corps in Darfur and then I saw this thing the other night on *60 Minutes*. They said that Pakistani girls *in New Jersey*—right here in *America*!—are being married off to old men and having twelve babies before they turn thirty."

[I am not Pakistani, at no point have I said I am Pakistani, and I am definitely not a "child bride" pushing out a dozen babies while preparing for med school essays and getting a four-year head start on the MCAT.]

Doctor: "Focus, Ali. It's probably just period pain. You know how freaked out the kids get these days. Dip her urine sample again, just to be sure. She did say the pain radiates to the left iliac fossa, so we need to quickly rule out two things. One, pregnancy . . ."

Nurse Ali: "And they tie the girls to these tiny beds in the basement that are really just a mattress and they make them pop out baby after baby and then they do this thing where . . ."

Doctor: "And two, possible ectopic pregnancy."

Nurse Ali: "Where these old women go to the houses to deliver the babies because they have to hide the child brides from the medical system because they're all illegal and . . ."

Doctor: "Never mind. I'll dip the urine. Grab the ultrasound machine. See if it's working today."

My two-ton MCAT textbook jammed with thousands of satisfying medical school prep questions pokes out of my tote bag. I hope the doctor spotted it earlier. Maybe she saw it and now understands that 1) I can comprehend that two lines on a damned pregnancy test means my life is over, and 2) I am not just Another Silly Girl who wound up desperately seeking help in the back of a truck because of One Bad Decision. My book should signal to her that I am driven, ambitious, and intellectual. I may have slipped up once but I plan on remedying this mess and I insist on Going Places. Okay?

I reach for the book and lug it onto my lap. Its heaviness on my thighs feels like one of my little brother's weighted blankets. I open it to a random page, the familiar sentences a comforting antidote to the traitorous, disloyal organs clenching and twisting deep inside me. I flick past neon-green, yellow, and orange color-coded highlights, peel away a pink Post-it note, and take my first deep breath in hours.

Section 4, Page 182, MCAT Practice Questions

Structure and Integrative Functions of the Main Organ Systems

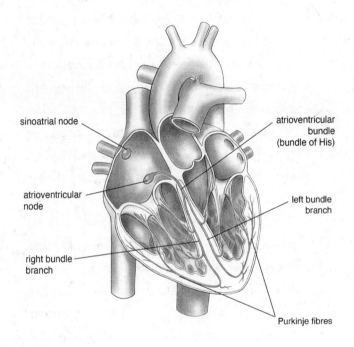

sinoatrial node

atrioventricular
bundle
(bundle of His)

atrioventricular
node

left bundle
branch

right bundle
branch

Purkinje fibres

Q: Which of the following statements best describes the
electrical pathway through the heart?

O **A.** Purkinje fibers → bundle of His → AV node →
SA node.

O **B.** AV node → SA node → bundle of His → Purkinje
fibers.

O **C.** JJ's smile electrified my SA node → which sent a zap of energy to my AV node, which → especially when he did that thing where he placed his hand on the small of my back and rubbed in tender, counterclockwise circles while whispering a line from a Rumi poem about honey flowing from a lover's lips [*Ugh, that boy was good*] → shocked into action my bundle of His and Purkinje fibers → and *this* is the electrical pathway that caused *my* heart to sizzle on that magical, impulsive afternoon, which made me forget the LLP and made me forget I wasn't taking the pill because they freaking banned all hormone medicines the previous month and all of *this* made me forget forget forget → and this is why I am sitting inside a taco truck hidden beneath a piece of blue tarp flapping off a crumbling wall next to a Walmart parking lot in north Dallas, wondering if One Bad Decision will kill me, or if I can make all of this go away with two pills chased down by a swig of mocha Frappuccino.

So, next question. Please?

Section 4, Page 183, MCAT Practice Questions

Q. A 17-year-old hijaabi girl with huge dreams and even huger regrets presents to an undercover mobile clinic in a Republican state with acute left iliac fossa pain, vomiting, worsening disappointment, and intermittent dizziness, persisting for six days. What advice do you offer the girl in this new, post-abortion world?

O **A.** Make a playlist for your funeral.

O **B.** Smile and shut up.

O **C.** Never step foot in your mosque ever again.

O **D.** Regret everything.

O **E.** All of the above.

Nurse Ali pulls back the curtain and hoists an ancient ultrasound machine onto the gurney, completely ignoring the MCAT book spread open across my lap. She dusts off the beige plastic box. "Reminds me of the machine I used when I was seconded to the Sudan with the Peace Corps," she says. "Didn't have electricity. Or running water. Or food. We had only small packets of chopped peanuts to chew on for days. The air was so thick with dust, you could hardly breathe." Her eyes mist up as she stares past me and into a daydream about all the Brown people she has saved.

I clear my throat.

"Your test," she says, snapping back to reality. She turns to flap the world's most useless curtain into place. "We ran a few. It turns out you actually are pregnant." She cocks her head and wrinkles her nose as if she's a curious puppy who wants to sniff out the foreign creature lying in front of her.

Actually pregnant? Is this a fucking joke? Tell me something I don't already know, Ali. In fact, tell me something *I* told *you* when I pulled up to this parking lot and slid under a tarp ten minutes ago. Why on earth would I risk my life in the back of a roving taco-truck-turned-undercover-abortion-clinic that's on the run from gun-toting vigilantes if 1) I wasn't pregnant, and 2) I might possibly be one of the 2 percent of unlucky pregnant people who suffer an ectopic pregnancy, which attaches outside of the uterus and might explode inside my fallopian tubes and kill me?

Satisfied that the pink curtain has secured our privacy (from the only other person in the truck—the doctor—who is minutes away from poking her icy hands around my unwaxed vulva . . . *Oh God, why didn't I wax last night?*), Nurse Ali presses a button to turn on the beige ultrasound machine. It looks like it was made when the Beatles were on the charts.

"Every student at the Warren Alpert Medical School at Brown University receives a handheld Butterfly ultrasound probe, which attaches to their smartphone and displays the images straight onto their screens," I whisper, knowing that I, Laylah P. Khan, will never see the inside of a medical school, let alone own a portable ultrasound scanner.

"Hmm?" says Nurse Ali. But she's too busy squinting at the flashing screen to understand me.

The machine exhales a long and pathetic *pffffffttttttt*. A spray of sparks flies toward Nurse Ali's dreadlock nest. She flaps her arms around her head as the relic fizzles to a slow and whimpering death. "Wowzers!" she says, lifting the ultrasound machine and smacking it on the bottom as if it's a naughty child. It responds to her punishment and rumbles into action.

"I got it working again!"

"Attagirl," the doctor yells from the other side of the curtain.

"The doctor will take a look at what's all going on inside of here, mmkay?" Nurse Ali waves a hand over my belly, which is covered with a white paper sheet. Then, without asking or explaining— which, technically, and medicine is always technical—makes this examination indecent exposure and assault, because you *have* to get a patient's consent before uncovering them, Nurse Ali yanks the paper off me, exposes my belly, reaches beneath the metal gurney, which I'm starting to realize was a food-prep table, and pulls out a spray can as big as her arm. *Is she about to tag me like a graffiti artist?*

Nurse Ali pops the cap on a can of Kirkland Signature Canola Oil Cooking Spray as big as her forearm. She sprays above my belly button like I'm a skillet she's getting ready to fry bacon. "We don't get the blue jelly anymore. They track it," she tells my belly button as she sprays. I squirm under the icy mist. "In Darfur, I had to smear the fat from a dead camel onto the belly of a teenager who was pregnant with triplets. No blue jelly there, either," she says, shaking her head. Her eyes mist over again.

And the Texas Ministry of Family Preservation isn't suspicious that you're bulk buying cooking oil spray at Costco? I want to say. But I bite my bottom lip. I've never considered that canola oil coming out of a nozzle aimed straight at your uterus might be freezing cold. But everything in this metal box is icy, and I'm less worried about looking like a bacon-frying skillet and more worried about where Nurse Ali is spraying. I inch my head off the table and peer at her gloved hands. She's so off target that she might as well be getting ready to scan the half-eaten poppy-seed bagel sloshing around in my stomach. I nudge the nozzle three inches down my exposed abdomen toward my fallopian tubes. Nurse Ali gawks at me as if I am an alien from another solar system, a whole different galaxy where Brown girls don't need White saviors and where we actually know things about our bodies.

I angle the cover of the MCAT book wedged by my side toward her, but she's too busy narrowing her eyes at the bangs beginning to creep out from beneath my hijaab. *I don't wear this because I'm bald! What the heck did they teach you about Muslim girls' anatomy in nursing school?!* But I don't say anything; I just tuck the disobedient strands beneath the fabric while Nurse Ali disappears behind the pink curtain in a huff.

The doctor pops her head around just in time to catch me rolling my eyes. "Hello, Lila! Mind if I take a look?"

"It's Laylah," I whisper. She rubs alcohol gel along her icicle fingers and approaches my greasy abdomen. She doesn't wear gloves, just picks up the probe, pushes it into the part of me that throbs, and furrows her brow as she peers into the black-and-white screen. "I introduced myself as Dr. Hogarth a minute ago, but you can call me Harriet," she tells the screen. "Now, let's see what's going on in there, shall we?"

She probes deeper, stops to spray more canola oil, and smiles.

"Well, that *is* good news."

"Good news?" I sit up and pray that I will see an unpregnant abdomen beaming in the full glory of its emptiness on the screen. But the doctor pushes me back down. "Lie flat." She digs the probe deeper, squints into the screen, and right then a loud *brrrrzaaaaaap!* rattles the machine and the image of my insides disappears. White and red sparks burst out of the ultrasound and send the doctor jumping back. We both scream.

"Well, shit. It's finally a goner," Nurse Ali says, poking her head around the curtain. "I might have some tools from my time in the desert that I can use to patch it up." She flings back the pink curtain, lowers the sizzling machine to the floor, and slides it with her foot into the corner of the truck. The doctor sits on the edge of the gurney/food-prep table, pulls a brown napkin from a metal dispenser emblazoned with TACOS EL SABOR! and drops it onto my belly button. The edge of the napkin grows wet as the thin brown paper soaks up the cooking grease.

The doctor speaks in one long sentence without stopping to catch her breath. "So there is some good news. Your pregnancy isn't ectopic and the cramps you say you're having are what we call implantation pain, which is pain associated with the fertilized egg attaching to the uterine wall. I know you said it hurts, but trust me, you'd be in agony if this was an ectopic pregnancy. The kind of lesser pain you have is actually a good sign. It means the pregnancy is happening in the right place inside your body."

Good sign? Lesser pain? Right place? There is NO right place anywhere inside my body for a pregnancy this side of my thirty-third birthday!

"So that's the good news."

She's said "good" three times. One more *g*-word and this bubbling pressure inside my head will explode through my ears, nostrils, and mouth in thick streams of hot smoke and I will blow this taco-truck-clinic-whatever-it-is into pieces.

"Is that clear? Okay, good. So, it's not an ectopic, plus it's early-ish, which means you can have a medical abortion, which requires taking two pills twenty-four hours apart. You can do that at home. Okay? Any questions? No? Good."

She doesn't let me get a word in.

"But I do have some bad news."

As if things could get worse. As if the LLP could swing any further off track. I stop wiping my belly with the scratchy napkin, look up at the doctor, and will her to speak and shut up at the same time.

"We don't have the pills."

"Oh, okay. That's okay. Who does?"

"No one."

"What? *No—?* No!" I knock the MCAT book off the gurney/food-prep table as I try to sit up.

"Studying to go to med school?" she says, bending down to pick up my textbook and finally noticing what's been in front of her the whole time. She narrows her eyes. "How old are you really?"

"I'm getting a head start." I snatch the book and clutch it to my chest. Bile rises up from my stomach like an acid fountain threatening to gush out of my mouth.

"You can get the pills. Right?"

The doctor shakes her head.

"*Nobody* has the pills?"

"Nobody has the pills."

"And you can't order the pills?"

"I can't order the pills."

"But why?"

"Because they've stepped up their game and found all the medication entry routes into the country. So right now no one has them. No one in Texas, Oklahoma, Arkansas, Nebraska. Not even in California and Oregon. We just did another round of calls last night to check."

"So what do I do? Where do I go? Can I call someone?" I flop back on the table, smacking my head on scuffed metal, where I imagine a sharp knife sliced avocados, red onions, and thin strips of beef and laid them to rest between fluffy taco shells. "I'm dead. Right?" I say to the silver ceiling. "Like, I'm actually dead."

That's when it happens. The last thing I remember is the doctor's face hovering over mine, the whites of her eyes growing bigger, her mouth forming a gaping black hole, and the clang of something metal crashing to the floor.

UNBECOMING!
THE BOLLYWOOD MUSICAL

FEATURING: Laylah Khan as *Hapless Maiden*! And
Joshua Jackson as *Dashing Fil-um Star*!

FADE IN:

EXT. FIELD OF BLUEBONNETS - DAY

Hapless Maiden runs into a field of bluebonnets,
twirls her red-white-and-blue lehenga, and dances
into the middle of a Texas-shaped flower bed. A dozen
maidens, played by her classmates on the fated school
trip, run to surround her. They dance along the
outline of the state of Texas in a traditional kathak
style as Hapless Maiden sings in the middle. Dashing
Fil-um Star, dressed in a blue sherwani, cowboy hat,
and cowboy boots, leans against a nearby tree.

                    HAPLESS MAIDEN
                (singing throughout)
            I was driving toward my
                    futuuuure,
            textbook open, legs closed,

fantasizing 'bout my big

dreeeeams,

when he strolled in from the

rodeo.

He said—

Dashing Fil-um Star runs from the tree into the
middle of the flower bed.

DASHING FIL-UM STAR
(singing throughout)
I can be your study buddy,
show you some anatomy.

HAPLESS MAIDEN
I said ain't got time for no
love, boy.
I've got my eyes on bigger
things.

HAPLESS MAIDEN   DASHING FIL-UM STAR
But we got drunk on   But we got drunk on
Blue Bell.   Blue Bell.

HAPLESS MAIDEN
He said don't make me wait.
We rolled around in

bluebonnets.
Next thing we know, I said
I'm late.

DANCERS
You're late?
I'm late!
You're late?
She's laaaaaate!

HAPLESS MAIDEN
I was speeding toward my
futuuuure,
to live a life all mine,
fantasizing 'bout my big
dreeeeams,
but RBG would not step down.

Ruth Bader Ginsburg appears in the center of the
flowerbed.

RUTH BADER GINSBURG
I said I want to keep my seat!

HAPLESS MAIDEN
We said that's selfish as hell.
And because she didn't step
down,

Roe v. Wade is dead.

                    DANCERS
            Roe v. Wade is dead?
                  It's dead!
                 You're dead?
                  I'm dead!
              She's deeeeeeeead!

HAPLESS MAIDEN   DASHING FIL-UM STAR
Cuz we got drunk on   Cuz we got drunk on
    Blue Bell.   Blue Bell.

                HAPLESS MAIDEN
          He said don't make me wait.
              We rolled around in
                 bluebonnets.
          Next thing we know, I said
                   I'm late.

                    DANCERS
                 You're late?
                  I'm late!
                 You're late?
             She's laaaaaaaaate!

Wall calendars, bullet journals, and a copy of
The Texas Teen's Guide to Safe Abortion fall

from the sky and fly around Hapless Maiden as
she dances in the middle of the flower bed with
Dashing Fil-um Star.

                    HAPLESS MAIDEN
               But with my planners and my
                         Guide
               and all the knowledge in my
                         head,
                 I can be my own hero.
               My dreams don't have to be
                         dead
                just because I was horny.
               And no one has to know why,
               because here come the pills
                   falling from the sky.

Abortion pill packets fall from the sky. Hapless
Maiden places a pill on her tongue as a bottle
of Topo Chico magically appears in Dashing Fil-um
Star's hands. School bell rings. A smiling Hapless
Maiden faints into the middle of the flower bed.
Asma appears with a perfect blowout, waving her
hijaab and dancing. RBG and Dashing Fil-um Star
scatter birth-control-pill packets and copper
IUDs over Hapless Maiden and into the air like
wedding confetti as the chorus girls dance around
the perimeter of the Texas-shaped flower bed.

"Lila? Lila!" The doctor hovers over me, shaking my shoulders. Nurse Ali stands behind her, jaw practically touching the ground. Okay, so I do this thing when I'm really, really stressed. I've been doing it since Mom and Dad divorced four years ago. The technical term for it is Dissociative Disorder (ICD-10 code F44.9), but it's not that serious to need an actual medical code, and you know how Western doctors love to pathologize everything—even (intense) daydreaming. They just don't understand that I come from a dramatic culture.

I haven't told Noor that my brain still does the weird Bollywood thing—I haven't told anyone. I should tell Noor because she tells me everything, but I don't want her judging me. It's not like it's a big secret anyway. Everyone saw me faint and disappear into the weird blackouts when I was twelve and thirteen. I learned to hide them so that they wouldn't think that I was *really* strange— even stranger than they already think I am, on account of the way I must write down multistep plans for Big Future Goals on calendars half the size of my bedroom wall, or the way I like to color-code my bullet journal with pink, orange, gray, blue, lilac, yellow, and green time blocks for: schoolwork, RICC youth club volunteering, MCAT prep, college essay research, weekly baking sessions with my nanima, and working on the Guide.

If they knew that I still have the blackout-Bollywood daydreams from time to time, I know they'd try to take away my driver's license. Not to mention the million ways a medical diagnosis could jeopardize my chances of becoming a doctor. Who wants an obstetrician standing between their legs one minute and laid out on the floor fantasizing that she's shimmying in a sari the next?

It's becoming more difficult to hide. I had figured out a way to manage it by avoiding caffeine after 11:00 a.m., doing four rounds of sun salutations every morning, chugging three cups of chamomile tea starting at around five-ish, and taking at least one nap a day. But last Friday, the same day I peed on the first damned pregnancy test, I was lying on the sofa and working on the Guide at Noor's house and she swears I blacked out with my eyes half open.

"So. Creepy. Dude," she said. "I was shouting at you, but you didn't even blink. It was only when I threw the cushion at your face that you sat up screaming."

I told her I had fallen asleep. "With your eyes open? Weirdo. You need to go to bed earlier. And give that massive book a rest."

Nurse Ali peers over the doctor's shoulder. "You blacked out!" she says. Always stating the obvious, that one.

"I needed a power nap. I'm just really tired." I look around for my MCAT book, lug it onto my lap, and squeeze my knees toward my chest.

The doctor pats my shoulder awkwardly. "We lost you for a second. Let's get you back up here. Look, I know this is a lot to take in. But the situation might change."

"Might change? Like I might magically unbecome pregnant?"

"Like, we might get a shipment of pills next week or next month. Who knows?"

"Who knows? *I* need to know! How many days do I have before the pills don't work and I have to figure out some way of getting a surgical abortion?"

"Ooh, you'd have to go to Mexico for a surgical abortion," Nurse Ali says, shaking her head. "I heard it's super pricey and they mix their meds with cocaine, and excuse me for saying this, but I do know quite a lot about Muslamic things because of my deployment in Sudan, and isn't all of this"—she waves her hand in what I imagine is the general direction of my uterus—"isn't all of this against the Shakira Law?"

Ole, ole, ole, hips don't lie, I want to sing, in my best Shakira voice. But I do not have the energy to educate this woman about the difference between a Colombian-Lebanese pop singer and Islamic jurisprudence. Not right now. Not in a taco truck. Don't nurses get cultural sensitivity training?

Nurse Ali unfolds her arms and leans in. "I know this must be so scary for you, what with your culture and the way it treats women and everything, but you can tell us. Is anyone coming after you?"

You mean other than the Texas Ministry of Family Preservation, the politicians who made abortion a criminal act, the hypocrite doctors who fought to make abortion completely illegal, and the gun-toting, Confederate-flag-waving vigilantes who want to kill anyone trying to get her life in order? I'd probably be safer in Pakistan, where you think every hijaabi is from and where abortion is actually legal in early pregnancy, I want to scream. But I don't. I squeeze my eyes shut to push back the tears. Must appear to be a Strong Brown Girl. I cannot let them see me cry. The last thing I want is to give them the satisfaction of rescuing a Pathetic Brown Girl.

The doctor clears her throat to interrupt the intervention. "The pills only work for a set amount of time." She looks over at Nurse Ali. "And that all depends on when she had her last period. Which was . . . ?"

Nurse Ali scrolls the iPad. "Last menstrual period began . . . Let me see here. . . . She said it was on March first."

"Bluebonnet season," I whisper.

"Huh?" says the doctor.

"Nothing. Look. I already told you when I had my last period. Just tell me how much time I have."

Nurse Ali mouths the numbers as she swipes the days on the iPad calendar and counts, "One, two, three, four." The doctor rakes her fingers through her urgently-in-need-of-a-touch-up hair and stares at me blankly.

"What do I do now? Where do I go next? Who controls the supply?"

She sighs. "Days like this, I wish I had a direct line to The Controller. Ultrasound on the fritz. Again. No pills. Only three disposable speculums and two boxes of gloves left."

"No, ma'am. We're down to one box of gloves." Nurse Ali corrects the doctor, which means she has to swipe the iPad calendar back to March and begin counting all over again.

"You probably know this," the doctor says, leaning forward and tapping my MCAT prep book, "but medical abortion using the two pills works up to seventy days after the first day of your LMP."

"That stands for last menstrual period," says Nurse Ali, pausing between each word, completely unaware that I, Laylah P. Khan, am the QOA: Queen of Acronyms. I swear to God I want to hurl my MCAT book at her head to see if I can dislodge the pile of culturally appropriated dreadlocks.

I take a deep breath and muster the courage to say something awkward but necessary. "I think you're actually . . . that's actually . . . inaccurate." I sort of whisper it as I look away toward the rack where taco sauces once hung. I want to tell them that I know for a fact that they are wrong because I have been knee-deep in research for weeks to write *The Texas Teen's Guide to Safe Abortion*. There's nothing like it out there. Not written for us, by us. There's nothing that really takes your hand and guides you, step-by-step, through the whole process from realizing you're screwed (pregnant) to figuring out how to track down a safe clinic, to avoiding the fake clinics called crisis pregnancy centers, and getting proper help. Most people don't think about abortion until they need one. So I know what Noor means when she goes on and on about how the Guide is radical and revolutionary, because even though everyone's an activist these days, no one's there to get down in the trenches with you and help when you need it most, especially if you're a teenager.

There's been a heavy price to pay for working on the Guide, and it's not even published yet. That's when the shit might really hit the fan. Studying for exams and writing college essays and volunteering and doing research have left me feeling suffocated. Some nights I crank up my desk fan and blast my face with cold air because it feels as if I am drowning in research papers, choking on medical statistics, and sinking into quicksand thick with textbooks. Not to mention the lead balls of anxiety that churn in my stomach when I think about cop cars pulling up outside the house, confiscating my laptop and textbooks, and dragging me out in handcuffs while Mom clings to my ankles and Adam screams *noooooo*. I bury those thoughts by jumping deeper into the data. My eyeballs scan pages and pages of depressing data about desperate people willing to do dangerous things. My heart aches. My brain wants to explode. Those are the days I drift into Bollywood-land.

The doctor and nurse stare at me as if I had been speaking in Gujarati. "It's based on the latest evidence. According to the most recent guidelines from the American College of Obstetricians and Gynecologists and the World Health Organization, yes, medical termination using the two-pill combination is successful up to seventy days' gestation. However, according to the Guttmacher Institute, 'medication abortion is approved for use up to ten weeks of gestational age, *but it is used safely off label at later gestation.*'"

I sound like the Guide because I am literally repeating a line I typed in section 2C. I worked on that part a week ago when I was already pregnant—but also delusional. I brushed off the nausea as a symptom of yet more anxiety and the cramps as indigestion. I had eaten way too much vanilla Blue Bell, emptied an entire bottle of caramel sauce, and gone a little over the top with the bottles of Topo Chico, all of which had left me as gassy and bloated as a beached whale. I had to switch out my jeans for sweatpants, leave the drawstrings untied, and burn Mom's special-occasion incense.

All of these facts and figures about pills, protocols, and success rates have been renting out space in my gray matter for weeks. But now they have bought the real estate, hammered a white picket fence into the lawn, and officially taken up permanent residence inside my cortex. Especially that wild fact that I explain in section 1B of the Guide, the part that lays out how pregnancy is calculated. It makes no sense.

> Even though you can't get pregnant until you release an egg, which can happen about 2 weeks after you start your period (if you have a pretty regular ~28-day cycle), doctors still count the beginning of pregnancy (what they call "gestational age") from the first day of your period, not from the day you ovulated and probably got pregnant. This means that everyone who is told they are 20 weeks pregnant is truly a walking incubator for an 18-week-old fetus. *The Texas Teen's Guide to Safe Abortion*, Section 1B

Wild.

Nurse Ali is gawking, again. I know I sound like a freaking know-it-all—and I try *so* hard not to sound like a know-it-all— but damn it, this is my *life*, and I need this nurse to count properly. I need every single day I can get.

"So, how long has she got?" The doctor turns to the nurse, who is so mesmerized by the fact that there is a brain rich with electrical signals pulsing beneath my hijaab that she's stopped counting and is staring in my direction. I can't help that I have this effect on people.

Dr. Hogarth reaches over and grabs the iPad from Nurse Ali. I clutch my textbook tighter and look up at the taco truck ceiling. I did the math early this morning. I've been doing the math every day since Friday. But in the back of this truck, with my butt numb on an icy table and my izzat puddled somewhere in the corner between a sizzling ultrasound machine and the place I had to squat and pee into a cup, my head is a swirl of numbers and months and dates. *I got my period the day the bluebonnets first bloomed . . . March 1 . . . which means I would have ovulated on or around March 15, the day of the bluebonnet school trip. Sperm can survive for up to five days inside the uterus, but let's say I conceived at the earliest possible date. Okay. That would mean I got pregnant on March 15. But they still count "gestational age" from the first day of my last period so that means I can take the pills up until . . .*

"I have to tell you something, Laylah." The doctor interrupts my calculations. "The Googmaker Institution might say you can take the pills after seventy days, but it gets more dangerous the later you leave it."

"*Guttmacher. Institute,*" I whisper.

The doctor leans in and speaks in a quieter tone. "It starts to get very dangerous, my dear. I want you to understand this. I don't want you taking the medical abortion pills any later than seventy days' gestation, and I doubt any provider in the state who is illegally procuring these pills will even give them to you after that. They don't want those problems on their hands. Nobody does."

Hot tears burn behind my eyes, but I will not let these strangers see me cry.

The doctor swipes the iPad screen. "Gestation began March 1. Today is May 4, so you've still got . . . three, four, five . . . six days to get your pills. Six days!"

She looks up at me. It's my turn to gawk. The doctor shrugs. "I've learned to be optimistic in these times," she says.

And I get it. I mean, thank goodness that Icicle Fingers and Gawking Bird's Nest are even here, because without them I'd be completely lost. They were the only underground safe clinic from the long list of safe clinics currently in the draft version of the Guide that I could actually track down. What a joke! The others switch cell phone numbers and change their encrypted internet handles every other day, sometimes twice a day. By the time I had located a different clinic, Seas the Day Seafood Truck, which I thought was stationed an hour outside of Fort Worth, the truck was six hundred miles away at the other end of Texas—practically in Mexico. I wouldn't be able to sneak away that far without Mom noticing, let alone Noor. *Shit. Should I tell Noor? I don't want to tell anyone, not even my best friend. I just want to make this go away and never have to mention it at all.*

"Try us again on Wednesday. I can't guarantee we'll still be in North Texas, but I promise we'll try to help if we can."

I cannot believe my life. A nurse armed with Costco spray oil and a doctor with grown-out roots who doesn't seem to know about the Guttmacher Institute are my last hope. And even they are coming up empty.

I pull down my shirt, button up my jeans, and rest my hands over my ovaries. My disloyal, traitorous, spoilsport, party pooper ovaries. *We had a plan,* I whisper to my organs. *We had a plan to make it out of Dallas and into the Ivy League. Do you want me to give up on my dreams?*

Nurse Ali pulls back the curtain and slowly unlatches one of the back doors. Her head disappears outside. "Coast is clear!" she says cheerily. I step down and out of the truck. The nurse reaches into her hair, pulls out a white card, and drops it into my tote bag. I just stand there for a second. Pill-less. I have failed Step 1 of my own damned Guide. It said: "Keep Calm & Get Meds." Not: "Have a Bollywood Blackout & Leave Still Pregnant."

Nurse Ali slams the door behind me before I can even crawl under the tarp.

By the time I walk to my car, the tarp has vanished and the silver truck is hurtling toward the George Bush Turnpike.

STEP 2

HANG ON TO YOUR DREAMS

To: The Program in Liberal Medical Education
    Brown University
    Providence, Rhode Island
    Monday, May 4

Dear Dean Williams:

My name is Laylah Khan. I am a second-generation Indian American, a proud, practicing Muslim, and a firm believer that science holds the power to change the world. I am applying to Brown University's unique Program in Liberal Medical Education because the combination of a four-year liberal arts program with guaranteed entry into Brown's medical school will arm me with the skills I need to save the lives of people from medically underserved communities.

My best friend says I'm not activist enough, that in this political climate I should be marching with her, pumping my fist outside the Texas capitol, driving to DC, painting banners. But I'm not sure that stuff works. I mean, look where it's gotten us.

I believe that as a doctor specializing in Obstetrics and Gynecology, I will be able to directly serve the people who most need my help. I believe that medical care, especially access to reproductive health care, empowers people and transforms not only their lives but the lives of their families and communities. It's like my best friend, Noor, reminds me about one of the philosophies of El-Hajji Malik el-Shabazz (also known as Malcolm X). Brother Malcolm said: "To educate a man is to educate an individual, but to educate a woman is to educate a nation."

That's why I am applying to your eight-year program. (Also because my artsy-fartsy mother is freaking out about me being a doctor. She thinks I can't have chosen my life path this early, and the "liberal arts" part of your program is the only thing making her chill out. She really thinks I'm under some invisible pressure to be a "good immigrant" and a "model minority," but it's not like that. I just really love medicine—and I'm not even an immigrant, technically. Also, I suck at art. Unless you can call splashing paint on a canvas "abstract art.")

My mom still harbors hope that I will become an artist like her. It's why she sent me to Booker T. Washington High School for the Performing and Visual Arts (instead of the Eddie Bernice Johnson STEM Academy, where I begged her to let me go). And while I do see the power of poetry and paint to change the world, I believe medicine is _my_ path to service. I have seen how amazing doctors can change lives and alter the course of history. Seven years ago, when we found out that my baby brother would be born with an extra copy of chromosome 21, my dad freaked out and left us. But my mom was empowered with all the information her obstetrician gave her about Down syndrome and she felt confident that she would continue with the pregnancy. Our lives were forever changed by that information because my brother, Adam, is the best thing that ever happened to my family.

I have dreamed of being there for others and standing by their side in their darkest moments ever since that day. I even know I want to subspecialize in emergency obstetrics so that I can be of service to people at risk of fatal complications during childbirth. With maternal mortality at record highs in America, I plan to open a clinic in a rural area to help the underserved. Acceptance to Brown's unique program would be the first step on this path to achieving my lifelong dream.

Sincerely,
Laylah Parveen Khan

What is the point of writing these essays anymore? Three days ago I found out I am a statistic, one of the 200,000 American teens who wind up pregnant every year. Who wants a pregnant hijabi applying to their university? The life I had planned is over.

~~STEP 3~~
STEP 1?

TELL YOUR BEST FRIEND

 Anonymous Seahorse
at 06:35

"Deleted Step 3"
Entered: Step 1?

 Anonymous Seahorse
at 06:36

Shouldn't this come before
everything?

CARAMEL-SCENTED CLOUDS waft over Noor's face and across the kitchen as she whisks sugar, water, and lemon in a copper pan. Blue flames lick the underside of the bowl. Noor turns the knob to dim the flames as the amber syrup bubbles and froths. This is our ritual. Play songs from *Sukkar Banat*, the classic movie about a group of women whose friendship centers on their beauty treatments in a Beirut salon; and squeeze ice-cold cans of La Croix between our legs in preparation for the burning but necessary pain that is to come.

"Here, take this!" I say, thrusting the candy thermometer toward Noor. My best friend waves her arm by her side, snubbing my scientific approach. "I just eyeball it, Lay. You can tell if the syrup is good from the smell and the color." She bends over to sniff the steam.

Noor turns off the heat and sets the pan in the sink. When the mixture has cooled to a treacly thickness, we will take turns mold-ing balls of wax between our powdered fingers ready to spread the stickiness across each other's skin—but not before I taste the caramel. "Just to make sure it's perfect!" I scream, dodging Noor's hand as she tries to swipe the sugary ball away from my mouth. I duck, she misses. "Since you didn't let me do a temperature check, I have to taste it to make sure it's perfect," I say, jamming the ball into my mouth and sucking the sweetness from my fingers.

"Maybe if your mouth is busy, you won't scream like last time," she says, shooing me into the living room, where the torture will take place.

Talking nonstop is also part of the ritual. Chatter distracts from the pain. But I am quiet this Monday evening, my insides bubbling with a secret I swallowed on Friday. The secret grows inside of me, lurches in my stomach, and sends bitterness shooting up my throat. I spit out the half-chewed ball of caramel and wrap the stickiness in a tissue. I shove it into my pocket. Another mess I have to hide from my best friend.

"Here. I wish I could spike yours with vodka," Noor says, shov-ing an opened can of fizzy water toward my chest. "It might make you less dramatic about a bikini wax. Then again, maybe vodka would make you *more* dramatic?" I slurp greedily to push down the bitterness. "Damn, girl!" She laughs. "You slurp La Croix the way Baba slurps beer." I guzzle and wipe the foam from my lips.

I laugh with her. A fake laugh. Everything about me is fake now. I put down the can, unbutton my jeans, lie back on the couch, and work up the nerve to tell my best friend everything. What really happened with JJ when we disappeared during the

Bluebonnet Bloom school trip. How I let myself get carried away because there were fields upon fields of endless flowers, the same shade of baby blue as my chiffon skirt, and the flower heads were freshly blooming, the unfurling petals turned sunward, just for us, and what was that if not a sign to open up, to let go? I could tell her how my billowy skirt was made for that spring day in the sun. How the scene was straight out of a Rumi poem. And when JJ read me a Rumi poem and asked—without stopping to take a breath—if I was wearing anything beneath my skirt, how I, breathless as well, smoothed the fabric against my thighs, took his hand, put it on my knee, and whispered that he should find out for himself.

"What's up with you today?" says Noor, eyeing me on the sofa with my crotch half exposed.

"What do you mean?"

"Normally you want to have a full-on debate about the pros and cons of getting waxed first versus second and then you want to go over the sixteen reasons why yanking off our pubes means we are caving to the patriarchy, but how being aware of this delusion makes us less-awful feminists—but still pretty bad feminists."

"Just want to get it over and done with. Anyway, I've been thinking. . . ."

"About?"

About how I failed to keep our promise of only having safer sex, how I destroyed the entire LLP with One Bad Decision, why I kept my missed period a secret, why I needed to believe that missing my period was a side effect of coming off the pill so abruptly, why I went to a taco-truck-clinic half hidden beneath a tarp by myself this morning, and why I lied and said I had to miss school because someone had to be home to let in the plumber.

"About the Guide."

"It's gonna be SO good!" Noor says, sprinkling baby powder over my thighs. I smooth the soft powder to a fine layer.

"But we need to rewrite step 1," I say.

"Because?"

"Because turning up at a safe clinic isn't as straightforward as we think it is."

"Huh?"

"Like, we can't just say, 'Hey, Panicking Pregnant Person! Here's a list of numbers and encrypted handles. Just give 'em a call or text 'em, why don't ya?!' What if all the numbers stop working? I mean, what if providers are constantly switching up their internet handles?"

Noor stops, her talc-covered fingers hover an inch above my crotch. "But that's why the Guide is a living, breathing document, Lay. We're not only printing it and handing out copies. I'm building a website so we can update the list and crowdsource solutions. That's the whole point, remember?" She pushes my thighs apart. I tense.

"Yes, I know that, but it's still too much to tell a pregnant person, who's probably alone and scared out of their mind and not thinking straight and freaking out and maybe in pain, to just call a number and turn up at an underground clinic alone."

"You said 'alone' twice."

Damn it.

Noor scoops a ball of wax from the pan and stretches it between her fingers. Fine strands of golden threads break apart into amber whisps. Her eyes narrow as she smears the wax along my thighs. She glances up at me.

She's looking at my under-eye bags.

Oh my God, she knows.

Yup, she definitely knows.

"Adam's not been sleeping this week so I'm a mess!" I blurt out, tensing every muscle in my legs and squeezing my eyes shut to brace for the pain and to block my best friend from reaching into the depths of my soul with her gaze. I feel bad for blaming my concealer-resistant under-eye bags on my seven-year-old brother, who, in fact, sleeps like a baby and snores like an old man with sleep apnea.

"Relax!" Noor smacks my leg with the back of her hand. "No sleep, huh? That would explain some of your weirdness. I saw this thing on TikTok that said if you lose just eighty minutes' sleep at night, it not only makes you sluggish and irritable the next day, ahem, but it makes you eat, like, three hundred more calories. Which would explain . . ." She points her chin over her shoulder, back toward the kitchen, where an empty Doritos packet, an empty Airheads box, a half-eaten burrito wrapped in foil, and two empty bottles of Topo Chico lay scattered across the table. It's a lot, even by my Olympic snacking standards. I open my mouth to tell a lie and say I skipped lunch or something, but instead hot gas escapes my mouth and I belch. "Oops." We both laugh.

"What is up with you these days?!" Noor giggles. "Ms. Perfect is even burping out loud! Reminds me of the old Laylay." She sighs.

Of course my best friend would know something is up. Noor's got spidey senses. Last year, I tried to hide a yeast infection and she sensed that something was wrong within thirty minutes of me coming back to school from the doctor with a tube of antifungal cream hidden inside the sports hijaab that I keep buried at the bottom of my bag on the off chance that I might engage in physical activity. Actually, Noor might have figured it out in more like ten minutes. We were sitting in the back of Ms. Sok's art class when she said, "Your eyes, Lay. They tell me ev-uh-ry-thing!" Noor pointed at my bag, beckoning to see what I had hidden inside, and when I refused to hand it over, she accused me of becoming stuck up and prim on account of spending so much time with the girls at the mosque. She snatched the bag from the seat and said, "Damn, Lay. Why you gotta be all secretive?" while rummaging through it. "Why don't you just tell me stuff? It's not like you're the first girl to get thrush." I yanked the bag back. "Ugh, Laylah! Why you gotta try and act all perfect and untouchable and undiseased all the time? Shit happens to everyone."

"Shhh," I said. "Somebody will hear!"

I unwrapped the sports hijaab and swiveled around in my chair to check that the coast was clear before flashing the tube in her direction and shoving it back inside my bag.

"Yup. Knew it," she said, rolling her big brown eyes, as if she were the one who had planned a future filled with making diagnoses. "It's because you sit and study for so long and you don't realize how long you're sitting. You need to move around more."

"That's not actually how it works," I said. "You're confusing thrush with urine infections. I got this because I've been eating too many of the rasgullah, rasmalai, jalebi, nankutai, and laddu that I make with Nanima."

"Well, I don't understand how you're sitting here with an itchy vag while your sixty-year-old grandmother doesn't have even one lick of diabetes!" Noor said. Then she answered her own question. "I'll tell you why. It's because your nanima is always going on long walks with all her grandma friends after their long-ass meetings. I don't know why she won't let you go with them. You're the one that needs the exercise!"

She sat up straight all of a sudden.

Uh-oh, here comes a wild idea.

"Why don't you join my basketball team?!" Noor leaned forward, as if this were her first time making the suggestion, as if it were a viable option for someone with two left feet and a height deficiency. The only place I have any coordination (and am closer to five foot seven) is in my Bollywood daydreams. And the only sport I play in real life, and for med-school-résumé purposes so I come across as a well-rounded medical student and not a full-time geek, is badminton. At least when I fail miserably at that, I'm only letting myself down, not an entire team.

"Thanks, Noor, but I have too much going on with the mosque youth group to join another club. Anyway, you don't even play for your basketball team since you became editor of the school newspaper. All I need to do is resist the delicious, coconutty, cinnamony, nutmeggy, cardamonny, syrupy goodness I bake with Nanima." I licked my lips dramatically.

Noor rolled her eyes again. "It's not that diabetes runs in your family, Laylah. It's that no one runs in your family!" she said, repeating the meme she loved to send me every time I complained that another relative who was anxious and confused about their newly diagnosed prediabetes was calling my mom and asking to speak with "The Future Dr. Laylah."

"True story, Lay. But those treats you make with your grandmother are amaaaaazing. The bright yellow round ones? What are they called?"

"Pendah."

"Yeah. Those old ladies need all that food, though. They talk for hours and hours and then they go on those crazy long walks. What do you think they talk about when they kick you out of the room?"

"Grandkids? Old-school Bollywood? I don't know. Nanima calls it 'gup shup.' Then she says, 'Betah, it was the Golden Age of Cinema. Not like this trishy, trashy modern filmy stuff!'" I had said, imitating Nanima's Indian accent. I felt immediately terrible for making fun of my grandmother, but Noor laughed so hard that Ms. Sok threatened to give us detention.

That was last spring. Life was simple back then. I hadn't made the One Bad Decision. My Big Future Plans and the LLP weren't lying in jeopardy about to be ruined because we lived in a joke of a democracy where nine judges—who we didn't even get to pick—drank coffee, took long lunches, decided my fate, and utterly trashed my future over a kale pesto panini.

"Three, two, one!" Noor yanks the wax off my skin, taking a patch of black hairs with it. I bite my lip. *Maybe now isn't the right time to tell her? No. Now is the perfect time. What's she going to do? Leave me half waxed? Smooth on one lip and hairy on the other? She'll have to carry on even though she's disappointed and angry that*

I went back on our safer-sex pact. Yes, now is the perfect time. I suck my bottom lip, inhale half the air in the room, and exhale. I'm ready to tell the truth.

"Drama Queen. It's not *that* painful," she says. "Not like that time you nearly ripped off my labia! Remember that? Three, two . . ."

I'm ready to tell her . . . but what will she think of me? What will she say? *How could YOU of all people be so reckless? How could Ms. Organized, Ms. Future Doctor, Ms. Perfect, Ms. Tells Everyone How to Be Healthy screw up her life because she got carried away on an afternoon school trip just because the bluebonnets looked pretty and the jock—the jock!—whispered some Rumi poetry in her ear in a field full of flowers the same color as her skirt? Sooo cliché!*

Shit. Maybe I shouldn't tell her. Not yet. Especially after she stared into my eyes when I talked about JJ the week before the bluebonnet trip. Noor had raised her eyebrows and warned me that some shit was about to go down. "Go down, like, how?" I said, confused. "Like *he's* gonna go down!" Noor said, collapsing in a fit of laughter. She had jumped up and down, her curls bobbing in the air, delighting at her own filthy joke. I crossed my legs. "Oh, bless your heart, habibti," she had said, stooping down to look at my blank face. "It's not complicated. All I'm saying is keep condoms in your bag. Simple." Which I didn't. Because "Give into the horniness" is not on the LLP for another three months. We weren't supposed to do it until after exams.

"One!"

I squeeze my lips together until I'm sure they are blue. Noor rips away a strip of hardened wax and presses her palm into my reddening thigh.

"Noor, I have to tell you something."

"Save it. I already know." She squints into the strip of wax, which is flecked with my little black hairs.

I prop myself up on my elbows. "Already know?"

Noor pushes me back down, reminding me of Dr. Hogarth this morning. *God, I hope I don't have a Bollywood blackout again.* I suck in more air and count to seven on the exhale.

"You are the worst keeper of secrets. Correction: You are the best keeper of *other* people's secrets, but you are the worst keeper of Laylah Khan's secrets."

"What? I mean, what do you know?" I stare at the Palestinian flag above the couch and wish it would wrap around me like the shroud I will one day be buried in.

"You gave it away on Friday, Lay."

"I did?"

Just say it. She already knows, so tell her what happened in the truck this morning. Tell her you tried to fix this mess and it didn't go to plan. Tell her this shit is not as straightforward as we think it is. It is definitely not as simple as opening a document and following steps one, two, three, four, five through eleventy million thousand. Tell her you need to rewrite the Guide for the real world. Tell her you tried step one and you failed. You, Laylah P. Khan, failed. At step one.

"I wish you'd just come out and say it. Stop trying to act as if life always goes according to plan. According to *your* plan."

I squeeze my eyes shut and suck in air, but the oxygen swells inside my chest and I can't breathe out. The edges of the room blur. The stripes of the Palestinian flag blur into a muddy mess. Air fills my lungs, but I still can't exhale. My forehead is on fire.

"It's not *that* hot in here. Damn!" She sprinkles more powder over my thighs, puts down the bottle, and fans my face and then my crotch with a copy of the *Dallas Morning News*. "So, anyway, I already know, boo. I can just tell when something is up with you."

I push the back of my head into the couch, willing the green velvet cushions to swallow me whole and spit me out in some other reality where I am unpregnant and still have a future. But the flag hangs on the wall and the sofa cushions just sit there. My face sweats from the shame of it. The shame of *it* and the shame of *being* ashamed and the shame of keeping this whole thing a secret for three days and lying to my best friend.

"The first clue was that you didn't go for two weeks. Or was it three?"

Go?

"Where?"

"That was a giveaway," she says, sliding her hand beneath my knee and scooping it up to butterfly my leg. She pulls my knee toward her face, angling it outward to reveal every crevice in my groin. I pull my knee back toward the ceiling. "Hey?" she says, furrowing her brow. I feel more exposed, more naked than I have ever felt in front of my best friend, even more than that time a yellow jacket stung me on the ass through my burkini at Jessica Klein's pool party. For three weeks straight, Noor would bend me over every morning, describe exactly how red the golf-ball-sized boil between my butt cheeks had grown, and offer to squeeze it.

She scoops another ball of wax. She smooshes, smears, and yanks. She pats and dusts. We stay silent.

"Okay, you're all done."

The air in the room is heavy with this unanswered question: How did my best friend find out if I didn't tell her?

"And then you stopped talking about Asma, and that's when I figured out your biiiiig dirrrty secret." I wince. I am so confused that I can't even concoct a dignity-protecting, shame-repelling lie. Noor dusts her fingers with baby powder, apparently reveling in my guilt and unknowingness. She is the chef and I am a lobster squirming in a pot of barely warm water. My outsides are turning pinker by the minute as I slosh around, acutely aware that any second now, this tepid bath will turn into my scorching death jacuzzi.

"They decided not to give you the job title promotion thingy you asked for, didn't they? Such a mess. They should have been calling you the head volunteer of the youth group for at least two years! I told you that mosque doesn't deserve you."

I exhale the air back into the room. My jaw softens. The water goes from a rolling boil to a simmer.

"The promotion? The promotion . . . at the mosque? Yes!"

"Sucks, but that's life. You've got enough on your plate, for real."

"Yeah? Yeah! Really sucks. But you're right. They would have just dumped more work on me anyways and I've got soooo much going on already. Especially with the Guide."

"LIAR."

"What?" I jump up from the sofa. "What are you going on about, Noor?! Stop interrogating me!"

"I knew it! You're a terrible liar! So defensive!"

The chef has thrown the lobster back into the boiling water. I can feel my face reddening. My shell begins to crack open.

"I. Knew. It. It's nothing to do with the mosque. It's JJ! Why are you pretending you don't like him? It's so freaking obvious. You know I saw you two slip away from the group when Mr. G was going on and on about bluebonnets. You were gone twenty minutes. Twenty-three actually."

"Did you time us? Do you time everything?" I flop back onto the sofa, pull a cushion over my face, and wonder if I should suffocate myself.

"Twenty-three whole minutes."

"Idommmfffmmmm."

Noor yanks the cushion away. "I can't understand you. Just say you've caught feelings for him and you're worried this is going to derail the Great Magnificent Laylah Life Plan."

"Fine! You want a confession so bad, here it is. No, I don't have feelings. Yes, we did slip away."

"Did you have a condom on you?" she says, squeezing her body between mine and the backrest of the sofa. Noor plonks her face on my shoulder and smiles. "I mean, like, did you have a condom already on you because you were planning it all along? I know you, Laylah. Bluebonnets, a warm spring day. It's fresh out of a Bollywood movie."

"No, I didn't have a condom." [Truth.] "And you said it yourself, Ms. Investigative Journalist Timekeeper. It was twenty-three minutes. Nothing's gonna happen in twenty-three minutes." [Big Fat Lie.]

"Fiiiine." Noor slumps onto her back, almost pushing me over the edge of the couch. "I thought maybe the future doctor had some gynecological adventures of her own and was getting ready to tell me all about it."

I turn onto my side, away from Noor, and stare into the pot of golden wax on the coffee table. I close my eyes and pray for the thick, golden caramel to spin into the shape of a tornado and suck me into the vortex and drop me somewhere far, far away from Texas.

"Hey, Lay?" Noor whispers over my shoulder.

"Yeah?"

"Are you being secretive because you're scared Asma will find out?"

"How would Asma find out?" I feel Noor shrug her shoulders behind me.

"I don't know. Feels like the Haram Police are everywhere these days." We lie together in silence. "Hey, Lay?"

"Yes, Noor."

"Promise me you won't turn all prissy and stuck up like Asma, yeah?"

"She's not like . . . Okay. I promise."

"They're already sucking all your time away. I don't want them sucking the personality out of you too. And promise me . . ." Noor turns on her side as if she's about to spoon me. She wraps her long arm around my waist and squeezes. "Promise me and swear on the Qur'an that you'll tell me if you catch feelings for Mr. High School Super-Star Sports Player, okay?"

I can't believe I'm lying. To Noor. To the person who tells

me everything about everything. To the person who dragged me into the bathroom stall in freshman year and showed me what she thought were "disease blisters" all around her bra strap, which appeared immediately after she made out with Becca Riley but turned out to be an allergic reaction to the new dollar-store laundry detergent her dad insisted they use, and not divine retribution for making out with a White girl. I'm lying to the person who FaceTimes me to ugly cry after she watches *The Bridges of Madison County* for the millionth time and wails, "What if Francesca made the wrong decision? Why aren't more people poly?" while I tell her, "Dude. Why are you even watching that ancient movie again?" To the girl who waxed evangelical about Lorals, the first-ever latex panties invented for safer oral sex for women, and who swore she'd never have unprotected sex—and made me swear too—and then told her father that the black rubber thong he pulled out from under her dresser when he was moving furniture belonged to me and was some kind of medical device I had to study for med school entrance exams. I will take Noor's secrets to the grave. I will lie for her, do whatever it takes to protect her. And I know she will protect me. But that's not what this is about.

The dishonor and shame of this whole mess are disintegrating my bones and turning me into a wobbly pile of faloodah. "Shame" isn't even the right word. This is sharam. It's much deeper and much, much worse. Sharam is not the regular brand of shame. Sharam is Cultivated, Holy, Glorified Shame. Sharam is a virtue. It's like a mindset woven into the DNA of Good Brown Girls everywhere. It's inside our brain cells. It speaks to us. It's taught to us so young that the voice of sharam takes on our own accent, our own tone, and it keeps us in check and aware of our place in the home and in society at all times. Sharam is the voice that says, *Who do you think you are? You can't wear that! You can't be that! You can't think that!* Sharam is the invisible force that pulls you out of your favorite fantasy, the one where you're standing in a silk hijaab the color of rubies at the podium of the Nobel Prize acceptance dinner in Sweden while giving an emotional speech about how women's rights are human rights. *Sharam* snatches you out of that glorious fantasy and tells you in a sneering voice that sounds just like your own, *How dare you dream so big? You? You conceited, egotistical, entitled little girl? Get ahold of yourself. You'll never win anything. Especially if people know your filthy secrets.*

"I have to go."

"What? Lay! What about me?!" Noor stands. Her sweatpants fall to her knees.

"Tomorrow? Can I do it then? I forgot I have to do this thing with Adam."

"Damn, Lay. What thing?" Noor looks quizzically into my face. She pulls up her pants, reties the drawstring, and puts her hands on my shoulders. "You're being really weird. Like, way weirder than usual."

"It's just so much going on. The fundraiser, the . . . the . . . everything."

"Take it easy. None of this is life-or-death stuff. Except for this." She looks down and pats her crotch through her sweatpants. "I was going to text Sara to see if she wants to hang tonight."

"I'm sure she'll love you no matter how furry you are."

"You're just saying that because you're nice and smooth. Are you going to see JJ? Is that why you're rushing? Or are you still avoiding him? Why are you even doing him like that?" I shrug. Noor looks at her feet. "Ugh, fine." She walks out of the room and yells from the hallway, "Do not forget to take this! My mom will be so mad if I forget to give it to you. It's for Adam."

I find her hunched over the first step of the staircase, struggling to pick up the world's biggest box of Lego. I lug it out of her front door. The two-ton weight feels as light as a feather compared to the heaviness of the guilt buried inside my stomach.

"I can't believe you did me dirty, Lay!" Noor yells, standing in the doorway, pointing both index fingers at her crotch.

"Stoppp! The neighbors will think we're up to something!"

She rolls her eyes. I turn back around to walk to my car and my knees almost buckle beneath the heaviness of my growing secret. Step One. *Failed*. Step Two. *Also failed*. And now, Step-Three-which-should-really-be-Step-One: *failed*.

At home, I grab my bullet journal and a dark gray pen. I sit on my bedroom floor in the almost-dark and shine my phone screen onto a blank page. The door cracks open and light from the hallway shines an elongated isosceles triangle of yellow light onto the beige carpet. Adam shuffles into my room dragging his blanket behind him. He pushes at my feet, huffing and puffing, silently trying to bend my straight legs until I scoot my heels all the way to my butt. He sits on my feet and presses his small back against my shins. My baby brother rocks from side to side and rubs the edge of the blanket across his cheek in the way that soothes him. And I do the thing that grounds me most. I make a plan.

(MODIFIED) LLP FOR WEEK OF MAY 4

DAY ONE	Do research to locate supply of pills. (This might mean calling people out of state. Tell them I'm doing research for the Guide.)	DONE ☐
DAY TWO	Call back numbers on the Safe Clinics List until someone answers. Keep trying to get appointments in case pill shipment comes in tomorrow, Wednesday, etc., etc.	DONE ☐
	Attend Tuesday night prayers and prep the girls for their fundraiser speeches.	DONE ☐
DAY THREE	Respond to edits of draft college essay and send edited version back to Mr. Smith for review.	DONE ☐
	Call back Tito's Tacos.	DONE ☐
DAY FOUR	Will have tracked down pills by now. (If not, TOMORROW is the absolute DEADLINE to tell Noor EVERYTHING.)	DONE ☐
	Complete section seven of MCAT prep book and type up handwritten notes. Review to-do list for the Guide.	DONE ☐
DAY FIVE	Mosque fundraising gala	DONE ☐
DAY SIX	Launch the Guide! And re: the other thing: ????????	DONE ☐

Signed,

Laylah P. Khan. Keeper of lists & secrets, hypocrite.
Coauthor of tips like "Tell a Best Friend!" but can't
even take her own damned advice.

NOOR

I SHOULD TELL Laylah. I should come clean and tell her everything. If I just explain that it wasn't even me who started it, then she might not be so mad. Nah, she'll be mad. She'll think I was trying to dig up shit and cause a rift. But I wasn't.

Keeping a secret is like telling a lie. And when have I ever lied to Laylay? (Answer: never.) I feel so bad. And she's running out of my house, practically tripping over the doorstep, thinking she's the one with the big, hairy secret. Instead, it's me. (I'm also the hairy one, since she bounced before doing my sugaring.)

I'm so scared of turning her world upside down and ruining our friendship at the same time. It's like my favorite reporter, the Gazan journalist Salma Abu Alyan, says: "Journalism has the power to build and destroy." I was about to learn the destroy part.

This is how it started three weeks ago. And I *swear* I wasn't trying to dig up any dirt.

"Pick a laptop, any laptop. They're all the same." I held open the door to the old-IT-classroom-turned-*Tribune*-HQ and watched my newbies file in. Newspaper newbies, that's what I call them. The eight eager ninth and tenth graders whom I recruited last fall to work as reporters for the *Booker T. Washington Tribune*— the three-time *Dallas Morning News* high school journalism award-winning *Booker T. Washington Tribune*. (Two of those wins were under my watch as managing editor.)

"Yes, Micah, that laptop is exactly the same as the rest. Okay, Magnolia. You can take your call since it's with a source, but hurry back, please. And the rest of you, pleeeease pick up the instruction sheet on your chair *before* you sit down. Thank you."

My newbies hugged and laughed as if they hadn't seen each other in years, even though I'd held a fact-checking workshop for the group just a week earlier. I kept one eye on them and one eye on the corridor. I glanced at my watch. It was exactly 4:00 p.m. If I had timed this correctly, then . . .

"Oh, hey, Noor."

Bingo.

"Sara? What are you doing here?"

I knew exactly what she was doing. Sara started saxophone class at 3:00 p.m. and walked past this room to get to her 4:00 p.m. jazz class. She had let that detail slip during lunch a few weeks ago when I was designing the journalism workshop flyer. I crossed out "Mondays at 5" and replaced it with "Tuesdays at 4." Save and print!

"Dance. Down there," she mumbled through a mouthful of granola bar while pointing down the corridor. She peered past me and into the class.

"This is my newsroom," I said, looking down at my boots while I humble-bragged.

"What are you up to?"

"I'm showing them how to be investigative journalists," I said.

"Wow. Like in *All the President's Men*?"

I loved that the most gorgeous girl in school liked watching old movies too.

Sara covered her lips with her fist, chewed aggressively, and swallowed. "Sorry, this is, like, my dinner and dessert in one." She waved her almost-finished granola bar in front of her face. I stared at a syrup-coated oat flake dancing at the edge of her perfectly shaped bottom lip. *Lucky oat.* Sara flicked her tongue across her lips and disappeared the crumb.

I snapped out of my trance. "So, what are you doing after dance? Cuz I'll be done with this lot in an hour."

"Meet you here?" she said. My heart fluttered. She chowed down the rest of the granola bar and handed me her empty wrapper. "You got trash in there?" she said, before waving goodbye and strutting away.

I pocketed the wrapper before anyone could see, and right as I was about to close the door and start the workshop, in walks trouble. Swaggers in, really. A ninth kid, let's call him Latif to protect his anonymity, because he's become kind of a source of mine, and you have to protect your sources even when they are irritating, smug little brats.

"Excuse you, but you're not in the newspaper crew," I said, watching the lanky new kid circle the table and eye the laptop Magnolia had marked as her territory by placing a melting Frappuccino dangerously close to the USB port.

"Yeah, but I'm joining today," said Latif, lifting his baseball cap half an inch off his head. He scrolled through his phone and turned the screen toward me. It was a photo of the flyer I had posted all around the school.

WANT TO UNCOVER GOVERNMENT SCANDALS?

EXPOSE LYING BUSINESSES?

Learn how to reveal the secrets the powerful don't want you to know!

FOIA*, PIR** and LexisNexis journalism workshop
4:00 p.m. every Tuesday in April/May in the
Tribune HQ (Old IT Room)

*Freedom of Information Act
**Public Information Request

"Omar showed me this."

"I've never seen you at any of my workshops." I waved his phone away. "And you have to fill in an application and interview to join the paper. It's a whole process."

"I *knooooow*," said the brat, pulling out a chair from under the table. "Kasim told me all of that. I'm joining. Today." He leaned back in the chair, spread out his long legs, and tapped the floor with his blue Air Force 1s.

"Fine. But we're out of newsroom laptops. Did you bring your own?"

He shook his head.

"Ugh, then you'll have to use mine. Move over to that spot." I unplugged my laptop and waited for Magnolia to come back to HQ. She jogged in mouthing, "Sorry."

"Let's get started. You've spent a lot of time with me and Mr. Goodman these past few months learning how to interview people, how to fact-check, and how to create a strong narrative. Now we need to talk about public records. Data. *Hard-core* data. I'm talking about the kind of stuff they want to hide from us." Latif rubbed his palms together gleefully. I wondered: *Why is this kid more eager than my own recruits?*

"You might already know that FOIA stands for a law called the Freedom of Information Act. That's what we're going to start with today. When journalists say they are 'FOIA-ing' someone, they're talking about one of the most powerful things we can do: file a FOIA request to the government to uncover all the things they want to keep secret. Or, for other places like charities and businesses, we file a public information request to the attorney general's office and get them to give us the info."

Latif flipped over the instruction sheet, glanced at both sides, and pounced on the keyboard. He was pounding the keys, *my* keys, while I was still explaining. "Can you wait? I haven't finished briefing you yet." But the kid stabbed away while my eager, obedient eight looked from the imposter to me and back at Mr. Stabby Fingers.

"Focus," I said, over the sound of Latif's clacking. "In the olden days, journalists had to type out a letter with all this formal blah blah blah, saying things like, 'This is a request under the Freedom of Information Act, or this is a public information request. I ask that a copy of the following documents be provided to me as soon as possible,' et cetera, et cetera. But because I love y'all, I've made a website. All you have to do is go to my website, fill in the blanks about what data you want and which agency or organization you want it from, and PING! Out pops a fully written letter. Email the letter, and voilà, you get your records! Well, sort of."

Latif was still pounding the keys as if my laptop had personally wronged him. Before I could tell him to calm down, he jumped up, grabbed his bag, mumbled a "Thanks!" and headed for the door. What did this numskull think he had achieved in seven minutes? I hadn't even talked through my four essential FOIA pitfalls or explained the detailed workarounds yet.

"I thought you wanted to learn?"

"I did. I do. But I've got it," Latif said.

"Got what?"

"The letter. I emailed it to them." He grinned past me at Omar.

Hold on a second. This kid had filled in the blanks, generated the records request, and already sent it to whichever agency he was trying to get information from?

"Wow. Okay. Well, come back in a few months and let me know what they say." I turned back to the group.

"Months?" The grin dripped off his face. He stood frozen in the doorway.

"Yeah, if they don't try to totally block your request, that is. Now, everyone, if you turn over to the other side of—"

"I thought they'd send me the stuff by Thursday or Friday?" he interrupted.

I tried not to smile, but I think I did. "Listen up, *everyone.* That's not how any of this works, okay? First, they'll try to block you, even though by law they have to respond to your FOIA request within twenty days. But what they usually do is—"

"Twenty days?!" Latif walked back toward my laptop and dropped his bag on the chair.

"Yeah, but even then, they'll try to make your life really difficult. Like they're punishing you for being a good journalist or something. They'll say that releasing the information you want jeopardizes national security or breaches confidentiality. Stuff like that. Which is why you have to preempt their bullshit."

"How do you even know this stuff?" Latif sneered. "Omar, is she right?"

Omar slid down in his chair and tucked his chin into his chest, fully aware that now was not the time to mansplain.

I inhaled a chest full of air and got ready to school this child. "Look. A FOIA request isn't just about emailing a letter and hoping they'll tell you the truth. The letter is just step one. You have to play the game. And the reason I know *this stuff* is because I've been studying it and winning awards for years." I turned around to gesture at the wall behind me, where plaques and framed certificates hung proudly. But when I turned back to glare at Latif, he wasn't even looking. He was busy lifting his bag and slamming his butt back into the chair.

"So, now, if you turn over the page, you'll see my four FOIA pitfalls plus my essential tips for a successful FOIA request. You need to look at these *before* you file a FOIA request." I looked over in Latif's direction. "It's not as simple as just sending a letter. You have to be *strategic*. You have to *think with a documents and records mindset*, which is my first rule for a successful FOIA request. Look at the back. No, Kasim. The *other* back. Okay, so what do I mean when I say you need to think with a documents and records mindset? I mean you need to think about *where* the powerful are hiding the data they never want us to find." I tapped the side of my head with my finger. "Powerful people are sneaky. You have to be sneaky like them. You have to think sneaky, too."

Magnolia raised her hand. Latif spoke anyway. "But I need to know *now*. This week."

Okay, this was getting weird. What was he working on that was so urgent? "Do you want to tell us what it is so we can help you? This is supposed to be a group workshop. Maybe we can all learn."

"I can't," he said, shuffling in his chair and looking down at his Air Force 1s.

"Look, there's no guarantee you'll get the data in a month

or even later. They could find a reason to delay and delay and deelaaaaay, or even block your whole request." He looked up at me with a furrowed brow.

"What's another way I could get information about someone?"

"What kind of data are you trying to get?"

"Like, if they've been arrested for fraud. Or . . . gone to prison?"

"Prison? Oh, you want to get personal? Well, when I won the award for investigative student journalist of the year for my exposé on the superintendent of the school district last year, I followed the money trail by using—"

"That's it. Money trail. That's what I need. What did they do with the money? How would I do that?"

The eager eight were looking concerned. Stabby Fingers was interrupting me during a workshop and everyone knew that was not okay. "Look, I'm trying to help you, but you need to come back next week when we get to the PIR and LexisNexis part of the workshop. Okay, everyone. Get back to your screens and your own FOIA requests."

Latif stood from his chair, grabbed his bag, and walked to the door. But then he just kind of loitered in the doorway. I helped Magnolia think about which agency was responsible for checking lead levels in school water fountains, but I could see Latif out of the corner of my eye, rubbing the toe of his sneaker into the carpet.

"Hey, Latif? Why don't you tell me what this is about?"

He walked toward the front of the classroom and looked off to the side at my poster of Ida B. Wells. "I just need to find out where a donation has gone. It's sort of . . . disappeared. I think someone stole it."

"Donation? Like, to a charity?"

"Yeah. Sort of. I think it counts as a charity? I don't know."

"Oh, so it's not a FOIA then. We have to go through the secretary of state or the AG. To get the charity's tax filings. And we can use ProPublica's tool, the Nonprofit Explorer, which tracks how much nonprofit staff get paid and stuff like that," I said. "There are so many ways to reveal the money trail and expose the fraudsters. I hate it when charities embezzle people's hard-earned money. Who is it we're going after?"

I walked to where Latif had been sitting, raised the MacBook to eye level, and inspected the keys Latif had stabbed. I could smell his stinky aftershave behind me. He was hovering over my shoulder, beginning to mumble an answer to my question. "I think they're a charity," he said. "They're called . . ."

Four letters. Latif hadn't even bothered to spell out the name of the so-called charity, but I knew it well. My best friend's face flashed before my eyes, and my laptop slipped from my sweaty fingers and landed on my toes with a leather-splitting crack. Everyone turned to look.

"Jesus!" Latif said, bending over to pick up my laptop. I stood frozen, staring into the middle of the classroom. "Your foot okay?"

"Is my laptop okay?" I snapped out of my daze and grabbed it from Latif, who was midinspection of the MacBook's underside. I needed to read his letter again. Did he really say RICC? Was that really Asma's last name spelled out in the records request?

Dear Sir/Madam:

This is a request under the Freedom of Information Act. I request that a copy of the following document(s) be provided to me: [*insert document titles here*]_____all financial records from the RICC [insert address here] ____ _____245 Anchor Street, Richardson, TX [*insert precise time period*] last summer to now. Especially everything to do with Mrs. Asma Khoury, who has probably been stealing thousands of dollars in donations from the mosque, from people like my dad, who raised nearly $12,000 for the RICC youth club from local businesses so that the mosque could take us on a very major trip and get the youth club new iPads, but we haven't been on any trips and we are still using the same dusty iPads and the money has disappeared and Asma keeps getting new cars and her husband is the imam, by the way, so that's probably how she doesn't get caught.

I wasn't even bothered that the boy had butchered my FOIA request form, forgotten to delete the blanks and prompts, added details that he couldn't prove, and confused a FOIA with a public information request. The whole thing was an unprofessional mess, and he had already hit send. But it was proof. Proof that my hunch had been right all along.

LAYLAH

JJ IS LEANING against the door to Ms. Chalabi's classroom, his nose buried so deeply inside the book of poems that I wonder, for the zillionth time, if the boy is shortsighted. Nothing, absolutely nothing, to do with medieval Irish poems about dying blackbirds could be that interesting.

I peek around the corner and jump back when I think he's about to look up. But his eyes are glued to the poem. He moves only to turn a page and tuck a stray dreadlock behind his ear. It's as if the hordes of students jostling past him don't exist.

I am trying my hardest to not exist, or at least to appear invisible. I'm moving in stealth mode, skulking around corners and slinking into class like a CIA agent, my black hijaab paired with oversized black sunglasses. But when I jump back around the corner to hide from JJ, I stumble into Hanna and send us both tumbling.

"Why are you walking backwards?" she says, pushing me off her and almost into JJ's view. "Class is *that* way." She takes a second to look me up and down. "You do know all this stuff just makes you stand out even more?" She lifts the sunglasses off the bridge of my nose. I slam them back down. "I don't know if you're trying to hide or something, but you look like those celebs who say they're avoiding paparazzi but then they go shopping in a baseball cap and glasses looking exactly like a Hollywood A-lister."

Hanna doesn't know that a black baseball cap sits at the bottom of my tote bag. I'm not wearing it because last week she said that a black cap over my black hijaab made me look like a skater-girl-slash-ninja. "Or . . . maybe she looks like a feminist mechanic?" Noor had said, squinting across the table, both of them talking about me as if I weren't there. "What's next?" Hanna had asked. "A balaclava? Ooh, is she working up to full facial coverage, Yemeni-style? My dad says that back in Yemen, my aunties have to wear these extra-long abayas so that the long train of fabric behind them sweeps the sand and vanishes any trace of their footprints."

"What? In case a man finds their footprints so distractingly sexy that he becomes obsessed and his life goes off the rails? Over footprints?" I tried to insert myself into the conversation, so that they would talk to me and not about me, but Hanna and Noor were only interested in hearing an explanation for my new all-black-everything fashion style. "Just trying to prevent skin cancer," I lied, pulling the rim of the baseball cap lower.

I couldn't admit that I had dialed up Operation Avoid JJ from a Level 2 to a Level 10 that very day, the day the consequences of my One Bad Decision had flashed on a white stick between my quivering thighs while I sat on the toilet. Level 2, which involved deleting JJ's texts without reading them and sliding into class when everyone was seated and it was too late and too quiet for JJ to interrogate me, had started in March, right after the school trip. That's when he changed.

Miss uuuu, he had started to text me, every single morning and night, followed by strings of blue hearts. It turned out that the One Bad Decision had multiple consequences, one of them was to transform JJ into an even bigger pile of mush. He had gone from respecting my need for independence to suggesting we do everything together. Wanna eat lunch now? Where are u? Hungry? I can grab you a slice . . . if you're busy? And then, three hours later: Have to buy school supplies for my lil sister at 4. Wanna come?

JJ knew my color-coded hour-by-hour schedule—I had shown it to him on our first date back in December in the hopes that it might scare him away. Instead, his eyes widened as he realized he had met someone as brutally organized as him. And yet, ever since that damned school trip, my phone was pinging with these random requests. What had happened to sticking to the program? JJ knew he was already a 2.5-hour Saturday slot on my weekly schedule.

It was my fault. I had let things get serious. We were supposed to wait until summer, but between the blue sky and the blue skirt and my "forgetting" to wear panties that day, we hit a June milestone in March. Overachievers. Now a steady stream of hormones was zapping through both our bodies, messing with our minds and changing the course of our futures.

I peek around the corner again. JJ's book is open but his face is looking up now, his wide smile beaming toward Ms. Chalabi, who is chatting away as she unlocks the door to her classroom. "Come on in, Mr. Jackson," I hear her say as she waves him through. JJ is always the first to class, always the first to finish the assignment, always the first to raise his hand. He's been that way since he arrived at Booker T. in September. In fact, it was in this very classroom on the second day of the school year that we exchanged words. JJ had raised his hand to answer a question—and every word that spilled out of those plump, pink lips was utterly misguided and inaccurate.

Ms. Chalabi was reading from *The Book of Essential Rumi* that day, her pages crammed with almost as many Post-it notes as my MCAT book (although hers were not color coded). She turned a page and stood from her chair as she spoke. "Now then, poets. Let's consider this next line. What does Rumi mean when he writes, 'This is love: to fly toward a secret sky, to cause a hundred veils to fall each moment'?" She flung her arms out wide and repeated the words: "'To cause a hundred veils to fall each moment'?!"

JJ's hand shot up.

Hanna and I glanced at each other and raised our eyebrows.

"Who TF is *that* and why is he in our *poetry* class?" she swooned.

"Oh, him? That's the athlete everyone's been talking about. I think." I pushed back a cuticle and pretended to examine my desperately-in-need-of-a-mani nails. But I knew exactly who the new guy was. I had spotted JJ at the welcome assembly the day before. He was fiddling with his dreadlocks, tying them up, taking them down, tying them up again. All the while, a gaggle of cheerleaders was giggling behind him.

But there was no entourage in Ms. Chalabi's poetry class, or "seminar," as she had us call it. JJ was surrounded by nerds who had spent the summer reading between the lines of a thick book of verse by the thirteenth-century Persian poet Rumi, who had become insta-famous for his quotes about love and heartbreak. I wondered when JJ had been given the book and when he had found the time to read it.

"Yes, JJ!" Ms. Chalabi said, pointing her book toward him.

JJ cleared his throat and spoke softly, his voice a deep rumble that had me leaning forward to hear. "I think Rumi's talking about when you're into someone so much and it makes you get rid of all the fakeness."

"Fakeness?"

"Yeah, like your ego and stuff. Cuz sometimes we let our head get in the way of our heart."

"Deeeep," said Hanna, snapping her fingers as if we were at a spoken-word open mic. I pushed her hands down. JJ fiddled with the dyed blond tip of a dreadlock grazing his chin. Ms. Chalabi was nodding as if the new boy had just given the perfect answer. I shook my head to rid the echo of his deep, soft voice and cleared my throat.

"Actually, no. That's not what Rumi means." I turned to Ms. Chalabi and pretended as if JJ wasn't there. She stopped nodding and pouted. Someone had to correct the new boy—the new boy with the muscles and voice that seemed to hypnotize everyone—and it wasn't going to be her. She seemed as smitten by him as everyone had been at assembly the day before.

"I know some people don't get it because they just see Rumi on Instagram and Valentine's Day cards and stuff and they don't really understand our culture, but what he's saying is actually way deeper than that."

"Well, to be fair, Laylah, Rumi was from the part of the world that we now call Afghanistan, which is where I was born. Or he might have been born in Tajikistan. Isn't your family from . . . India?"

Wow. As if I haven't been her favorite student for the past two years until this fake-geek-of-a-jock turned up. As if being Muslim isn't its own culture. Why is she dividing us? We're from the same *general* area.

"Actually, my great-great-great-great- . . ." *Shit.* I had lost count of the greats. "My family's originally from Persia," I said, as it dawned on me that Nanima had been talking about *Iran* when she said our people arrived in northern India from Persia generations ago. I had zero connection to Afghanistan. A guilty bead of sweat trickled where my hairline touched my hijaab. "Anyway, the point I'm making is that Rumi's not talking about lusting after an IG baddie or trying to bag the captain of the cheerleading squad." I paused so that the class could take in my words. "This isn't a poem about loving a *person*. He's talking about loving *God*. The divine."

"Oooh, snobby! Even for you!" Hanna whispered with a cackle. She slid down in her chair as if disappearing beneath the table was a better look than sitting next to me.

"Well, Laylah," Ms. Chalabi said. I could tell from her tone and curled upper lip that she was about to side with the new kid. "When we seek with an open heart, we might find the divine in other people."

Hanna snapped her fingers and inched back up her chair. "God is a womaaaaan," she sang into my ear. I pushed her away.

"But that's not what he's saying! You can't just make things up! You can literally see in the next line that Rumi is talking about God because he's talking about when you die and meet your Maker! Look, he even says it: 'First, to let go of life. Finally, to take a step without feet.' Don't you get it? 'To let go of life'?"

JJ's hand shot up. Ms. Chalabi smiled and nodded.

"But love can feel like that."

"What? Like death?"

"Like a small death," he said, looking at me. "You know, like you kinda lose yourself when you really fall for someone, and all this stuff that you thought was important in your life doesn't feel that important anymore. Cuz you love them so much. You know?"

No, I didn't know. What was this guy going on about? Was everyone from Houston this soft?

"That's literally *not* what Rumi is saying. But go off."

I was so over it. I was ready to find Noor and tell her that this new guy thought he knew everything about poems and love and our culture and it was only the first week of school and he was already ruining poetry class and becoming Ms. Chalabi's pet, which should be *my* role, naturally, since I'm the one who has to put up with a poetry professor for a mother who's been schooling me about radical enjambments since I was a baby.

But I couldn't escape, not even at the end of class. When the bell rang, JJ stood blocking the doorway with his sports bag in one hand and his half-open backpack filled with too many textbooks in the other. He smelled of deliciousness: sandalwood mixed with cedar and vanilla.

"Hey!" he said, as I tried to get past him. I resisted the urge to sniff the air like a puppy and focused on rearranging my facial muscles into an expression of deep annoyance. JJ spoke as if we were meeting for the first time. As if we hadn't just spent the past hour locked in a heated debate about his ignorance of Rumi. "Cool stuff you were saying about this guy!" He waved the book in front of his broad chest and flashed a blinding smile. "You know a lot, huh?"

"She knows soooo much," Hanna said, rolling her eyes and elbowing me at the same time.

"So, like. Do you wanna head to the food hall now, or . . . ?"

"Nope. Got somewhere to be," I said. I squeezed my eyebrows together and glared so he would move to the side. JJ stepped to the right just enough so that I could squeeze past all six feet and two inches of his muscular frame. I tripped over the strap of his sports bag, but I disguised the stumble by jogging along the hallway, as if I always jogged out of poetry class. Before I knew it, I was sprinting down the hallway to find Noor.

Mom called it. "Compulsion and repulsion are two ends of the same circle."

"Huh?"

She jabbed the potato peeler in my direction. "In the time you've been talking about him, I've peeled nearly one pound of potatoes and you haven't helped one bit."

I lifted a dusty loop of potato peel and dropped it back onto her pile.

"I didn't talk about him for *that* long. Anyway, aren't you bothered that he's misinterpreting ancient Persian poetry?"

"That's the beauty of poetry, Laylah. It turns each one of us into a translator. We bring our own life stories and perspectives to the page. We each decipher our own meanings. You two should study the same poem together and compare notes. You'd be surprised what you can glean from another poet's reading."

"He's not a poet! He's a jock!"

Black mustard seeds popped in a pan. Mom was making Adam's favorite finger food, Bombay Aloo. "You know, one of my favorite poets, Donald Hall, says that athletes have a ten-minute attention span." She zigzagged a wooden spatula across the pan. "But not this guy. It sounds like he could be on his way to the sporting leagues *and* to an Ivy League school. Impressive. Why don't you invite him over for dinner one night?"

"Absolutely not."

I blame Rumi. One full semester of Rumi, to be precise. The Sufi poet had stretched his arms from thirteenth-century Persia to twenty-first-century Dallas and fucked with my heart. That's how this happened.

In the last poetry class of the semester, JJ would not back down. Not even my eye rolls and pouts could deter him. Not even me flicking through my leather-bound bullet journal and thrusting it in his face to show him the highlighted pages filled with sticky notes and scribbles that left no space for him. "Look. There is literally no time for a date."

"There." JJ stabbed the page with a finger. I snapped the journal shut.

"Where?"

"Ouch!" He laughed. "Look, you've been saying no for months. You can't keep saying no!" He extended his hand. I stared at his palm. What was I supposed to do with those long fingers? Was this, like, a lady-in-waiting thing? Was I supposed to take his hand so we could ride his chariot to NorthPark Center?

JJ watched me watching him. He put his hand to his chest and looked up at the ceiling. "'Let yourself be silently drawn by the strange pull of what you really love,'" he said in that voice as smooth and sweet as honey, the voice that made my insides vibrate.

JJ knew what he was doing. He must have asked Hanna or Noor, because he was reciting lines from one of my favorite Rumi verses. I shoved my bullet journal in my tote and agreed to one date—but only one.

STEP 4

KEEP THE FAITH

LAYLAH

"BUDDHA? AS IN Buddhism?" Noor scrunches her face in confusion as I mumble on the phone. I bite my cuticles and wait for the voice on the other end of the crackly line to explain why a clinic needs to know which deity I worship. Noor shrugs. She hasn't left me alone all morning, and now it's lunchtime. I had hoped to eat my pizza slice alone, make as many calls as possible to locate the pills, and secure my own appointment for any day before Sunday.

But there is to be no alone time this Tuesday. Noor sits opposite me at the back of "our" art room. (We claimed the coziest of the second-floor art rooms as Laylah-Noor territory in ninth grade, when I realized that flinging acrylics at a canvas and calling it "abstract" was the only way I could succeed at this high school for the arts. I should have been at the Eddie Bernice Johnson STEM Academy all along. I begged Mom and Dad to let me go there, but they wanted me to be "well-rounded," whatever that means.) Noor's eyes flit between her laptop screen and my face as I try to make every call sound like research for the Guide and not a desperate plea for personal, lifesaving help.

"Not Buddhism, honey!" The voice on the other end erupts into a hearty laugh, which turns into a hacking cough. "Buda! *B-U-D-A*. It's a town south of Austin." I mute my phone and mouth an explanation to Noor to get her off my back. She needs to focus on her own laptop screen and work through her list of tasks instead of watching my every move. "It's a *town* called Buda. *B-U-D-A*." I whisper.

"Sheesh. I thought having a Paris, Palestine, and Italy in Texas was bad," she says, turning back to her MacBook. "OMG! Did you know there's even a Utopia? I just googled 'Texas weird place-names.'"

"How long will you be there?" I ask.

"What was that, sweetheart? Oh, yes, we're here for another . . . how many? She said four hours." The voice on the phone relays a message from a person I can faintly hear talking in the background. "Four more hours and then we have to be on the move. Been here twenty-four hours already. Where to? Wait, let me check. . . . Head . . . ed . . . east . . . to . . . morrow. Should be . . . un . . . certain by Thurs . . . day." White noise crackles, and the cheery voice breaks into a robotic rap.

"Sorry? You're uncertain about Thursday?"

"No, no! We'll be *in* Uncertain by Thursday. Prolly by early evening."

Buda? Uncertain? This has to be some kind of prank.

"But to answer your question, I just triple-checked, and nope, no pills. Nada. Hahaha." The voice in the background chatters away while my messenger of bad news guffaws through the phone. "She said we'll be driving through a town called Nada tomorrow! Nada is on our way to Uncertain!" Another throaty laugh conspires with the great state of Texas to mock my messy, out-of-control life.

I hang up the phone and annotate the online directory. "A29— aka Bella's Bundts: No pills as of Tuesday, May 5." I hit reload to update the Google Doc, as if eager eyes are scrolling through the twenty-six-page document already. But it's not live yet. The big launch is on Saturday, less than four days away, and Noor has been harassing me since I got home from her place last night to run a fact-check of every clinic phone number and encrypted internet handle that we found on a now-abandoned online message board that had listed details for dozens of clinics. If you can call a bakery-on-wheels a clinic. Noor thinks I'm calling each number to fact-check before we add it to our Guide. She doesn't know that I need to call every single one to find out who has pills or at least access to someone *somewhere* who has them, because the LLP and my future life, if I'm going to have one, depend on it.

I think back to Dr. Hogarth's grown-out roots, the way she tried to scare me off taking the abortion pills after seventy days, and decide she didn't know what she was talking about when she said that absolutely no one has the pills. It cannot be true. Someone in Texas has to have them. I just wish the pill-mailing system that was in action before all the bans fell into place was still working. It would save me the stomach-churning process of having to physically track down and drive to a mobile clinic. But everything medical gets intercepted in the mail these days. There's no point even fantasizing about help landing in my mailbox.

I scroll through my texts just in case I missed an alert from one of the sixteen clinics I left messages with this morning. But all I see is the last text from Noor. "Skip third period and meet in our art room." That was the message that had snapped me out of my 7:00 a.m. panicky daydream. But I can't stay here much longer or I'll miss English, and I have to speak to Mr. Smith about my college application. He's in charge of the FLI program for First Gen/Low-Income students who hope to be the first in their families to go to the Ivy League, and I have to see his edits so I can give him an updated version to send to some committee next week. The great state of Texas has to review the entire application before deciding if they'll support my application to go to Brown.

Eighteen, nineteen, twenty, done. I scroll down the list of clinics, stuff the pizza slice into my mouth, and do the math as I chew. That leaves seventeen clinics to call. So far, twelve out of twenty have had defunct phone numbers or were unresponsive, making them impossible to locate. They may have gone dark for a few days, only to pop back up next week, three hundred miles away and using a different phone number. I leave messages for the rest.

We've put in so many weeks of effort that I dare not question whether the Guide is a good idea anymore. The last time I wondered out loud about the danger of us writing it, Noor jumped down my throat and accused me of "giving in to the patriarchy."

She rummages through her bag for a scrunchie and piles her curls into a pineapple on top of her head. This means business. She must be going *innnn*. Noor crosses her legs on the chair, reminding me of the way Nanima scooches one leg up or sits cross-legged like a yogini, her gold toe ring flashing.

"Everything okay?" I mumble through a mouthful of dough and unseasoned tomato sauce.

"Mmmm." Noor inches closer to her screen. "I just keep seeing this name. Have you ever heard of someone called The Controller? Like, with a capital *T*. The. Controller?"

"Yeah, I've heard that name."

"Really? Where?"

My heart stops. It was yesterday. Dr. Hogarth's voice rings through my head. "Days like this, I wish I had a direct line to The Controller."

"Er . . . actually, no?" I stutter. "I don't think so?"

"So . . . you haven't heard of it?" Noor's eyes stare straight through my skull and burn into my frontal lobe. She looks back at her screen and my brain stops frying. "Suddenly, I'm seeing it Every. Where." She scrunches up her nose.

I shake my head and scroll down the list of numbers I still have to call. In less than fifteen minutes, the bell will ring for fourth period. But Noor slides my laptop to one side and spins her own MacBook around. "Look." She gets up and walks around to stand behind me. She rests her chin on my shoulder as she reads from the screen.

"At the heart of this underground movement is a figure so powerful, it conspires with illegal organizations, corrupt law enforcement officers, and unfaithful religious and Republican leaders, leveraging its vast networks to smuggle illicit hormones across the border, to traffic unethical healthcare providers from one end of the country to the other, and to deploy unscrupulous tactics to break our laws and kill our babies. Some say The Controller even has a foothold in the all-powerful Texas Ministry of Family Preservation."

"She sounds badass," says Noor.

"How do you know it's a she?"

Noor purses her lips. The website font is thick and angry. Noor keeps scrolling.

"Wait! Hold on a second. Go back up. Right up. Okay, there. Oh my God, Noor! Why are we reading the *Daily Bugle*? It's right-wing AF!"

"Because even though ninety percent of their reporting, if you can call it that, is complete BS, some of it is factual. And they know some things that we don't. You can't just dismiss stuff so quickly. You have to read *broadly*, Lay." She switches to her solemn journalist voice, as if I'm one of her devout newspaper underlings. Noor stretches her arms out to her sides and waves them around as if she's grabbing all the news that's flowing through the air. Then she brings her hands together in a ball shape. "You're like this, Lay. Look. Look at me. You're trapped in here, inside your cozy little echo-chamber-comfort-bubble-thing, where you only read the news you like. I mean, I'm not saying the *Daily Bugle* is actually—"

"News I *like*?! I don't like any news! Who *likes* the news these days!?"

"What I'm saying, Laylah, if you listen, is if we only read the stuff *you* like, we wouldn't have heard about this Controller. Sometimes you have to read these crappy sites to find the little grains of info they sprinkle into all the junk. Who the hell is this Controller person?"

"It's no one! It's obviously some boogeyman they've invented to put the fear of God into their paranoid readers." I look up at Noor. The pineapple on her head is slowly flopping toward her left ear. One arm rests on her hip, and the other hand clutches her chin.

"Nah. It's *someone*. I've seen it on too many of these sites."

"They make shit up, Noor. You say that yourself. Stop reading these—"

She swipes her laptop away from me and walks back to her spot. My phone buzzes right as the bell rings. A text from JJ. I delete it without reading it.

"You better not be leaving, Dr. Khan," Noor says in her sternest voice, the voice I imagine she reserves for interviews with politicians and school principals. I shove my laptop into my tote and stand. "Noooo," she wails, flopping her head onto the desk.

"Okay, who's being the Bollywood drama queen today?" I say.

"I'm serious, Laylah. Where are you going? We've only got three more days."

"Four," I correct her. No one is counting down the minutes, hours, and days more accurately than I am.

"Fuck. Fourth. Period. We *have* to finish this. I need to find this Controller. *The* Controller."

"We've got more important stuff to do. Look at the list! It's so long!"

"But who is this Controller person? I have to find them."

"And if it leads you to some trap designed especially to catch girls like us? What do we do then? It's like you're *trying* to forget how dangerous all of this is." I fling my tote over my shoulder and zip up my backpack.

"I mean, it is kinda fun. You have to admit."

"No, it's not *fun*, Noor. None of this is *fun*."

"But it *is* kinda fun to think we're fucking shit up and finding a way to work around their ridiculous laws."

"How is it fun? Their laws are ruining our lives!" I realize that I suddenly sound very personally affected. "And who are you even texting right now?" I am trying to sound less angry. "Your phone keeps beeping." Noor puts down her phone and looks away.

"Sara," she whispers. Then louder, "I mean, if you're not going to help me, then I don't see why I can't bring her in."

"What? You only just started crushing on her, Noor. And she won't even understand the way I've organized the sections in the Doc or how to work through the to-do list in the right order."

"It's numbered."

"She won't get it."

"She can count, Laylah."

Silence.

"We'll figure it out."

"We? Okay. Fine. Do what you want. But don't forget that she's a loudmouth," I blurt out, sounding a lot like a loudmouth myself. "If she gets us caught and we both wind up in prison, I'm blaming you and your horniness. You better explain *that* when NPR interviews us and asks us what we think about being called domestic terrorists."

"I'll tell them we're freedom fighters," says Noor, fingering a stray curl that has fallen across her face.

"Sure. And tell them we went to prison because you had a crush and were desperate to impress this Sara, and your silly little crush couldn't keep her mouth shut and probably made a viral TikTok about the Guide and tagged us all and got us caught."

"Actually, Sara is very anti–social media. You would know that if you gave her a chance."

"Promise me you won't tell her!"

"Fine!" Noor doesn't even look at me. "You can go now," she says sourly, her mouth pointed toward her keyboard. She even has the nerve to shoo me away with her hand. "Guess you won't be working on this tonight. Since it's Tuesday."

"I'm never *not* working on this!" I yell. She doesn't look up, not even to glare at me for raising my voice. She just smirks at her phone and shoots off another text. Most likely a sext or a complaint about me, her former best friend.

"Be smart, Noor." I walk toward the door and turn back to her. "Think with your head, not with your . . . other thing," I say. *Me.* Laylah Khan. *I* say that. The wannabe obstetrician who has lost the courage to accurately name body parts. The wannabe doctor who effed everything up because she couldn't think with her own head. That One Stupid Time.

I open the door as words fall from my lips and scatter to the ground. The letters rearrange themselves to spell: Laylah P. Khan, Future Nobody, the Worst Best Friend, and the Biggest Hypocrite in the World.

NOOR

SCIENTISTS SAY THAT listening to your gut is unscientific, that you shouldn't follow a hunch, that only hard facts can prove a thing is true. Those same scientists are finally admitting something journalists and Palestinian moms have known for centuries: The gut is our second brain; intuition, a superpower that can be developed over years; a nose for trouble, an organ that can be trained so that one sniff of a bad thing and the hairs on the back of your neck and arms stand dead straight and you know right away that the room isn't cold. Oh no, you know that something bad is brewing.

Scientists don't say it like that, of course. They use fancy words. Laylah taught me these words back in middle school, the same day we had a special guest speaker visit our class. While we filed into the room past a smiling Mrs. Dickey, Laylah explained that scientists were calling this second brain the "enteric nervous system." I preferred to call it the "belly brain." She went on and on about how a gazillion "brain chemicals" that we thought only affected the brain in our *heads* were swirling through this second brain in our gut, up and around our intestines. "That's probably why your mom's stomach hurts after she has those dreams. Right, Noor?"

Mom had passed down her ability to sniff people out. Sure, I didn't have dreams that predicted my grades, which cousin would marry next, or what sex the baby would be, but Mom's intuition was braided into my DNA. It's how I knew Asma Khoury was a fraud from the start.

"This is the new youth club leader at the Richardson Mosque. And she's the wife of the imam," Mrs. Dickey said, gesturing to Asma, who was wearing a pink T-shirt emblazoned with FEMINIST in purple letters. "I didn't even know Muslims could be feminists!" Laylah whispered quite loudly to no one in particular.

Asma adjusted the turban she had matched to jeans just baggy enough to be halal, yet slim enough to pair with sky-high stilettos the same shade of purple as her headwear. "It's the *Youth Leadership Program* at the Richardson *Islamic Cultural Center*," she said, screwing up her nose. "And my relationship to the imam isn't important." She turned to face us and parted perfectly painted red lips to reveal bright white teeth. "At the RICC, we say all people are equal."

Feminism wasn't our experience of the RICC. Our families went once a year for the annual Eid party, where Aunty Fatimah complained that it wasn't right for boys and girls to be separated, and Baba texted selfies from the men's prayer hall to say he was missing me. We weren't even allowed to enter through the main entrance with Baba and my brothers. "They should delete the *I* in "main" or just call it the *male* entrance instead of the main entrance," Aunty Fatimah would say. We squeezed into a shabby women's prayer room through a side entrance and ate crusty cookies while the boys ate cake in the main worship hall. Our small room smelled of damp socks.

Neither of Laylah's brains was remembering these facts that day that Asma visited our class. She was leaning forward over her desk, drinking in the turban and the red lipstick and the T-shirt, hanging on every word uttered by her soon-to-be role model. She was forgetting why I had stopped going to the mosque six months earlier. "It was because of *her* husband! The one who shouted at all the girls! Remember?" I elbowed Laylah, but she scooted away.

Almost a year earlier, Baba had insisted on sending me for Arabic lessons at the RICC. Baba didn't even go to the RICC to say Friday prayers, but when he heard through an uncle that the mosque was offering free Arabic lessons, he signed me up immediately. (Baba's favorite word is "free.") I was mad at first. Mad that my Saturday mornings had been given away without my consent and mad that my brothers didn't have to attend classes on the weekend. But for reasons I can explain, I began to wait anxiously all week for those weekend Arabic lessons.

Saturdays became synonymous with sacred girl time. Before I knew it, I was jumping out of bed and eagerly slurping my cereal on

Saturday mornings, while a curious Baba raised his eyebrows at me over his newspaper. I didn't dare tell him that the only two words I had learned in two months of lessons were "kubla" and "busa."

It was wild to me that it was in the holiest of places that all of us girls felt the most free, the most protected from silly boys. Boys were forbidden from the basement of the mosque (although now that I think about it, why were the girls relegated to the window-less basement?). But we were still too young to see the injustice, so we made it our own. We even discovered a secret room, its entry-way hidden behind a bookcase.

Each Saturday I would walk along the musty basement hallway, fling open the door to the classroom at the far end, and be swept away by the girly scents: fruity lip glosses mixed with strawberry candy, which mingled with the Victoria's Secret perfume the older girls drenched themselves in. The fumes made me high. The next two hours were ours. No one came to the basement to check on us. No one cared what us girls or our teenage "teacher," who spent the two hours scrolling Muslim TikTok got up to. Hijaabs came off, braids loosened, and new hairstyles tried out. That basement classroom was the first place that I felt the gentle scratch of nails on my scalp and playful pinches on my hips and cheeks from other girls. After our teacher had given us handouts with labeled body parts in English and Arabic, we would scatter into the corners in threes and fours and practice our new anatomical words. Then we would mash our faces together in a game called Make New Colors, which involved mixing the glosses on our lips in creative ways, while the girls watching whispered "shafah," the Arabic word for "lips." We would creep into each other's laps and drape abayas over scissored legs so the teacher wouldn't see that one girl's thigh was jammed beneath another girl's pelvis. I'm sure the teacher had played the same games when she was younger. Occasionally, she would look up from her phone, roll her eyes at our sticky, giggly faces, and keep on scrolling and taking selfies.

One day, when I was having my hair braided by a girl called Sameera, my legs spread into a V shape and nestled within the triangle of Sameera's longer legs, a tall man flung open the door and stormed into the room. A row of four or five older men huddled behind him. "No men allowed in here!" our young teacher said, tucking her phone beneath her abaya and pulling her hijaab forward.

"You don't tell me what to do!" the tall man bellowed.

A shorter man rushed forward and stuttered an apology. "These girls are just . . . ," he tried to explain. But the tall man kept screaming and my stomach churned. I pushed my back into Sameera's chest.

"What is this mess?" the man screamed. He pointed around the room at the girls huddled against the wall. There was even a card game going on in one corner.

All hell broke loose in the basement. Our feminine sanctity was shattered. The tall man happened to be the new mosque leader, Imam Khoury, and he was being given a tour of the mosque by the elders. That was our first introduction to Imam Khoury. After he screamed at us for dishonoring *his* mosque (there was no mention of it being God's house or *our* space), he disbanded the girls' Arabic classes (boys could still go to their lessons in the grand room with the big windows) and said that every girl in attendance that day had to report to him for punishment on Monday at 6:00 p.m.

Fuck that, I thought. I had basketball practice anyway. It would be three years before I stepped foot in the mosque again.

So, call it the sixth sense, premonitions, enteric nervous system, whatever. Call it straight-up resentment since her husband was unfair to us girls while she was proudly calling herself a feminist. But on that first day of meeting Asma, I knew the twisting feeling in my belly brain was the truth.

Laylah's gut was lying to her. She sat looking googly-eyed at Asma, who used the word "feminist" at least sixteen times in that one hour, described herself as a "mipster" (a Muslim hipster), and told us how it was Islam that brought feminism to Arabia. "Contrary to what you might have heard, Islam gave women and girls rights at a time when baby girls were being buried alive just for being female. Tell that to the Islamophobes!"

"Yeah!" Laylah said.

"If she's so pro-girl, then why doesn't she admit her husband is a misogynist?" I whispered to Laylah. "He said that girls deserve—"

"Shhhh!"

When Asma finished her talk by inviting our class to the youth club's Tuesday-evening Chai and Chat, adding, "We'll have chai tea lattes and cupcakes," I really knew the whole thing was sus. What kind of sellout Brown person says "chai tea latte"? ("Saying 'chai tea latte' is like saying you want milky-tea tea-milk," Aunty Fatimah once told me, when she heard Laylah ordering at our favorite coffee shop. "The 'latte' is redundant.")

By that evening Laylah was googling "Muslim feminists," "Islamophobe clapbacks," and trying to talk me into going to the mosque. "No chance, girl. They act nice one minute and they're screaming at you the next, telling you you're gonna get punished and that girls are more likely to sin and so they need more punishment. Shit like that."

"That was ages ago," Laylah said.

"That doesn't make it okay. Even your mom said it was verbal assault! Anyway, since when were you into religion?"

"It's not just about religion, Noor," she said, as if I'd missed the point entirely. "It's about being spiritual and manifesting your goals."

The next week she announced to Aunty Fatimah that she was going to Chai and Chat. While I reminded Laylah that we could eat better cakes and cookies at her nanima's house, her mom took to calling Chai and Chat by her own names. First it was "Cupcakes and Conversion," then it was "Baked Goods and Brainwashing." My fave was "Pastries and Propaganda." That nearly sent steam shooting out of Laylah's ears and nostrils. That girl can be so extra.

"Shouldn't you take up soccer or something?" I said, a month into her sacrificing her Tuesday evenings for the youth group. I was seeing a little less of my best friend every week and hearing more and more about Goddess Asma (although it would have been blasphemy if she'd actually used that word). But Laylah loved that Asma in her jeans and different styles of hijaabs was "disrupting" the silly narratives about Islam and Muslims. And I get it.

Everything is confusing when it comes to religion. There's hate from the outside, and we have to fight back against that. But then there's all the messiness from our own people on the inside, and I don't want to defend that just because we're trying to protect our cultures and traditions from the Islamophobes.

I stopped giving Laylah a hard time about going to the mosque once I realized it had become her second home, a place she loved—and it was steadily becoming a part of her identity. I supported her when she started wearing hijaab, and even when she started volunteering twice a week, cutting into our art time—unlike Aunty Fatimah, who would go off on these long lectures about the harms of organized religion. "Spirituality is a personal pursuit, Laylah, betah," she'd say. "Be wary of people who attach political ideologies to love of God, or love of nature, or love of anything good." Aunty Fatimah would tell us stories about the religious schools in India where girls were abused and no one did anything because the imams were immune to prosecution because of their status. "They used their faith as a shield against accountability," she told us.

I went back to the RICC just once with Laylah on a day to feed the homeless. I hardly brought up the fact that I couldn't bring Ruby, my girlfriend at the time, who wore a double-axe necklace and possessed an entire wardrobe of rainbow-flag shirts and sweaters. "I can't even talk about her being my girlfriend," I complained, packing cans of string beans into a box. "So, like, how progressive is it really?" Laylah said it was fine to talk about relationships in the women's section of the mosque (*Why is it even divided by binary gender in this day and age?!*), but I knew the mosque people would say stuff about me afterward, and I wasn't trying to have the self-appointed Haram Police come between me and my best friend.

It soon became clear that Asma was much more than the leader of the youth club, or *leadership program*, of the RICC, as she insisted on calling it. She was also the top boss of North Texas's Haram Police, as I liked to call them. Laylah would sometimes repeat things Asma had said about someone's manicure, abaya length, hijaab style, or Arabic pronunciation.

So even though it had been four years since I'd spoken to Asma, by the time Latif barged into my workshop and said she was stealing donations from the mosque, I felt I knew her inside and out and could imagine that she was capable of doing something hidden and evil. My stomach twisted into a tight knot. His hunch was the truth. Sure, he was a smug and annoying brat. Yes, he was bringing me a rumor, a single data point about missing money, something Mr. Goodman would have brushed away if I had told him that this needed to be investigated. But I knew things Mr. Goodman didn't. Latif's allegation concerned Asma—do-gooder Asma, whom the aunties adore because she's so hip and young but still religious. Do-gooder Asma, who visits schools to recruit Muslim girls to join the mosque while saying she's a feminist but never complaining that the women's section of the mosque looks like shit or that her husband has double standards for girls. And she claims to give one-fortieth of her salary to charity every year, but she drives around in a bright-blue Porsche.

That didn't mean I agreed with Latif's plan of action for what we were calling Operation X. Especially when Latif told me that the scandal involved not only my best friend's heroine but someone way more powerful. A week after Latif barged into the FOIA workshop, he found me in the newsroom and spilled some more tea.

"I think I can trust you."

"Obviously."

"But you might not believe this."

Mr. Goodman looked up from his phone to see what we were talking about. "Who are you? Noor, are you working on the water fountain story?"

"Yes!" we replied in unison. I glared at Latif. "This is a new volunteer, Mr. Goodman."

Latif smiled the fakest smile I had ever seen. "You'll never guess who's met up with Asma twice this past week."

I shrugged.

"Humairah Hilal."

"I know that name. Wait. The congresswoman? No way."

"Yes way."

"They meet up? For what? Where?"

"At the mosque! Isn't that crazy that a *congresswoman* is coming to the mosque so much, Noor?"

"Well, hold on. She *is* Muslim. Isn't that like saying it's weird that an alcoholic goes to a bar?"

"You really need to work on your analogies. Or metaphors, or similes, whatever. Anyway, Humairah Hilal isn't a real Muslim. She just acts Muslim to get our votes. That's what the aunties at the mosque say."

"Well, there you have it. That's why she came to the mosque twice this week. Because there's an election coming . . . umm, no. Wait." I search the date on my phone. "She's good for another year. The election isn't till next November. But, Mr. Haram Police, *you* don't get to decide who's Muslim and who's not. Neither do the mosque aunties. I hate that shit about you mosque people."

Latif huffed. "If she's a real Muslim, then why isn't she going to the prayer room when she comes to RICC? And why not meet with the imam? You know what she does after she parks her car? She runs straight up to Asma's office and stays in there for, like, twenty minutes."

"Asma? What would she want with . . . ? Bro, are you *spying* on them?"

"No. Yes. Sort of."

"What do you mean?!" I grabbed Latif's arm and yanked him out to the corridor. "Getting a snack!" I yelled at Mr. Goodman as we walked out of the classroom into the chaos of the hallway. He was absorbed in scrolling on his phone anyway.

Latif confessed it all. He had been so convinced that Humairah Hilal—Texas's first and only Muslim congresswoman—was in cahoots with donation-stealing Asma that he had set up a temporary Wi-Fi router in the mosque, ready for the congresswoman's next visit. When she returned on a Sunday morning, he patiently waited for HH's cell phone to connect to the fraudulent Wi-Fi so that he could hack it and permanently connect to her geolocation services.

"So, you know where she is? Right now?"

"Right now . . . she's at . . . Pink Box Donuts." He pinched his fingers and pulled them apart on his phone screen. A blue dot hovered over a strip mall in Arlington. I smacked his phone away so that no one passing us in the hallway would see the criminal activity.

"That's so fucking illegal!"

"It's only accurate to one hundred feet!"

"She might be in the CVS! It's an invasion of privacy!"

"Sometimes it freezes!"

"Who taught you all of this?"

"YouTube. Anyway, weren't you the one teaching us how to investigate private records a few days ago?"

"A FOIA request isn't an illegal invasion of privacy, you num-skull. You need to block that YouTube channel."

"I was only watching it to find ways to locate our missing money. I learned a lot. Her location ain't the only thing I can see." Latif tucked his phone into a pocket and whispered into my ear. "I can read her texts." I put my hand over my mouth.

"Only outgoing texts! Only outgoing texts! And I can't see what number she's texting them to. So don't freak out." He hopped on his tiptoes. I covered my face with both hands.

"You're so dead if anyone finds out."

"You mean, we're so dead. Anyway, no one will find out. And why do you seem more bothered about what I'm doing than what they're doing?" He inched away from me and looked over my head down the hallway. "What I'm doing is justified. What Asma and HH are up to is illegal."

Besides eating donuts, we knew little about what HH was up to. But we did know that she planned to meet someone, maybe Asma, at a strip mall in Plano this very afternoon. Latif is already there, at the far end of a parking lot behind some bougie cheese shop. He's been texting me nonstop for the past ten minutes. Where are you? HH just pulled up! What's your ETA??!! HH is talking to someone on her phone. She's in her car! You'll have to walk into Betty's Cheese Shop and ask to exit through the back door. Sneak into my car. I have the perfect spot. Where are you?!?!?!

I'm lying on my belly opposite Laylah, who is furiously swiping her phone screen and frowning and calling up clinics to find out if they're open. I pretend I have a lunch date with Sara and call an Uber so that my car isn't spotted anywhere near the stakeout.

The Uber drops me outside the CrossFit, but I walk into the cheese shop Latif mentioned. Here, I text him, as a gray-haired White lady emerges from behind the counter and shoves a cracker loaded with red-flecked cheese toward my face. "It was made in Waco!" she says, smiling and rubbing her hands down her apron. I toss the whole cracker into my mouth and start to chew. "It's ghost pepper cheddar. Very spicy," she says. "But you'll be able to handle it." I stop chewing to ask what she means by that, but I swallow the bland-as-paper cheese and ask for a favor instead.

"Can I use your back door?" I edge toward the counter while she looks me up and down. Betty, at least I think she's Betty, puts her hands on her hips. Before she can say no, I stride toward the back entrance and peek through the glass. Latif was right. Only HH is here, still sitting in her car at the other end of the parking lot. Neither of Asma's cars is here, not the flashy Porsche or the Subaru. I look for Latif's car and spot a blacked-out . . . *Wait, is that a Prius? A . . . matte-black Prius? With blacked-out windows? He's supposed to be incognito!!! Ugh. This child!*

I slip out the back door, crouch, and sort of crouch-walk over to the passenger side of Latif's highly conspicuous vehicle. Betty is standing behind the glass window peering out at me.

Latif opens the door from the inside. "What the fuck is this car, man?" I say, squeezing into the passenger seat.

"Shhh! Don't swear!"

He turns to the backseat, where an elderly lady in a tight head-scarf and black robe holds silver prayer beads midair. Her lips are parted as if my cursing interrupted her prayers.

"Sorry, Nani," he whispers. "Ye Amreekan lurkeyen buhot boree heh."

"Latif!" I hiss, through gritted teeth. "WTF?!"

"What?! My dad made me pick up my grandma from the hospital! What was I supposed to say? 'Sorry, Nani, I can't take you straight home because I have to spy on a congresswoman first'?"

"Are we spying on a congresswoman!?" an eager voice calls out from the back. Huddled in the corner, behind my seat, his nose smooshed against the fogged-up glass, is a young boy, just as lanky as Latif but probably no older than eleven. "I want to sit on that side," he says, pointing over the praying elder. "I want to spy on the congresswoman."

"That's my cousin Abid," Latif says, squeezing the steering wheel and staring straight ahead. The vein in his forehead bulges. "Had to bring him as well. He got kicked out of school this morning."

"What are we doing? Why do you keep looking at that car? Who are *you*? How long are we staying? Can I take a piss now?" says the kid. The old lady swats him across the head. "Sorry. I mean, use the toilet."

"I swear to God, Abid! No more questions until three! What did I tell you? Put your Beats back over your ears!"

My mouth is agape. I don't know what to say.

"You should say 'salaam' when you meet an elder," Latif whispers.

I turn around. "Assalamu alaikum, aunty."

The old lady mumbles something, and I look at Latif.

"She said you smell like cheese."

I wipe my mouth with the back of my hand, then cup my palm over my lips to smell my breath.

A car pulls into the lot. A white Camry bumping house music. Two gym bros emerge lugging bags over their shoulders. I can smell their sweat and cologne from inside the car. The smell might be a mix of Latif's and Abid's funk and body spray.

"Ugh," I whisper, sliding down in the passenger seat and crossing my arms. "I can't believe you brought your grandma and a child to a stakeout!" I hadn't thought to spell this out when we were planning the surveillance operation last night. "Latif, do not bring an elderly religious lady and an inquisitive eleven-year-old with a weak bladder who will spill all our secrets about Operation X," was not something I thought needed to be spelled out.

Latif grumbles under his breath.

"What is it?"

"What was I supposed to do? My nani had her hip replaced six months ago, and her appointment today ran really late," he whispers. "Doctors are really bad at time management."

I shake my head. "And this car, Latif. You told me to leave mine a mile away and you came here in *this*?"

"What are you going on about?! This car was made for spying!" He turns his head to stare at the congresswoman's shiny black Bronco. "Where do you think Asma is? The text we intercepted said one forty-five, right?"

"*You* intercepted," I muttered. "And we don't even know if she's meeting Asma. It could be anyone. This might all be a waste of time."

Abid bounces in the backseat. "How do you spy on text messages? Can I look at your phone? Can you see what I'm texting right now?" He has one hand on the clunky headphones he has lifted away from his right ear.

"Shut it, Abid!" we say in unison.

"You better not be texting anybody!" Latif yells, trying to yank the phone out of Abid's hands. The kid recoils into the backseat and clutches his phone for dear life.

The old lady recites her prayers louder. "Bismillah. Subhanallah. Astaghfirullah," she says, shaking her head and passing the beads of a turquoise tasbeeh between her fingers.

"Does she go to the mosque?" I ask Latif.

"Practically lives there. Like your bestie. Have you told her about . . . this?" Latif waves an arm around the car. His nani pats him on the shoulder and says something softly. "She's asking if you go to RICC. Shall I tell her you're a lesbian heathen?"

"Don't say that! Anyway, I'm not a lesbian. I'm pan."

I pull down the mirror and look back at the praying lady. She looks familiar, like she could be the aunty from back in the day when RICC was my happy place, before it became Laylah's second home. Somebody's grandma would send coffee-flavored milk-shakes for all the girls with this chick from Arlington, and we'd be high on caffeine and sugar in the basement for the next two hours.

"Tell her I used to go to the mosque *all* the time." I stifle the smile starting to spread across my face.

"I need to go to the toilet," Abid says, kicking the back of my seat. "Now."

I glare at Latif. We could be here for hours depending on how this unfolds.

But then . . . "Look!" I hiss. "That's Asma's Porsche!" Right on time, a blue SUV pulls up and parks next to the congresswoman's truck. I spot a HOOK 'EM University of Texas Longhorns bumper sticker on the back.

"This is it," I whisper. Nani and Abid shuffle over to the left side of the car and practically glue their faces to the window. The old lady smacks Abid, who has pulled his headphones down to his neck and is leaning over her to get closer to the window. "Oi! Watch her hip!" Latif yells.

"Shhhh! Everyone, be quiet."

Asma gets out of her car first and leans against the driver's-side door. Damn, I can't see her if she stays there. HH hops out and walks to the front of her truck. Asma joins her, and the pair lean their butts against the hood of the Bronco and talk as if they're old pals meeting up for a midday chat, not a congresswoman and a religious leader plotting to spend all the money they're stealing. We take photos manically.

"Not you!" Latif yells at Abid. "What are you taking photos for?"

"Ugh. I wish we could hear what they're saying."

"Yeah, but this is evidence that they're up to *something*," says Latif. "Something they're trying to keep secret."

Asma looks around more than HH. Their heads nod, shoulders shrug. Then a handshake and an awkward sideways hug. And just like that, the drama is over. The congresswoman gets back into her truck and drives away. She has the same Texas Longhorns bumper sticker as Asma.

"That lasted a minute. A whole fucking minute." I lean forward and touch my forehead to the glove compartment. "Sorry, Nani."

"Ho-lee shit." Latif taps my shoulder frantically.

No sooner has the congresswoman slipped out of the parking lot than a black Cadillac with blacked-out windows pulls into the spot on the other side of Asma's car.

"Who is *that*?" I say, reaching over Latif to get a better look.

"That car is badass," he says.

No one gets out of the car. A window is lowered, a thick package wrapped in brown paper pokes out at the end of a mysterious arm, and Asma, who had been standing by her driver's-side door, is beckoned over to collect it.

"Pictures! Take pictures!" I yell. And both Abid and Latif snap away while I zoom in with my phone camera, hit record, and squint at the slightly blurry screen to see what on earth is going on. Asma walks toward the extended arm and bends over to look into the car. For about twenty seconds there is chatter through the open window but no grabbing of the package. Then, as Asma goes to take it, the arm retracts, almost disappearing the package back inside the car.

"What the . . . ?" I say, barely remembering that there is a praying elder in the backseat.

Asma is shaking her head and a few seconds later the hand emerges again. Asma takes the package with both hands, looks around, pulls it to her chest, and hurries around to the driver's side of her car. The blacked-out Cadillac backs out the same way it came in. Asma watches it drive away.

"Did you get the license plate?" I say to Latif.

"*O-D-3 6-L-W*!" Abid shouts.

And in the few seconds it takes for me to write it down in my notebook, Asma's Porsche drives away.

"Do we follow them?"

"No. Let her go. We know where to find her, and we don't want anyone to see that we're onto her."

"She'll be at the RICC tonight acting like nothing is up," he says, shaking his head.

"I need to run this plate and connect some of these dots. Drop me around the corner."

Latif's nani pokes my shoulder. I turn around. "Kuch ghurbur hoh ruhee heh," she says, shaking her head and pointing the tasbeeh toward where Asma's car had been parked. "Woh larkee burah raaz chuppah ruhee heh."

"She said something fishy is going down," says Latif, turning to smile at his grandma. He looks at me with big eyes. "My nani's kinda psychic, you know. She has premonitions in her dreams and stuff. She said Asma is hiding a really big and really bad secret."

LAYLAH

MY GRANDMOTHER SMOTHERS me in kisses and squeezes my shoulders. "Nanima's being extra sweet because she needs your car, Laylah, betah," Mom says, sifting through poetry books scattered across the kitchen table. "I told her, of course you'll say yes."

"Whaaaaat?! I hate it when you make decisions for me! You know I need my car!"

"Laylah," Mom says sternly, in that tone that makes me feel four years old again and as if I've just taken a bite out of her most expensive lipstick and cut up the new curtains with a large pair of scissors. It's the tone that lets me know I am about to be in deep trouble if I utter another word. Maybe if I wrote a poem about not giving my things away, she would understand what it felt like.

"You're robbing me of my independence! Why can't she have *your* car?"

"Laylah! Bas! I'm teaching every day this week. You know that."

Adam leaves the kitchen and returns with a toy truck. He pokes it into Nanima's thigh, and she turns to smoosh his cheeks.

"Don't worry. I'll drop you at the mosque now and one of your religious friends can bring you back home," Nanima says cheerily. "My Love Bug will be in the shop for another week, and I can't keep Ubering around town. I have so many places I need to go."

"But there's a mosque fundraiser on Friday," I wail. "I'm responsible for picking up the banners from the printshop. And then tomorrow I have to shop for the ingredients and bring them to your house for bake night," I remind her.

"That's okay. I'll use your car to take you wherever you need to go and then I'll do what I need to do. Simple." Nanima smooshes my cheeks as if I'm seven.

Right when I desperately need to be able to jet at a moment's notice, they are robbing me of my autonomy and I can't say a thing. "Don't know why you drive that silly Volkswagen Beetle anyway," I mutter, heading toward the kitchen door. "It breaks down every month. And didn't you know that car was invented in Germany for Hitler?" I drop in a random historical fact.

"Laylah!" I can feel Mom's eyes piercing the back of my head with that icy glare. "Don't guilt-trip your grandmother with Nazi history. She's been through a lot."

"Been through a lot *how*? You *always* say that! What does it even mean?!"

"Laylah Parveen Khan!"

"Fine! It's fine!" I stomp upstairs, grab my laptop, planner, and mosque tote, and sit in the passenger seat of my own car. Nanima is busy chatting it up with Mom in the kitchen, taking her sweet time, forcing me to honk the horn.

"Areh! You can't beep at your own nani!" she yells, lifting the skirt of her baby-pink sari as she steps out the front door. "This is Dallas, not Delhi!"

But when she gets into my car, Nanima puts it into reverse and honks the horn twice, hooting and hollering at the same time. Mom covers her face with both hands and waves us off from the doorway.

My grandmother is a riot. Every day that she's lived in Dallas—she moved here before I was born—she has worn a sari. The brightest fuchsias are saved for Wednesday evenings when she packs her house full of guests and packs her guests full of sweet treats that she and I spend the afternoon baking. The other women often wear pink saris too, as if they're in a girl gang.

Our weekly ritual grounds me, even if it's got nothing to do with Major Career Goals. My nanima is fun and witty, and I love it when she makes us take a midbaking tea break to drink freshly brewed masala chai and devour whichever batch of the various goodies cycling in and out of the oven is ready for our taste test.

We pretend to be judges on the *Great British Baking Show*. "Excellent bake," Nanima says, in an English accent, tapping the browned bottom of the pastry with her nail while all ten of her gold bangles jingle.

"Perfect crumb," I add, sinking my teeth into a still-warm nankutai.

Nanima swears I get As in chemistry because she taught me how to carefully weigh bicarbonate of soda when I was only eight. She says I will make a great surgeon on account of the hand skills she taught me when she showed me how to cautiously knead dough so as to not overwork it, which breaks apart the gluten protein in the flour and makes the dough tough and hard, not soft and stretchy.

"Don't forget to pick up two bags of powdered cardamon from the Patels' shop tomorrow," Nanima says, zooming down the turnpike.

"How can I forget? You'll be dropping me at the shop after you pick me up from school. Remember?"

"Oh, yes." She laughs and turns up the radio. The news anchor switches from a story about a monkey that was stolen from the Dallas Zoo to a law that will devastate our lives. "Senate Bill 601 moves toward a vote next week. The bill proposes tougher sentencing for those who aid any person in the termination of a pregnancy, instituting minimum mandatory custodial sentences and introducing the death penalty, in some cases." I turn down the volume. Nanima turns it back up.

"So, what is this thing happening at your mosque center on Friday?" she says, when the newscast switches to an alert about rising egg prices.

"A fundraiser."

"They need money to convert people to your Islam?"

"*My* Islam? Nani, didn't you take shahadah and swear your belief in God too?"

"Not really." She shrugs. "It was decided for me when I was a baby and I just went along with it. But you know, my father was always a rebel, so he gave me this name because it's also a Punjabi Sikh name," she says. "Clever man. 'Parveen' means someone who is highly skilled. An expert."

"But you told me Parveen was a Persian name that means a cluster of stars!" My grandmother's stories are forever changing.

"Yes, yes," she says, flapping her hand. "Stars. Expert. It means all those things. But my point is, my beliefs were decided for me, without my consent."

"Well, it's different for me. No one in our family supports me being religious. But I don't care. I made this decision for myself." I cross my arms.

Nanima glances over at me with curious eyes, looks forward and smiles as if she's very pleased with the smooth tarmac on the road. "Nothing wrong with that," she says, still smiling. "Nothing stronger than a woman with conviction! And I'm sure they are doing wonderful things with the donations." She keeps one hand on the wheel and flexes the other, showing off the little bump of a bicep that pokes out from beneath her sari. She says years of kneading dough and whisking cake batters have made her super strong.

Nanima takes my hand from across my chest and squeezes it. "Anyway, religion is about more than just worship. It's about belonging to something bigger than you. And I'm proud of you for making your own decision, lalee." She calls me by the sweet nickname she has uttered for as long as I can remember. "Lalee" means "beloved." "You're a strong young woman."

I wince. If only she knew that I am crumbling on the inside like an underbaked cookie. I turn my head to look out the window, hoping she won't see the frown on my face.

Nanima breaks the silence. "Thank you for the car, lalee. Sharing is caring. I've got so much to do this week."

"It's fine. Here. Take this exit. And if you turn on this street, yes, the first one, you can drop me at the back. It's easier to get to the women's entrance that way."

"Ah, the famed women's entrance." Nanima sighs. "Did you know there's a Facebook account called Side Entrance that documents all these terrible, tiny side entrances and silly little spaces women are fobbed off within mosques around the world?"

It shouldn't amaze me that my grandmother is social-media savvy. I do in fact know about this account because she told me about Side Entrance back when it was on Tumblr.

"Gotta go. Love you. See you tomorrow," I say, hopping out of the car and blowing her a kiss. I almost bump into Asma dashing out of the infamous side entrance as I walk in.

"Oh. Hi," she says quietly. The whites of her eyes are tinged pink and she's not wearing her trademark Fenty MVP lipstick or her extra-white and extra-confident smile. "You're early for youth group."

"Yeah, I'm on my grandma's schedule. And I have to get stuff ready for the girls' speech-writing session." Asma looks me up and down, and I'm suddenly aware that my shoulders are rounded and that a few strands of hair have escaped my hijaab. I stand up straight and tuck the wayward hair.

"I have to grab some stuff," she says, looking past me. "Go get the cakes from the kitchen, put them on the stands, and put the stands on the tables in the girls' lounge. Please." I can already sense that something is wrong.

I find the cupcakes and stands in the kitchen and neatly arrange them in the peach-colored room where we hold youth group every Tuesday. When Asma barges into the girls' lounge ten minutes later, she slams cupboard doors, practically grunting with each fling, and even though the drawers on the new cabinets have that fancy soft-close feature, she still tries to bang them shut, then sighs when they roll to a slow and gentle close. She roots out a stack of yellow legal pads and notebooks tucked at the back of a cupboard and drops a tall pile of them onto the wobbly Ikea table, which sends my entire display of cupcakes, baked by some overworked aunty, flying cherry-frosting face down onto the peach-colored carpet. Globs of pinkish-brown buttercream flecked with bright red maraschino cherry halves trickle off the silver cupcake stand that someone has lovingly donated to the mosque and which now lies at a jaunty angle on the floor.

Asma slumps onto the wobbly plastic chair that accompanies the wobbly table and clutches the sides of her turban as if she's trying to squeeze her head. The carpet has only just been replaced after a yearlong battle in which we tirelessly fought for the increased representation of women and girls on the Richardson Islamic Cultural Center's Governance Committee. Instead, we've been granted a peach-and-white refurbishment of the women's areas, including a new industrial kitchen with not one but four restaurant-style stainless-steel ovens.

"I'll clean it." I crouch to pinch dollops of frosting and mounds of crumbling cupcakes off the carpet.

"Leave it, Laylah. Just give me a minute." Asma pinches the bridge of her nose, slides down the chair a few inches, and lets out a long sigh.

I walk with hands full of soggy cake to the kitchen, the largest of all the women's area spaces, which is conveniently loaded with mops, brooms, and all manner of cleaning supplies. I dump the mess from my hands into the trash and grab a pink cloth and a bottle of carpet cleaner, all the while wondering why I can't seem to make her happy. Asma has not been herself since November. Jokey, witty, and quick to pass down eyeshadow palettes she's no longer using, or pinching my cheeks and playacting as if she's one of the aunties, is how she used to be, how I'd known her to be ever since we met when I was in middle school and she was newly in charge of the center's youth outreach program. But something happened a few months back that made her grouchy and hot tempered. The recent decision to not allow women on the committee and to fob us off with carpets and more ovens only made things worse.

The aunties have been appreciating the four-oven kitchen in a way that Asma and I wished they wouldn't. "See, knew you'd love this stuff," Imam Khoury had said one Sunday morning as the aunties whisked and whipped and brewed and baked, the lights on every oven blinking with pride, the smell of browning butter and vanilla essence floating through the kitchen, along the corridor, and down the stairs to the grander first floor, which housed the men's communal areas. "Good investment this," he had said, pointing around the kitchen. Asma elbowed her husband in his side and pursed her lips.

"Get out of here, Habeeb." The imam rubbed his side. "We were fighting for an equal say about how this place is run. Not three extra ovens to fuel your prediabetes."

"It's not just ovens! It's carpets as well," he said. "And my sugar is fine now. The doctor said I can eat six cakes a day if I like."

I try not to smear the pink frosting deeper into the thick pile of the peachy carpet. "You're going to need the other spray bottle." Asma sighs, unpinching the bridge of her nose to peer down at me crouching among the pink and brown mess. There's no pleasing her these days. I'm either "doing too much" or "not using enough initiative." She loves to say, "I shouldn't have to tell you *everything*, Laylah. You need to figure things out for yourself. Don't you want to be a doctor someday?"

Asma leans her head back in the chair and stares up at the newly plastered ceiling. "My head is pounding," she says. "I can't seem to shake this headache."

"I can lead youth group. If you like?" I wish I hadn't ended the sentence on a question. *Ugh. I need to sound like I can take more initiative.* "I *will* lead youth group today," I say, sounding overly aggressive.

"Fine. Make sure you rehearse properly for the girls'

performance on Friday. It needs to be perfect. Lots of people will be here. Even our congresswoman." She gets up and slams the door behind her.

I have ten minutes before the girls' group will start piling into the room. Ten minutes to rescue my future. I pull out my to-do list and call Tito's Tacos. The line is dead. I call back Bella's Bundts, just in case. No answer. I call a clinic in New Mexico, two in Oklahoma, and one in Nebraska. They all answer, but no one has pills. By the time Sulayha walks in with Amina, my eyes are watering and I am ready to sob.

"What's up with you?" Sulayha says, pulling out a chair.

"Allergies."

The next forty-five minutes are a blur of me lying through my teeth about how everything is perfect and how there is nothing more urgent in my life than planning our five-minute presentation for Friday's fundraiser. "I'm soooo nervous," Amina says, turning her notebook toward me. Two pages are plastered in a blue scrawl, her script for a one-minute speech about the importance of listening to the voices of young Muslim women in Texas and protecting our right to practice our religion safely.

"You'll be so good. Talking nonstop is your superpower," says Sulayha. Everyone laughs.

"Not when there's a congresswoman in the audience!" Amina clutches her notepad and winces.

"Oh my God, did you see that Humairah Hilal was hanging out with Matthew McConaughey at the Texas Film Festival last week?" Zeba swoons.

"Yeah, and I heard she's friends with Beyoncé's mom and they go shopping together in Houston all the time."

"Ooh, maybe she'll bring Ms. Tina and Matthew McConaughey here on Friday!" says Amina, her nerves disappearing into a haze of celebrity fantasy. "And maybe he'll see my speech and put me in a film!"

"We could be the first hijaabi extras in a Matthew McConaughey movie! What color hijaab you gonna wear? I'm gonna wear my black one, to keep it classy, you know, but then I'm gonna wear the headband over it, the one with the crystals."

"Okay, calm down. No one from Hollywood is coming with the congresswoman on Friday."

"She's a sellout anyway," sighs Zeba.

"And, Amina, you'll do great. We've got your back." I force a smile, hoping to cheer her up, but the girls slump in their chairs and the energy dampens when I say a Hollywood star and Beyoncé's mom will not be walking into our mosque to drink chai and support a fundraiser.

"It's going to be great! I'll go first. Then Mona's going before you and Sulayha's speaking right after you. And you can even put your notes on the podium. The important thing is that your voice is heard," I say, adding more enthusiasm to my pep talk.

"Don't worry," Zeba whispers loudly to Amina. "I'll film your speech on Friday and put it on TikTok and tag Matthew McConaughey. And Beyoncé."

"Film me!" says Sulayha. "I'm going to tell them how they need to make a law to protect girls in hijaab from being harassed."

"Duh, that's already a law," Mona chimes in.

"Yeah, okay, but I mean like a law-law. A proper law. One that actually does something. And I'm going to tell the congresswoman that she needs to give us more money so we can have a proper library, not that tiny room, and a bigger girl's bathroom with a full-length mirror."

"Please don't mention bathrooms," I say.

Sulayha shrugs.

"Yeah, we need *two* full-length mirrors and some extra hijaab pins because I always lose mine when I take it off to do wudhu," says Amina.

"Okay, so everyone listen. Big question." Zeba clears her throat. "Who do you think would look prettier in hijaab: Beyoncé or Rihanna?" Zeba turns her phone screen to show edited photos of the singers in headscarves styled in the Emirati fashion.

"Let's take a vote!" Mona yells.

I slip out of the room to check my phone, in case any of the clinics have returned my calls. I pace the hallway between the girls' lounge and Asma's office. All my apps show zero messages. My voicemail box is empty.

"It's those fucking hormones! I can't stand you like this!" I freeze. Asma's husband's voice trickles out from beneath the door of her office. There is no one in the hallway but me, no one on this floor except for the girls in the lounge and Asma in her office.

"I hope you get pregnant ASAP because those shots are driving you loopy. How the hell could you do something so stupid?"

Pregnant? Shots? But isn't IVF illegal?

"How else am I supposed to get the meds, Habeeb? You think because Baba's a pharmacist that we can just concoct this stuff in the kitchen? I have to get them somewhere!"

"And jeopardize my whole organization?"

"*Your* organization?"

"I could lose everything because of this."

"Quite the opposite. If you calmed down, you would understand the situation."

"Oh, I understand the situation, Asma. You made an executive decision, on your own, and it's a stupid one. Idiotic, even for you."

I hear shuffling and sniffing. "Okay, okay, spell it out. Look, okay, calm . . . calm down! It's fine, it's fine. Yes, yes. I want us to have a family as well."

More sobbing.

I tiptoe toward the office, inching carefully along the hallway until I can hear the crying clearly. Asma speaks between sobs. "It wasn't as bad as last time. It was a doctor in Austin." Her voice quiets so that I can't make out the name she mentions. ". . . sent me, and she told me to tell the doctor that—"

"I told you never to speak to her. She's putting all of us in danger."

"I had to! You think it's going to happen by magic!?"

My phone vibrates in my hand. It's Bella's Bundts! I swipe right to answer and run down the hallway and into the empty kitchen before I speak breathlessly into the phone.

"Hello?"

"Hello!" A deep voice bellows through the phone. The woman

on the other end clears her throat. "Okay, you're there. Good. Good that you called and left that message. Change of plans and everything. We ended up in Utopia and now we're headed your way."

"Really?"

"And good news. We've got the pills. Meet us in Arlington tomorrow morning. I'll text the coordinates and exact time in the next hour. Okay? Hello? You still there, hun?"

My cheeks are wet and my throat is blocked by a lump bigger than a cupcake stuffed with maraschino cherries.

"Yes," I whimper.

"Okay, good. So look out for the message. Next hour. Our systems will go dead after that until the morning. Be sure to leave your phone at home. Got that? Phone at home. Okay? Good. We'll see you bright and early." *Click.*

I steady myself against the gigantic oven, hold on to the thick steel handle, and try to stay standing. But the weight that rolls off my shoulders and crashes onto the kitchen floor turns my thighs to pudding. I sink to the ground, sit cross-legged on the floor, press my back against the cold oven, and give thanks. *Things always go to plan as long as you have a plan.* Tears drip down my cheeks. I just knew I could make this go away. Alhamdulillah. Everything is going to be okay.

STEP 5

EXPECT THE UNEXPECTED

Peaceful Protester Blinded, Children Injured by Police

By Noor Awad

DALLAS—An elderly woman and two children were seriously injured during a peaceful protest against new plans to criminalize the possession of all hormone medications in Texas, including drugs used for the treatment of menopause and some types of cancers. The bill was announced just fifteen weeks after hormonal birth control was banned. A crowd of more than one hundred protesters gathered outside Dallas City Hall early Sunday evening. Among them, women in their seventies and eighties, and younger women with children. One protester, Elaine Matthews, 69, of Denton, was permanently blinded in the left eye with a rubber bullet shot by police using military-grade weapons, which were aimed at protesters and journalists. Matthews, a Black woman, was taken to Parkland Hospital for emergency surgery. The children, ages 6 and 11, received treatment for serious burns, likely a result of tear gas canisters thrown into the crowd by officers, some of which landed directly on the crowd. New Dallas Police Chief, Priti Malhotra, the department's first South Asian femme leader, said the use of force and "nonlethal" weapons became justified when a small group of protesters, including half a dozen women in their seventies, attempted to enter City Hall. Organizers of the event, affiliated with the group Citizens for Health Justice, said protesters were attempting to enter the lobby to seek shelter from police, who had begun throwing tear gas canisters into a peaceful crowd. "We needed to get the elderly women and kids away from the tear gas," said Swati Patel, an organizer with Citizens for Health Justice. "That's why we went in the building. The kids were choking and gasping for air, but then the police started to shoot." Human rights organizations across the world have lambasted the violent response to such gatherings, saying that if similar abuses of power by militarized police forces occurred elsewhere in the world, the United States would intervene to protect civil liberties. Texas lawmakers and law enforcement officials continue to defend the use of deadly force by Dallas PD against elderly women and children.

-30-

NOOR

"THE PROBLEM WITH that story is that every single one of your biases was coming through. As usual. That's why it's still causing us so many problems. You should never have published it without my permission. I've told you over and over again that you must . . ."

Mr. Goodman loves to hover over my left shoulder, editing as he reads, blah-blah-ing as his coffee breath clouds my judgment. I should back my chair into his groin and storm off, but apparently that's unprofessional behavior and he won't write a recommendation letter for my newsroom internship if I do it again.

"Seriously, Noor." [Here he goes.] "Don't let your lack of journalistic objectivity get in the way of your damned good reporting chops. I gave you major credit for getting to that protest last month before even the *News* sent its reporters. I saw your Snapchats from the riot at five o'clock, when the rioters were only just arriving. How did you know they—"

"'Riot' is a racialized term, Mr. Goodman. Would you call them rioters if the crowd had been mostly White women? See, this is *your* problem. You don't even realize that your colonizer mind can't see how . . ." [DEEP BREATH. Shut your mouth, Noor.]

The problem with your editing skills is that your man bun is tied so tightly that it's starving your brain of the oxygen needed to separate your biases from your ability to edit my story, is what I want to say. But instead, what I say, very politely, with a sweet smile and after unclenching my shoulders, is: "Mr. Goodman. That story is five weeks old. Why are we going over it again? And since you want to keep going over it, please show me where in this story you see anything but carefully reported facts."

I can't believe this dude is sighing dramatically and actually leaning into the screen to point things out! "You almost got us shut down, Noor. That's why we're going over the story *yet again*. If you can't prove to me that you understand what you did wrong by reporting with such bias and hitting publish without my permission, then I can't, in all honesty, let you continue working for the school newspaper. Now then, let's start here with your need to include the race of the rioter, I mean protester, who was shot, as if that's relevant."

"She was sixty-nine! They blinded her! So you want to know her age but not her race when you know damned well race has everything to do with what's happening?!"

"This is not a race story, Noor! Race doesn't have to be in every single graf that you write. Calm down. And what is 'femme'? Like a femme fatale? You can't say the police chief is a femme fatale! And look at this. Your use of quotation marks around 'nonlethal weapons.' Then you say the police fired at journalists, which is ludicrous. Then there's this part about tear gas exploding directly on people. That's not what Channel 11 reported. Their reporters said that police were attacked. . . ."

"Channel 11 is a Blue Lives Matter news organization that routinely misreports police scandals and unethical practices in DPD. I do not recommend it as your news source for issues related to law enforcement in Dallas. But you're a journalism teacher, so you already know that."

I take a sip of my now-cold coffee and swish it around my mouth, a failing attempt at keeping my tongue busy. Mr. Goodman sighs and smooths the frizzy edges of his slicked-back hair. Maybe he knows his man bun is dangerously tight.

"Look, Mr. Goodman. The reason I got there before other reporters and was keen to publish is because I needed people to see that major news orgs were sitting out this story. It's not an accident that they rarely send their people to cover these peaceful protests that turn ugly because of the police. They didn't even bother to cover that town hall in Vickery Meadow last week, where that one mom got four thousand signatures demanding an investigation to find out where that sleazy mattress-salesman-turned-antiabortion-law-funder Norm Miller really gets his money. They didn't even cover that other protest outside City

Hall last month that ended up a complete shit show. They're trying to shut us down because we're making the so-called real news orgs look like the scammers that they are. It's like all the editors in town are either asleep or on Miller's side. Like they just wanna let him fund these fifteenth-century bills to outlaw twenty-first-century medicines." [Ooh, that's a good line. I should write that down to put in a story.]

"If you don't care about yet another school newspaper getting shut down because of its abortion coverage—which, I really wish you did care, Noor. I know you heard about the executive editor of the *Austin High School Tribune* losing his job and his teacher's pension because of that story they ran . . ."

"Don't fall for their scare tactics, Mr. Goodman."

". . . then you should at least give a damn about your *own* career. You could have a bright future ahead of you if you just calm down and stay neutral. No editor in this city wants a reporter who's difficult to work with. When Arlo Malveira calls to ask me if this is the year you're finally ready for a summer internship in his newsroom, what he's really asking is, 'Can this girl get the job done without causing a scene or winding up in prison? Can she report the news without becoming the news?' And I really don't know what to tell him, Noor. That mess from last summer got in the way of what could have been your second internship and a bunch of clips that you really need for your applications. Then *this* mess happens. Nobody wants a reporter who ends up part of the story or gets the paper shut down."

"Whoa, whoa, whoa! Nowhere am I in this story!"

"You are jumping up and down and flapping your arms between every single line in this story."

"Flapping? Like a chicken? Never mind. Listen, I turned up. I took photos. I even made a reel and posted a TikTok. I reported the facts. I can literally show you that the police fired directly at peaceful protesters and even toward me. Look at my TikTok! I've even got video of one of those silver canister things hitting a woman's arm, and she wasn't doing anything but holding up a sign."

I grab my phone out of my satchel to show Mr. Goodman that I have the receipts, but he's reaching for his bag like it's time to leave. It's only 4:45 p.m.! What happened to his commitment to reporting the facts and working the twenty-four-hour news cycle that he's always going on about? He seems to forget that *student* journalists have ousted university presidents and uncovered major scandals.

"I have to go. But you'll do well to keep in mind that a decent journalist reports both sides. Stop making everything about race. You have to learn to interrogate your own biases, be objective, and get past your judgments of the police."

"The police in riot gear with military weapons who blinded a sixty-nine-year-old woman? Those police?"

"We don't know if she's permanently blind yet," he says, opening the door. He stops, his hand still on the handle, and turns back to look at me. "I don't want to do this, but you're forcing my hand. I'm going to have to take you off this beat. Run some stories on the youth center in South Dallas. The one that's about to be bulldozed. I'll find someone else to cover the new repro laws."

"Not the rec center, Mr. Goodman!" I stand and pretend to faint back into my chair, pressing the back of my hand against my forehead like I'm one of the Bollywood actresses in the movies that Laylah loves to watch. "The rec center! Wow, the biggest story of my LIFE, Mr. Goodman! Thank you for the honor and opportunity to change the world and speak truth to power by reporting on the rec center while the state is literally murdering pregnant people using your taxes. Why, thank you, sir!"

I glance up at him from behind my hand, frozen in my dramatic *I am fainting* pose, but Mr. Goodman has put his pretentious sunglasses on so I can't see how far his eyes have rolled back into his head.

He sighs, again. "Calm down, get serious, then we can talk. See you at eight a.m."

"Bothsidesism is gonna be the death of us!" I yell, as he closes the door to our office-cum-newsroom. "Or at least the death of *me*," I mutter.

Man, if that dude was alive during that Watergate scandal that he loves to teach us about, his bothsidesism-loving ass would have let that lying, cheating President Nixon stay in power. That is not the kind of ass-kissing journalist I plan to be.

When I'm sure he's halfway down the corridor, I take out my notebook and run the plate of the mysterious Cadillac and wait for the database to spit out the results. *O-D-3 6-L-W. Come on. Come on. Come on. Show me what you've got.* The car is registered to a Mandy Louise Hunsinger in Abilene. I do a quick search on Mandy. Registered nurse. Currently works at UT Southwestern, which means she most likely lives in the Dallas area. Which means the address she gave the DMV is incorrect. No big deal. People forget to update their details all the time. I find Mandy's Instagram account. MandyLouRN. Yoga pics. A bulldog called Bernie. Lotus pose in Kessler Park. Cute bikini pics from a girls' trip to the Four Seasons in Cabo. That's when I see him. Lurking in the back of a photo behind Mandy and three equally red-faced blondes in sparkly minidresses. Standing behind the women is a face familiar to every Texan. I grew up with that smug smile all over my television screen on Saturday mornings.

Norm Miller's mustache and his greasy little goatee interrupted my cartoons every ten minutes with promises of "Catch the Best Sleep of Your Liiiiiiife!" While I slurped Cap'n Crunch and waited for the cartoons to return, Norm swung a lasso around a mattress and jabbed the air with a meaty finger. He used to point to his first store in a strip mall in Fort Worth in those commercials. That single business quickly ballooned into a chain of stores that spread across the state and turned into a symbol of Texas as sacred as Blue Bell ice cream and Dr Pepper. There are Norm's Mattress Stores all over the state, from Amarillo to McAllen, Texarkana to Juarez. He nearly caught a case a few years back when there were allegations that the mattress stores were really a front for money laundering. I mean, how many mattress stores does Texas need? But Norm has walked out of court with a smile and jabbing that meaty finger in the air every time new allegations were thrown at him. He's transformed himself into an icon of Texan success— and a multimillionaire. No one could miss that face, even blurry and in the back of an Instagram post.

I scroll through more pictures from what seems to be a bachelorette party in Cabo, but I don't see Norm. Maybe he was just photobombing that one pic. I scroll and scroll. He probably has no connection to a nurse named Mandy, whose blacked-out car is registered in Abilene but happened to pull up next to Asma's car with a package in a parking lot less than a minute after the congresswoman had driven away. Maybe the photobomb was just a random coincidence.

I want to stop scrolling. I want to see if Sara's finished jazz class and is ready for something to eat. But last week, in social studies, when we were arguing about the small earthquake that rattled the school that morning and if it was caused by fracking or something else, Ms. Halls told us about a problem-solving rule called Occam's Law. The rule says that the best explanation for a problem is the simplest one. "Say you hear the sound of hooves clopping along the road outside of school," Ms. Halls had said. "Clop, clop, clop." She added sound effects as she curled her hands into hooves. "What does that mean? Well, that could mean there's a camel outside, or a gnu, or maybe a mountain goat."

"Or a zebra!" shouted Sian from the back row.

"Could be. But since we're in the middle of Dallas, do you really think there's a camel, a zebra, a gnu, or a mountain goat running along the road?"

"Yeah! This place is a circus!" Sian shouted.

"Well, Occam's Law says that we should take the most obvious explanation as the one that's most likely to be true. So, yes, you can consider all the options—maybe there really is a zebra outside. . . . I mean, someone did just steal a monkey from the zoo—but the sound of hooves most likely means there's a what outside?"

Horse, horse, horse, I mutter, scrolling Mandy's Instagram page on my laptop. Norm's face in the background of one of Mandy's posts might be a coincidence, but Occam's Law would say that . . . *Bingo!*

It isn't Norm's face with its oily goatee or that stringy mustache that I spot. It's that meaty sausage finger. I would recognize that lump of flesh anywhere. "When two hearts beat as one," Mandy has written beneath the picture of her hand next to Norm's, their fingers curved and touching to make a heart shape beneath a setting sun. *Scroll.* "Special moments with that special some-one. What life is all about," reads the caption beneath another photo of their hands. This time their hands are resting on a white tablecloth scattered with red rose petals. Not only do I recognize Norm's finger in the photo, but that same finger that used to jab the sky now grazes the part of Mandy's hand, right at the base of her thumb, that is tattooed with PROVERBS 31:25 in black ink. "And she laughs without fear of the future," I say out loud, reading the verse from a Google search.

Clearly someone's not afraid of the future if they're chilling on a beach in Cabo, enjoying sunsets and fancy dinners with the second richest man in Texas . . . who happens to be a married father of four. But why was Mandy's car used to transport a mys-terious package to Asma? Was one of Norm's cronies trying to avoid a car registered to Norm's business being flagged? Or was

Mandy driving the car that day and doing Norm's dirty work?
Is she involved in all of this? And does she really think she's slick
putting Norm's hands in her IG pics?

"Boo!" Hands grab the tops of my shoulders and I let out a yelp.

"Damn, Noor! It's just me. Why are you so tense? Your muscles
are like concrete!"

I slam the laptop shut and turn to look at Sara's glowing face.
Her cheeks are rosy. Her brow glistens. She's fresh out of jazz class.
We were supposed to meet at the front entrance. I didn't realize
that it was already ten minutes past the hour.

"I waited for you."

"I'm sorry. I got busy."

"Yeah, busy scrolling IG. Who you stalking?"

"No one."

"Didn't look like no one."

"I . . . I can't say anything."

"Another blonde caught your eye?"

I pull her onto my lap. Her gym bag wedges between our bodies awkwardly.

"Not at all. You know I only have eyes for you."

"Isn't that exactly what you said to Jessica last year when you
cheated on her?"

"It wasn't cheating! Don't believe all the rumors about me. It
was a complicated situationship."

"Someone said y'all were in an entanglement."

"Ugh. Something like that. Seriously, people talk too much."

"Mmm-hmm. So, tell me. Who was the blonde?"

"I really can't say. It's related to an investigation I'm doing."

"Ooh, I love a woman of mystery." Her soft fingers brush away the hair falling across my face. She leans in. We're not supposed to have our first kiss like this. I had planned it all in my head. First, dinner at a new phở restaurant in Oak Cliff, then an evening walk through the park near the Trinity Bridge to watch the city lights shimmering in the background. That's where this was supposed to happen. Not in my newsroom, where the smell of Mr. Goodman's coffee breath still lingers.

Sara leans in another inch. I bite my bottom lip and invite her to mess up my plans. She presses her lips to mine and we float all the way to the Four Seasons in Cabo.

LAYLAH

DON'T TEXT YOUR EX. *Don't text your ex. Don't text your ex.*
But what if your ex doesn't yet know he's your ex? What if he was
never really your man in the first place? Not from your point of
view, anyway. Then can you . . . ? Never mind. *Don't text your ex.*
Don't text your ex. Don't text your ex.

I write this mantra in my Notes app to stop myself from reply-
ing to JJ. I shouldn't even have my phone with me. Bella said twice
to leave it at home, but since my car was donated to my grandmother for the week, I have no choice but to call an Uber. Bella's
Bundts is still twenty-four minutes away, and I need to get JJ off
my back in the next minute so I can turn it off. He's "worried" and
"confused," he says. Which makes sense because I've been deleting his texts without reading them. But this one, the one flashing
across my screen right now, mentions Noor. *Have they been talking*

about me? I click. I'm gonna reach out to Noor . . . just to see if you're okay. A blue heart emoji vibrates on the screen (blue, like the skirt I wore the day we . . .).

The driver speaks loudly into his phone in a dialect of Arabic that I cannot understand one bit, not even after all these years of hanging around Asma. A notification pings on my phone. A text from *Do NOT Text Him Back!* This one contains the word "Friday." I have to click on it, too. Or Friday? I could come to your fundraiser event, habibi?

Don't text your ex. Don't text your ex. Don't text your . . . It's HabibTi, I respond, almost without thinking. With a T. If you're speaking to a woman. Ugh, he got me. I haven't even figured out a way to stop him from talking to Noor or coming to the mosque. Instead, I'm unable to stop myself from correcting his English spelling of the Arabic word for "lover"—even though my phone should have been off two minutes ago.

Oh, hey, habibti! he texts back in an instant. Then another: I know you're busy. So . . . see you Friday? Hayati. I freeze. *Shit. How do I keep him away from the mosque that day?* Mom will be there and she adores JJ. I would hate for him to tell her that I've been avoiding him. We merge onto the highway while I compose a text. No, Friday's too busy. And don't text Noor. . . . She's got a lot on right now. But I don't hit send, not yet. Three dots appear on the screen. I wait for his response. Maybe he'll realize that he's being pushy. Maybe he'll back off and say he won't come on Friday and he won't talk to Mom or Noor. My finger hovers over the send button as I drift into a memory of JJ repeating a Rumi poem about flowers, line after line, as he tried to memorize the verses.

Our first date began at noon in a coffee shop but turned into an almost daylong affair. It was the week before Christmas, the stores were in full winter-wonderland mode, and I had embellished a pearly white hijaab with a fluffy headband, even though Dallas was sixty degrees and sunny.

"I do not need glasses!" JJ insisted as he squinted at the menu of the hipster coffee shop in the Bishop Arts District. Black-framed glasses would look gorgeous on him. I imagined sliding a pair over his nose so he could fully earn the secret nickname I had given him. "*That* is the definition of chic *and* geek," I had said to Hanna as we watched him from a distance back in September. "But a super-sexy chic-geek." That day I had circled the outline of his stocky frame, from the broad shoulders to the thick binder of notes gripped in his hands, to the loosely laced OG Jordans, with my pencil. Hanna giggled and swatted my pencil down when JJ looked over.

Now we were peering at each other over the tops of overly complicated coffee menus. "They have banana milk?" JJ said, screwing up his nose. "Do bananas make milk? For real, how would you milk a banana?" He furrowed his brow, and I swallowed a laugh because I was playing it cool and sophisticated and definitely not about to wrap my hands around an imaginary banana to show him how I would squeeze it.

By the time we had downed our first round of banana-milk mochas, I was throwing my head back and laughing so hard that my stomach hurt and my mascara threatened to run down my cheeks. I blotted the tears with a napkin.

"Stop making me laugh!"

"Fine. You want me to get serious?"

"Actually, no. I take that back. Keep making me laugh."

"Did you know—" He paused.

"Go on."

"I just need to make sure you're ready for me to hit you, the future Dr. Khan, with a heavily scientific fact."

"Ready."

"Okay. Did you know that the stuff in your tears changes depending on why you're crying?"

"Stuff in your tears? Do you mean the chemical composition?" JJ flopped his head toward the table as he laughed.

"Sure. Like the ingredients of the tears, is what I'm trying to say."

I bit my lip to stop from smiling, but I could see that JJ was distracted. He fixated on my bottom lip.

"So, you were saying?"

"Was I . . . ? Oh, yeah! So if we took the tears that were running down your face just now, they'd have salt and stuff in them. But if you were crying because you liked me so much and you were so emotional about how much you were into me, those tears would have more protein in them."

"I like how this science lesson has strayed into me liking you territory."

"Yeah, you like that?" JJ smiled and lifted the dreads away from his forehead. A golden beam of sunlight seemed to be aimed directly at our booth. The light bounced off the table and danced on his left cheek.

"Did you say 'protein'?"

"Oh, yes, back to my science lesson. And this is the dope part. Your tears, the 'I'm so into JJ' tears, would contain more protein, and that makes them heavier and that means they'll fall down your face more slowly than laughing tears or cutting-onion tears. And because they fall down your face slower, it means someone— me—is more likely to see those tears and give you a hug."

"That's so amazing how the body knows that—"

"Can I get a hug?"

He put both his palms on the table as if he was getting ready to lift himself out of the other side of the booth.

"I . . . um . . . I . . ." *What happened to being slick and in control, Laylah?! You're getting played by a guy who obviously planned to make you laugh and then hit you with a science story about tears and protein just so he could get a hug.*

It *was* very slick though.

"Sure," I said, looking away and trying my best to act nonchalant. JJ walked over to my side, slid onto my leather-covered bench, and turned to face me.

"Kinda tight for a hug," I said. There was barely a centimeter between his bulging right bicep and the table. He smiled a childish kind of smile and opened his arms as best he could.

"Fine." My right arm was wedged against the back of the booth so I slipped my left arm over JJ's shoulder and leaned in for a quick . . . *Damn, is his chest made of memory foam?* JJ pulled me in for a tight squeeze. My face filled with vanilla-scented dreadlocks and golden sunshine.

The Uber trundles over a pothole, and I snap out of the memory, my finger still hovering over the send button.

"Miss? This is it? This is your drop-off?" The driver looks around at the barren parking lot, not noticing the tarp flapping in the distance. *Shit.* I forgot to turn off my phone twenty minutes ago! And what the fuck was I thinking bringing the Uber this close to the truck. I was supposed to drop the pin half a mile away and walk the last ten minutes. I drop my phone in my lap and press my palms against the side of my head. *What is wrong with my brain?*

I want to be sick. "Yes. This is it." I crack open the door, look back at the driver, and watch as his head turns in the direction of the tarp, seemingly in slow motion.

"Something is under there?" he mutters. "Is that a . . . truck?" He turns back to look at me and we lock eyes. "Where exactly are you going, miss?" He waits for an answer. "This area looks no good for a girl like you."

I step out of the car so fast that I trip over my own feet and land with my palms on the concrete. Tiny rocks dig into my hands. I should have told him this was wrong, that the GPS had led us astray in the derelict part of Arlington, that we should turn around and hurry back to some other place with people and coffee shops and traffic. Instead, I pick myself up off the ground, slam the door shut, and mouth through the window that he should drive away.

STEP 6

ALL YOUR SKINFOLK
AIN'T YOUR KINFOLK

 Anonymous Armadillo
at 05:26

Need to reference that this was first said by the writer Zora Neale Hurston and say it's a phrase that comes from Black American English.

NOOR

THE BACK ROOM of Rudy's BBQ on McKinney Avenue is empty this Wednesday lunchtime. Except for the pair huddled over racks of meat. The sign on the front door says CLOSED, but the people inside are important enough for the joint to be open and the pits to be fired up five hours before the doors open for the ordinary folk of Dallas.

The screenshot flashed across my screen thirty minutes ago: Hey, Asma, will let you know how it goes. Meeting at Rudy's soon, probably done by 1ish. Latif forwarded the message with an eyeball emoji followed by about fifty red exclamation marks. "Why TF is the congresswoman texting Asma about a meeting? Who is she meeting at the BBQ spot?" I read and reread the intercepted message and texted Sara that we would have to switch our lunch plans to dinner.

By the time I get to Rudy's, they are already halfway through a rack of ribs. I crouch at the side of the restaurant between a bush and a brick wall, my knees digging into gravel as I peek through a window. This surveillance op is doing a number on my legs, but it's worth every minute of pain to get a glimpse of what Asma's new BFF is up to in a place that definitely does not serve halal BBQ.

HH wears a white shirt with a bright orange scarf neatly tied around her neck. Her hair is blown out to perfection, as usual. Loose brown waves frame her oval face. She'd be hot if her politics weren't so dirty.

The burly man sitting opposite her is hunched over his phone. The brim of a cowboy hat obscures his face. I can see her lips moving, but he seems to be silently sucking on a rib. A delivery truck trundles past, and I duck as it grinds to a halt, its brakes screeching at the back of the restaurant. I jog to the corner and crouch, knowing that a back door will be opened any minute. Within seconds two men in bloodstained aprons are passing wooden crates filled with dead animals from the truck to the restaurant. I peek around the corner. When they stop to sign paperwork near the driver's door, I run into the back entrance, past an office, and make it all the way past the long, window-lined kitchen and to the back of the dining room to a row of aprons hanging from a line of hooks on the wall. That's when he spots me.

"Hey! You! What you doing in here?"

He's a cutie, the cook, the butcher, whoever he is. Jet-black hair slicked up into a mohawk, a pencil behind his ear, and long, thick eyelashes. His apron is stained with splatters of brown dots.

"Hey! New girl. Just grabbing this." I lift the apron and smile a jolly smile.

The man moves closer. He smells of cigarettes. "New girl?" He leans against the wall and watches me slip the apron over my head. My fingers fumble behind my back as a million excuses race through my mind.

"Here. Do this for me," I say, turning around. If I'm going to be bold, I figure I might as well act extra bold and make an accomplice out of this stranger. He ties a knot and whispers, "Ten minutes. To do whatever you're doing here." He slips his number into my pocket before disappearing into the smoky kitchen.

I walk to the end of the hallway and enter a tiny, dark space, just big enough to fit two or three people. It stands between the kitchen's double metal doors and the dining room. It's more of a curtained entranceway than a room. Thick black curtains on both sides keep the light and smoke away from the restaurant's two diners. I nudge the heavy fabric aside. There they are. Hunched over plates of ribs. They are silent now. But soon they will talk, and I need to hear every word that is spilled.

The cutie seems to understand the urgency of my situation. "I won't tell anyone if . . . ," he says, over my shoulder. I look back and he is standing behind me in the dark space with his finger over his mouth, his phone pointed toward me. I input my digits switching all the sevens for nines and get back to business. "Don't text me yet. I need my phone to stay quiet."

At the far end of the restaurant, past the two diners, stands a bar, just left of the hostess stand. A row of upside-down glasses is stacked neatly next to a silver pitcher. I roll my shoulders, crack my neck, take a deep breath, and move the curtain aside. I stride straight to the bar, make no eye contact with the diners, grab two glasses and the pitcher of ice water, and walk toward them.

"We already have water," says the man. "We asked her for tumblers. For Scotch." He doesn't look up from his phone and his face is still obscured by the cowboy hat, but I would recognize that voice anywhere. "Catch the Best Sleep of Your Liiiiiiife!"

Norm Miller looks up at me. His cheeks are flushed, his forehead sweaty. He glances to his side, and when I look down at the red leather seat, a metal flask is wedged between his thigh and a rolled-up newspaper. He waves me and my useless pitcher of water away. "Actually, I'll take a refill," HH says.

"Not drinkin' with me, Mrs. Muslim?" He laughs as I pour.

The congresswoman smirks. "Oh, you know, Norm. Not trying to break *all* the rules!"

She waves the pork rib in his direction, parts her lips, and bares her teeth. A rib slowly enters her mouth. She sucks the strings of flesh off the bone. I hold my breath to keep from shaking, mop the small puddle of water I've created around her glass, turn on my heel, and practically run back to the dark room.

Norm Fucking Miller and Humairah "I'm Not a Sellout" Hilal. Together. Eating in secrecy. Eating *pork* in secrecy! What is the congresswoman doing with the sleazy mattress salesman?

I guzzle big gulps of ice water straight out of the pitcher to cool the heat rising through my body. Norm belches. I peek through the curtain and see him leaning back in his chair, his fingers interlaced over his belly. He is shaking his head and muttering. I stick my head out a little farther.

"Nice car you got out there. And congratulations on the new campaign office," Norm says. "Swanky."

HH wipes the corners of her mouth with a red napkin and rips open a square packet to pull out a wet wipe. She drags the white tissue along her fingers and reaches inside a fancy leather purse.

"What do they call that style these days?" says Norm. "Hipster? I don't know. I can't keep up with the young ones."

"Thanks," HH says. I don't know if she's grateful for his complimenting her new car and office or if she's trying to say that she's one of the young ones. (She isn't.)

"New donor?" Norm puts the bottle of Scotch on the table.

"You know how it goes, Norm. Always hustling."

"Who's fronting all the new stuff?"

"I'm always working hard to represent the Thirty-Second District and to garner additional support to better the lives of my constituents."

Norm shakes his head. "Might need to hustle a little harder."

HH lowers the lipstick that she hasn't yet applied to her lips and stares at Norm.

"You know what I'm talking about, congresswoman. Your ratings."

"Oh, those." She uses her phone as a mirror and paints her bottom lip. "Fluctuation comes with the territory."

"You gotta be a fighter! More assertive." Norm punches the air. "You gotta read the temperature of the room." He sticks out his tongue and licks his finger slowly. He stares directly at HH while holding his finger in the air, as if checking the direction of the wind in this dark and still restaurant. "Mmm, the temperature tells me the people of District Thirty-Two want a congresswoman who will protect the rights of the family. The rights of the unborn."

"I'm all about that, Norm. You know I am. I ran—and won—on that message." HH sounds tired and weary. As if she's repeated the same line over and over again.

"It's not what I'm hearing you say now."

"Then you're not hearing me right."

A sinister smile stretches across Norm's face. He leans back farther in his chair.

I walk slowly from behind the curtain and stride to the bar to look for whatever glasses you're supposed to use for Scotch.

"Go on, Mrs. Congresswoman. Sorry, Ms. Congresswoman. What is it that I ain't understanding about your request for an amendment?"

"I'm saying there's a difference between the two things, a big difference, and you're getting them mixed up."

I have no idea what a Scotch glass looks like, so I grab the thickest, heaviest tumblers I can find. I polish them on my apron and walk over to their table. Should I have put them on a tray?

"On the one hand, you have single women sleeping around and making reckless choices and using abortion as a quick fix to undo their recklessness. That's over here." HH puts the cap on her lipstick and stands it on one side of the table. "But over here . . ." She slides the bottle of Scotch over to the other side of the table. "Over here you have good Texas folks wanting to use IVF to grow their families. The current laws ban abortion, for sure, but they also, accidentally, I would say, outlaw the destruction of all embryos, even those created by a loving husband and wife who need IVF because they're struggling to have kids naturally. So we've inadvertently banned IVF. Do you see that? And I know you've seen the birth rate, Norm. We have a problem on our hands."

"That problem you're talking about is being addressed by the bans," says Norm. HH shakes her head.

I put the tumblers on the table and suck my teeth at the absurdity of their logic. The double standards are sickening. They look up at me. "Umm, anything else I can get you?" I say, reaching for the last crumpled napkin on the table.

"No." Norm looks at me a little too hard. He lifts a glass to eye level and turns it this way and that. *Keep your mouth shut, Noor! Do not let your emotions get in the way of your investigation. Do not let your emotions get in the way of your investigation!* I turn back toward the dark room and pull back the curtain.

"And who the hell are you?"

A gravelly voice hits me as soon as I enter the dark space. My eyes are still adjusting to the light. I size up a short woman with a screwed-up face holding a tray with two tumblers. She glares at me. "You're not Sandra. Anyway, Sandra's not s'posed to be here now. No one's s'posed to be here." She shoves the tray at me. Her arms fall to her side, and I see that she's shaped like a square.

"Hi. . . . I'm Laylah?"

"Well, you're not supposed to be on now."

"I . . . umm."

The cute butcher emerges from behind the back curtains. "Oh, hey, Laurene! She's the new girl. She's just helping out."

"What new girl? I didn't authorize no new girl." Laurene glowers. Her small pink eyes narrow into slits as she turns on her heel and walks past the cutie and back toward the kitchen.

"That's the manager," the cutie whispers, taking me by the elbow. "And those are VVIPs in there. Not just VIPs, so she's extra paranoid. She's supposed to be the only person serving them. You gotta get out of here before she . . ."

"Carlos. Hand me her ID," Laurene calls from behind the curtain.

"Oh hell no, Carlos!" I whisper.

"Shhh, this way." He takes me by the elbow and marches me out through the curtains and to the far side of the restaurant. HH and Norm are sipping Scotch out of the wrong glasses and probably talking about important things that I absolutely need to hear.

"The front door is locked so you need to exit from there," he says, pointing to a fire exit at the side of the bar. "Run, before Laurene comes looking for you. I'm going to tell her you were confused about your new shift time. Go!"

"But your apron!"

"Just get out of here!"

I take long strides to the emergency exit and fling open the black doors. I run toward my car, my heart racing, and drive past HH's shiny black Bronco. I'm halfway to Richardson and repeating every little thing I heard them say into my Voice Memos app before I realize that the butcher's apron is still looped around my waist.

LAYLAH

"THE THING ABOUT putting a Bundt in the oven is you have to position it juuuust right." Bella leans over the oven door, slides a tray of Bundt tins onto the top shelf and shuts the door. "Do you know the secret to making a Bundt cake, Laylah dear?" I shake my head and hold on to the sides of the tiny metal stool I'm balancing on.

"The secret is in the science." Bella puts her hands across her lower back and stretches, pushing her nonexistent belly toward me. For someone who bakes cakes for a living, she looks like she barely eats them. "You see this?" She reaches for a round black tin shaped something like a flower. "All these rounded edges and this classic hole in the middle mean a greater surface area of the cake is exposed to the heat. That means you have to make Bundt batter dense but very, very moist. And you have to cook a Bundt cake for longer. Lucky for me, I'm one-eighth German, one-half perfectionist, and three-eighths a chemist. At least, I did my bachelor's in biochemistry at UT back in the seventies."

She wipes her hands down her beige apron. The thick calico is emblazoned with BELLA'S BUNDTS and a cartoon of her smiling face. She studies me while sliding beige oven mitts off her hands. I hope Bella is as scientific and thorough about ending this pregnancy as she is about baking Bundts.

"Carly's the medical one," she says, pointing over her shoulder to the front of the truck, where a mousy, middle-aged woman in denim dungarees rummages through a backpack. Carly's hair is thick and curly, her skin tanned, but I can't tell where she's from, and I can't ask the dreaded question, *Where are you from?* What I really want to ask is, "Is she a doctor?" But I imagine Bella throwing her head back and letting out a throaty laugh. *Is she a doctor? A doctor? Like you've got any choice, missy!*

"I run operations to keep everything safe and running smoothly. Carly will administer the pills in a moment and talk you through the steps. But first, you are approximately sixty-six days pregnant like you said on the phone? Correct?" I nod. So does Bella. "Okay, give or take a day or two, of course. And you left your phone at home and no one knows you're here, correct?"

"Yes," I say, liar that I am. I would have left my phone at home, if I wasn't forced to take an Uber.

"Okay, great!" Bella smiles like the cartoon version of herself. "Then we're all good to go." I fan myself against the rising heat.

"I have to bake, dear. It calms my nerves. Plus, the smell of baking makes this whole operation . . . safer, shall we say? Who's going to mess with two little ladies selling cakes, eh?"

Carly steps over the division between the driving side and the bakery/clinic side of the truck. She looks flustered. Gray-blue circles sag beneath her hooded brown eyes.

"Hello, Laylah. It's good to see you but sorry to meet under such circumstances." Carly slides a second stool from under a small table and sits. I try to smile. "So, here we have the pills." She reaches into a square pocket at the front of her dungarees and pulls out a small white box. She waves it in front of her chest and the tablets rattle like Skittles—life-changing, future-saving, sanity-restoring Skittles.

"Probably the only mifepristone and misoprostol this side of the Mississippi." She puts her palm on her forehead and kneads the skin above her brows. "No exaggeration. Bella here is trying to cook up her own batches, but she hasn't quite perfected the recipe. Anyway. You take the miffy today and the miso tomorrow. Now, they typically come in a blister packet, but these pills are rolling around inside this box without any other packaging. So, I'm going to show you what's what. First, you take this one—" She opens the box and rolls a small yellowish tablet with MF carved into one side into the palm of her hand. "This one today. Bella will grab you some water. This is the mifepristone, or miffy as we call it. It works by stopping your pregnancy from progressing any further. It can cause some bleeding. But even if you bleed later today, you still have to take the misoprostol thirty-six to forty-eight hours after you take the miffy. Okay?" I nod again.

"And these are the tablets for tomorrow." She angles the opened box toward me so I can see the four peach pills nestled inside. I name each one of them. Freedom. Med School. Hallelujah. Joy. I'll name the miffy . . . Life Saver. That's when it dawns on me. "But why are there—"

"Four? That's because . . ." She sighs. "That's because you don't swallow these. If these were oral misoprostol, I would be handing you a single tablet."

"*If* they were oral?"

"Right. These are the only ones we could get. You're going to have to insert all four of them vaginally in thirty-six to forty-eight hours' time. I'll talk you through how to do it. It's straightforward, I promise. Do you have a friend who can—"

"No."

"Oh. Okay. So after you swallow this one now . . . Bella? Water? Thanks! After you swallow this one now, you insert these four into your vagina tomorrow night. Okay?"

I nod.

"The way the four miso pills work is they soften your uterus to empty the contents. That can cause bleeding and cramping. Usually the cramping occurs before the bleeding. Okay?"

I nod. *Just gimme the damn pills, woman.*

"Here."

She places the yellow tablet in my palm, and I close my fist around the little circle that will make everything go back to the way it was. Life Saver.

"Bella? Water! Tomorrow, at around eight p.m, wash your hands, then lie down and insert these four pills one by one into your vagina as high up in there as you can. Push with your finger all the way up. Then, I want you to stay lying down for thirty minutes. You might pass clots in those next few hours, and you can put a pad in your underwear. But I don't want you to fret, okay? This treatment is safe. The two medicines combined end pregnancy ninety-five percent of the time."

I know the stats. The stats that have taken up rent-free lodging inside my crowded brain. But said to my face in the back of a truck by a complete stranger as the scent of baking cake batter wafts up my nostrils, "95 percent" sounds like a wonderful promise and heart-break at the same time. *Why isn't it 100 percent? Or even 99.5 percent?*

Bella crouches in front of the small fridge. I see her reach for a bottle of water, but her outstretched arm freezes. She doesn't take a bottle of water. She leaves the fridge door open, walks to the front of the truck, and peers out of the driver's-side window. Carly turns to watch her. Bella pulls down the shade and fiddles with a radio that hangs from the roof. Then she kneels on the passenger's seat to look out the opposite side.

"Can I just . . . ?" I say, pointing past the doctor to the open fridge. I could try to swallow the yellow pill without water, but that's guaranteed to make me gag, and I'm already fighting nausea and a stream of bile rising up my throat in waves. "It's fine. I can just grab the water my—"

A revving engine cuts me off. Bella and Carly whip around to look at each other.

"Did you?"

"Yeah. You?"

"Definitely."

"Are you certain?"

"Yes! I shut off *all* the transmitters and *all* the phones back when we passed Waco. You saw me! I pulled out the map and navigated using only the paper from way back then," Bella says.

Carly stands and shoves the white box at me. I make a fist around it as the growl of engines grows louder.

"It sounds like they're circling," she says.

"They are."

"Are you sure they're coming for *us*?"

"Well, honey. We're the only fucking truck in this piece of wasteland, and we're being circled. So I'd say yes."

I squeeze my fist tighter. BANG! A piercing sound reverberates through the truck. I grip my pills tighter.

"What the hell was that?!"

"Could be one of their engines backfiring," says Carly, jumping into the driver's seat.

"Or it could be . . ."

"Don't say it," Bella yells from the passenger side. "They found us! But fuck if I know how."

"Who is *they*?" But the pair are busy opening and closing compartments and passing . . . Wait. Did Carly just pass Bella a sawn-off shotgun?

"Hold on tight, kid," Bella says, cocking the barrel. "They've tracked us down. We've got to move."

"Hold on to what?" I say as the truck lurches forward. Carly floors the accelerator. My stool topples toward the oven, and I open my palms to brace for the hot metal.

"Nofucknofucknofucknofucknooooooo!" The pills fall to the

ground. Life Saver rolls toward a crack between the oven and a cupboard. I reach for it as Carly slams the brakes. My palm shoves the pill deep into the crevice. "Noooooooooooo!"

"What's happening back there?"

"The pill!"

"Hold on!"

"I dropped it!" I try to stand, fall to my knees, and pound the floor with my palms. I put my face flat to the ground and peer into the crack between the oven and the cupboard. Bundt tins crash into the glass oven door as Carly smashes the brakes and makes a sharp turn.

"You need to SIT DOWN and hold on to SOMETHING or you'll hit your head!" Bella screams.

"Where's the box?" shouts Carly.

I crawl toward the box wedged beneath the small fridge.

"What's going on back there?" Bella yells.

The last pill in Texas. Was in my hand. Is now deep inside some unreachable crack. I crawl toward the fridge. How did I come this close? *This* close? Why didn't I just stuff it into my mouth without water? For safekeeping. I swear to God I will shove those misoprostol pills into my vagina right this minute. Shotguns and vigilantes and car chases be damned. The truck lurches again, and I flatten myself against the floor. Carly slams the gas as Bella screams new directions. I reach out my arms as if I'm making snow angels with my cheek pressed to the floor.

"Left, left, left!" screams Bella.

"Hold on!"

I lift my head. Bella cracks open her window and slides the barrel through the narrow gap.

"It's that troop from Huntsville," she says.

"What do you see?"

"Blue truck. Red truck. Two in each. No plates."

She presses her cheek into the grip of the gun and peers along the barrel.

"Bella. Do not. Remember what happened last time? I swear to God, Bella. Do not."

"Not doin' it. I swear. Not doin' it. Just keeping them in my sights is all," says Bella. I hear a sharp crack, and I can't tell if Bella pulled the trigger or if something hot and sharp came flying at us, piercing the truck's metal skeleton. A beam of light shines through a jagged hole. I wiggle the crushed cardboard box this way and that, gently pulling it out from beneath the fridge. When a whole inch is sticking out, I grip the box with my fingers. *Screeeech.* The truck slams to a stop and my hand shoves the box beneath the fridge until not even a glimmer of white sticks out. I get onto my knees and slide my fingers under the fridge as the truck starts to move again. With one hand I lift while the other sweeps. There it is! But just as I grope for it again, we accelerate so hard that the fridge slides onto me, pushing me back and onto my butt. It slides back to the wall and I sit up to see the box poking out half an inch. Back to square one. I will not let it out of my sight this time.

I curl a finger around the visible edge and slide the box out from under the fridge. Another inch is exposed. I grab it with glee.

Half a box emerges from under the fridge. Half an empty box. My
heart drops. The oven door flings open. The back doors swing
wide letting in the sun. Sizzling cake tins fly out of the oven, one
smashes into my back. I try to reach around to feel if my spine is
still intact. The Last Pills in Texas have disappeared. Everything
fades to black.

UNBECOMING!
THE BOLLYWOOD MUSICAL

FADE IN:

EXT. ARLINGTON PARKING LOT - DAY

Car chase. Goondas (Bollywood villains) in ripped
white vests, red bandanas around their sweating,
grease-stained foreheads, half-chomped cigars in
their mouths, hang out the windows of a battered
blue Ford truck. They fire pistols at Bella's
Bundts. Bullets ricochet off the metal. The back
door of the van flings open, and Laylah Khan,
dressed in a white-and-gold gharara, emerges with
a shotgun. Laylah clings to the swinging truck door
with one hand and fires at the goondas with the
other.

                    GOONDA NUMBER 1
              (in Hindi with English subtitles)
                 तुम्हें यह गोली चाहिए?
                 You want this pill?

Goonda number 1 lassos a comically large
mifepristone tablet the size of a bicycle wheel

that is rolling around the parking lot. Goonda
number 1 laughs in the villainous Bollywood style
and flings the lassoed pill into the air.

GOONDA NUMBER 2
(shoots gun at the lassoed pill flying
through the air., and a chunk of the
tablet falls to the ground)
You American girls think you
can control everything!
You should be ashamed?!

Laylah fires her shotgun at the lasso, freeing the
damaged pill from the goondas. The pill smashes to
the ground and rolls toward her. The goondas' car
gains on Bella's Bundts. Goonda number 1 lassos
Laylah around her waist and pulls her to the
ground.

GOONDA NUMBER 1
We've got you now, you
besharam American girl!

Laylah's gharara balloons like a parachute,
elevating her from the ground. She frees herself
from the rope and uses it to swing toward the
rolling abortion pill, lands on it, and takes a huge
bite. She laughs manically, pill crumbs falling from

her mouth. She fires her shotgun at the goondas'
car, sending it careening. She lands on the ground
and dances around the mifepristone pill.

                    GOONDA NUMBER 1
                 You won't get away that
                         easily!

                        LAYLAH
            (singing to the tune of "Fame")
                       Sharam!
               I'm gonna live my own life.
               I'm gonna learn how to
                       survive.
                I don't need no one to
                       save me.
                No one will see me cry!

A dozen female dancers in saris holding plate-sized
mifepristone pills dance in the style of dandiya
and gheet, using the pills as dandiya (traditional
dancing sticks). They dance in a circle around
Laylah.

                        LAYLAH
                       Sharam!
                I'm gonna fix my mistakes.

                    No, I'm not gonna cry.

                 You don't rule my uterus.

                  I control my own life!

Laylah takes another bite out of the mifepristone
and then another.

FADE TO BLACK.

NOOR

"WHAT DO YOU mean, it was a waste of your time?" Latif bites into a shawarma as big as his head. Ketchup squirts down his fingers.

"Bro, who puts ketchup in shawarma?"

"Who walks around in a dirty apron in the middle of the afternoon? You look like you killed a goat," he says, his mouth open as he chews.

"It was part of . . ." I crumple the apron in my lap, the one I wore into the shawarma shop because I was too busy texting Sara an excuse about why I didn't turn up like I said I would and so I forgot to take it off before I was face-to-face with Latif. ". . . a disguise. Sometimes you gotta switch things up, you know?"

"You look like my uncle on Eid morning after he's slaughtered an animal." Latif looks over at his uncle standing behind the counter, handing a normal-sized shawarma to a teenage girl. "So why was it a waste of time?" He licks the ketchup from his fingers. I've seen enough of men eating meat to last me a lifetime. I dip a fry in chili sauce and turn my head to stare at the wall covered in Bollywood film posters.

"You saw the two of them talking and trying to keep it a secret, right?" Latif says, talking with his mouth full. "That's big. Don't journalists love that type of shit?"

I slide down in the plastic chair until my face is level with the pile of fries heaped in front of me. I pick one off the top and drop it into my mouth. "All I heard them talk about was IVF." I should be spending time on the Guide, not running around after HH, trying to figure out her secrets.

Latif clears his throat. "But at least you know she talks to him. On the down-low. Must have been something important."

"Anyone coulda guessed they talk to each other. That's not a scoop." I dangle a second fry above my mouth. Latif's uncle looks over at me. I sit up straight and eat like a normal person. "She's a congresswoman. Of course she talks to Norm disgusting Miller. He's one of the biggest political donors in Texas. She has to get her money from somewhere. Although . . . we should check if she declares that she takes money from him cuz I'm pretty sure she was trying to distance herself from him last year. You know, so she could get Muslims and Brown people to vote for her. Why was she texting Asma about this meeting? That's the question."

"Was HH trying to get money from him? At this meeting?"

"I don't know. I don't think so. She was saying something that was pissing him off actually."

"Like what?"

"Something about IVF. She was using her lipstick and a bottle of Scotch to explain to that woman-hating hemar that people should be allowed to get rid of embryos as long as they're married and doing it as part of IVF, but that other people, like single women, belong on death row if they try to have an abortion. Cuz good Christians should be allowed to have big families, but no one else should get any help with family planning! You know, typical antiabortion bullshit."

"Shhh. My uncle will kick us out if he hears you say 'abortion.' Or 'hemar.' He feeds enough Arabs to know what that means."

"Are you forgetting that abortion is acceptable in Islam? And Judaism. It's these evangelicals who are batshit rabid about making it illegal. Don't they teach you that at the mosque?" I roll my eyes. Of course they don't teach that. The imam is too busy making sure he's in line with whoever is in power to teach the truth about Islam. Luckily, they're not all like him. "Did you know there are these badass imams and rabbis who have gotten together and they're using this old-ass law called RFRA, I think it stands for Religious Freedom and something something? Anyway, they're so amazing and they're using the law to say that by making abortion illegal in Texas, it basically makes it impossible for Muslims and Jews to practice their religion, and so the bans are persecuting us."

"Wait a second. 'Us'? Are you admitting publicly that you're Muslim now? Mashallah, sis."

"Oh, hush. It's complicated." I sigh. "I'm *culturally* Muslim. Anyway, that's not the point. Norm Miller *is* a fucking hemar. I can't stand his slimy face. If I'da known that's who HH was going

to meet up with today, I would have taken an antacid. He's a disgusting fucking hypocrite and a—"

"Stop swearing! Look, I know you're into your women's rights
stuff and everything," Latif says, leaning toward me and lowering
his voice, which only makes his uncle look over at us and narrow
his eyes. "But you gotta cool it. You're getting too emotional. And
what does any of this have to do with the stolen donations?"

"Ohhhh, I'm sorry, Latif. Is it bothering you that I'm talking
about ABORTIONS? Are ABORTIONS just women's business,
Latif? Awww, did no one ever teach you how many men had
their asses saved by their partners ending pregnancies that would
have ruined their futures? Hmm? No? Well, let me tell you about
ABORTION, Latif. And let me start by explaining that it's not
only women who get pregnant, okay? It's anyone with a uterus,
and that includes people who don't identify as women. Okay?"

"Okay! Okay! Can you be quiet? You'll get us found out. Look!"

Latif's uncle walks over with a basket of freshly baked tandoori
naan in one hand and a two-liter bottle of coke in the other. He
places both on the table and nudges the bread closer to me. "She's
not eating enough," he says to Latif.

"She's a vegetarian," Latif says, his eyes wide. "I know, Uncle!
Pagal, right!" Uncle puts a hand on my shoulder, shakes his head,
and walks away.

"Keep it down," Latif hisses.

"Don't tell me how to speak."

"You're hungry," Latif says, sliding the tandoori naan even
closer to my chest. "And hangry."

I bare my teeth at him like I'm going to bite his hand off. He leans back in his chair and laughs.

"What else did they talk about?"

"Nothing. Just the IVF stuff."

"A whole meeting about IVF? Maybe it *was* a waste of your time. It doesn't help us track the missing money." He taps the lid on the bottle of coke.

"They probably talked about all the important stuff after I left. I was only there for ten minutes before I got chased out by the creepy woman who wanted me arrested, remember?" Latif shrugs. "Ugh, if only I could have stayed longer. They started drinking right as I was running out. I just know they were about to get down to business and spill all the tea."

Latif ignores the Styrofoam cup next to his plate. He tilts back his head, angles the coke bottle over his face and pours a steady stream of fizz into his mouth. "Areh! Yeh hooligan kyah disgusting kam kur ruhah heh?!" Uncle shouts from behind the counter. He hurries over with another Styrofoam cup.

"You're so nasty, Latif."

He burps in agreement.

"It was pretty scary having to run like that, you know. The owner would have called the cops on me. What would I have said to the cops?"

"Was the cowboy guy asking her anything? Or telling her to do stuff?"

"Norm. Not really. He was just making snide remarks about her new office and her new car. But I still don't get why she texted

Asma about *this* meeting. Why admit to her that she hangs out with slimeballs like him?"

"What new car?"

"I don't know. I guess the one we saw her in that day must have been new. He was saying something about that. And he said her new office is fancy, but kinda like he was pissed about it."

"Does she get all the money for that stuff from him? Or people like him? I don't really understand how politicians make money, to be honest."

"They get it from all sorts. HH is forever fundraising. You've seen her commercials. And she probably has loads of wealthy donors. White people loooove to say they support her." I unscrew the cap on the coke. "Norm was asking her about a new donor, actually. Maybe he's jealous because he wants to be her biggest donor so he can control her."

"Who's the new donor?"

"She wouldn't say."

Latif taps his foot under the table. "I just wanna know why we didn't get our trip. Did I tell you we were supposed to go trekking in Costa Rica? My mom even bought me this backpack that ties in the front, sort of like a waistcoat thing. You can get a lot of stuff in it, and it comes with a built-in camel pack. You know those water pouches with the straw?"

"You're obsessed with that trip. Let it go."

"*You* let it go."

"Let what go?"

"Your hatred of Asma." Latif's eyes narrow.

"My what?" I sit up straight.

"Why do you hate her so much?"

"I don't hate . . . Look, you have to think about someone if you're gonna hate them. I don't even think about her. I'm only talking about her because you brought up the donations and the thieving. You're the one always going on about her."

We sit quietly and watch the line at the counter grow. I tear a piece of fluffy tandoori naan and dunk it into a pot of white-and-green sauce. The yogurt cools my mouth. My phone buzzes with an email alert showing that Laylah has added comments to the Guide in the Google Doc. The Guide we're falling behind on because I'm chasing my tail on a waste-of-time investigation. I put my phone face down on the table and dunk more tandoori naan into the yogurt dip. My phone buzzes again.

"Who's that?"

"Stop being nosy."

I sneak a quick look. It's a missed call from a 713 area code.

"Seven-one-three is . . . ?"

"Houston?" Latif shrugs.

"JJ?"

"The athlete? Why's he keep calling you? Are you Muslim *and* into boys now?"

"Oh, hush. It's probably some drama with . . . Never mind." I clear the missed calls from my recents list, put my phone on Do Not Disturb mode and slip it into my bag.

"It's not just me who missed out," Latif says, as if he's explaining it to his shawarma. "You have to think about all the kids who missed out. There's this one boy, Jamil, and his family has never even . . ." Latif's words trail off and mingle with the voices of the diners at the next table. I can't think about the mosque kids at a time like this. *Laylah.* Laylah is all I can think about. Doesn't she deserve to know that her feminist role model is up to no good with a two-faced politician who is in bed, or in a BBQ joint at least, with the poster child for the Texas Ministry of Family Preservation? Even if I'm not a good enough reporter to figure out what the connection is, shouldn't I tell her that *something* is going on? That Asma isn't who she appears to be? Shit. Laylah was probably working on the Guide on her laptop during her breaks at the mosque last night, inches away from Asma, who she doesn't realize is . . .

"Holy. Fucking. Shit." I drop the fry on the plate and sit up straight. Latif freezes with his half-eaten shawarma between his lips.

"Holeeeee . . ."

"Spit it out," he says, dropping the wrap on his plate so that the whole thing unravels into a soggy heap.

"I've figured it out!" I stand and press my palms into the table.

"And?"

"Asma. HH. Mandy Lou. Norm Miller. That's how the money is moving! *That's* how the money is moving!"

"Shhh! Wait, what?"

I sit and speak softly. Latif leans forward to listen. "Whoever gave that package to Asma was in a car that belongs to a nurse, yeah? And that nurse is having an affair with Norm Family Values Miller, yeah?"

"Yeah. But what are you saying? That he's giving the money to her? A nurse he's dating?"

"No, listen. So they're talking about the IVF stuff at lunch, right? And she's pissing him off. HH, I mean. Acting like she doesn't even need his money. Well, maybe she *doesn't* need the second richest man in Texas's wallet anymore. Maybe she's found *another* money source."

Latif wrinkles his forehead.

"Your donations!"

He gasps. "So that's how she's driving around in that nice new car! They're all lying thieves." He slams his palms onto the table, and the shawarma heap collapses even more as if the lamb personally wronged him. "Wow. You've figured it out. Now we know where the money's been going."

My stomach churns. Maybe the fries were cooked in animal fat. Maybe I stood too close to Norm, close enough to smell the pork on his breath. Latif shakes his leg beneath the table. "Fucking haramzada."

"Can you stop doing that thing with your leg? You're making me nervous."

"I can't believe she would take all that money people donated and give it to those politicians. Politicians? Instead of kids who need to go on a trip?" Latif angrily tears off a piece of shawarma and chews hard, his foot still tapping the floor. Teenage boys are the most annoying creatures on the planet. How anyone could get close enough to kiss one is beyond me.

My stomach rumbles. "Well. We can't say we *know* this for sure."

"You just said."

"There might even be mosques involved. But we have to *prove* it. We have to nail her."

"The missing donations, you mean."

"Yes. Exactly. We have to figure out why money would go from the mosque to HH and how Mandy Lou and Norm are connected. We have to prove what's really going down at the mosque. We have to be right."

"We *are* right. You're the one who's always going on and on about that Okey law."

"Occam's Law?"

"Yeah! The simplest solution is the most likely one? Something like that." He reaches for the bottle of coke again. "Cuz if that law thing is right, then you're right, and the best way to explain the missing money, the secret meetings with HH and Asma in a parking lot, and HH's new stuff is that *our* money is going from Asma to HH to get all that new stuff. Haramzada." He whispers the last word while looking over at his uncle, and for the first time I notice a blue collections box on the counter next to a glass shelf filled with trays of pistachio-dusted baklava. The label on the blue box reads: PLEASE KINDLY DONATE TO THE RICHARDSON ISLAMIC CULTURAL CENTER (MASJID) YOUTH GROUP.

I pull my bag onto my lap and dig out my keys. As soon as I prove these details, I can finally tell Laylah that her heroine is not who she appears to be.

LAYLAH

THE VOICES SWIRLING above me are muffled. I can't see their faces, only blurs of blue and white. I lift my head off the ground. An invisible weight pushes it down. Through a film of tears, I see a hazy Bella standing over me. A phone dangles in one hand, a shotgun in the other.

"But it's in airplane mode, right?" I hear Carly say. "So she couldn't have . . ."

"We have no idea when she switched it over to airplane mode. That's the problem. Coulda been a minute before she knocked on our door. Or ten seconds. Her location could have been known right up to the docking point in Arlington, and they could have triangulated her identity as a seeker by piecing together her search history and any calls she made to us or other clinics that they were monitoring, which would mean they're still onto us. We just scared them off for a second."

"Fuck."

Fuck. I squeeze my eyes shut. "Life Saver," I mumble.

"Huh?"

"What did she say? Life . . . what?"

"Oh, honey. We're long past that point. We need to get you outta here before their backup arrives. We have a hideout we need to get to, but we need to drop the truck off first, and we can't have you with us."

Carly crouches near my shoulder and slips an arm beneath my back. "Here, sit up."

"The pills?"

"Just look around, hun." Bella sighs. I rub my eyes, which only dislodges a contact lens, making the wreckage appear even blurrier. "Here. Water."

Water. If I'd just had that water a second earlier, I would have gulped that tablet down and been halfway on the road to ending this nightmare.

"We need to get her on her feet and out of here," Carly mutters.

Yeah, you already said that. I touch the back of my head. A knot throbs at the base of my skull.

"Where are we?" I rub my eyelid and blink frantically, trying to get the lens back into its rightful place. A perfectly formed Bundt cake sits at my feet, as if it were placed there as a gift. All around it lies mayhem. Lumps of cake, empty cake tins, metal oven racks, napkins, and boxes are strewn across the truck. Two holes pierce the wall.

"Are those . . . ?"

"Mmm-hmm."

"We're in Poetry, about thirty miles east of Dallas. We need to drop the truck at Sulphur Springs for repairs, but we have to leave you here."

"Poetry? Where's my phone?" Bella hands me a crumpled mass of glass and metal. Spiky shards cut into my palm. "Can I use your phone?"

Bella puts her arm around Carly's neck and turns her away. They crouch over a map and ignore me. "The message said to avoid the 35, 205, and Market Road 1565," Carly explains to Bella in a whisper.

"Who's giving the safety guidance today? Is it coming from . . . ?" Bella's voice trails off into a whisper as she reaches into her pocket, pulls out a phone, and extends it in my direction without turning around. There is only one phone number that I remember by heart.

"Tell them to meet you in a park called Fish Poetry," she says, without turning. She points a finger at the map. "I think we should drop her there, then head up Poetry Road to the 276."

"But look over here," Carly says. "The Campground Cemetery is better. It's more hidden. Let's leave her there."

"I'm not sitting in a cemetery," I say, as the phone rings. They keep plotting their escape route on the paper map. Neither of them turns to look at me.

By the time my car pulls up in the distance, I have been staring at the crystal-clear pond for two hours. A small wooden bridge connects the mainland to a small island in the middle of the pond. I have crossed it ten times, walking back and forth along the creaking wood, stopping only when a truck pulled up half an hour ago. A tall White man emerged with two coolers and a fishing rod. I have been sitting quietly on this bench ever since.

"Lalee! What are you doing all the way out here?!" Nanima shrieks. I walk toward her as she gets out of the car. "And where is your phone?" I keep one eye on the fisherman to my right. He squats and fiddles with something in a cooler box, probably bait, but everyone looks like a possible vigilante these days. I imagine one cooler is filled with slimy, wriggling worms and the other with location-tracking devices and shotgun ammunition.

"When did you get here? I would have come sooner, but I was all the way in Richardson helping your mom with Adam. I didn't plan to pick you up until three thirty, and that would have been from your school."

"With Mom? Did you tell her you were coming to get me?"

"But of course."

I groan and bend my neck to look at the sky. "Did you tell her where I was?"

"What's the problem? Is there some secret?"

"No! No secret." I scan the fisherman's truck for any giveaway signs of his politics, but the lone bumper sticker says LONGHORNS! HOOK 'EM! I wonder if he was at UT when Asma and HH were there.

"Well, if there are no secrets, then there are no problems!"

Nanima says cheerfully. "Get in the car and tell me everything about everything. All these years in the DFW and I've never even heard of this town. Poetry. Looks very . . . White."

I eye the black van that seems to tail us as soon as we pull onto the main road. It overtakes us and speeds away. Another truck takes its place, and I imagine a whole chain of trucks are out to get me, trading places as they follow me to Nanima's house. I look over at her. She seems to be eyeing the traffic just as carefully as I am.

"Tell me everything. What's in Poetry?"

"Nothing major. Just doing research."

"All alone?" She squeezes my arm. I brush her hand away.

"The friend who dropped me was supposed to come back to take me home, but she had an emergency and then my phone stopped working and I had to borrow someone's phone to call you."

"She okay? She need help?"

"She's fine."

"Here, let me see if I can fix your phone."

"I lost it."

"Oh. So, what were you researching?"

"Poetry. The town. History. And stuff."

"Well, you made me come out of my way, but that's no problem because I passed that very nice spice shop over on the east side on my way over. We'll pass it on the way home. We need to get some extra-special spices for our bake night tonight. Having an extra-large gathering. Lots to talk about. So tell me more about this research."

"What have you been doing with my car today?" I peer over to catch a glimpse of the odometer. I want to put Nanima in the interrogation seat instead.

"Oh, you know, life stuff. Hey, about this special gathering tonight. You're welcome to stay, but I know you have lots of studying to do, so tell Noor to take you home as soon as we're done baking?"

"She's busy."

"Areh, everyone is busy these days. But that's okay. You can take Uber."

"I don't have a phone."

"Here. I brought you this one." A brick of a phone magically appears out of a fold of Nanima's sari.

"It's an Android. I don't even have a charger for these." A loop of gray cable emerges from another set of sari pleats. "How long are you going to need my car? I really need it back."

"Just until Monday. Tuesday at the latest. Inshallah."

"Inshallah? That's what you say when you mean you don't actually know."

Nanima chuckles. I hear Mom's voice in my head. "Laylah. Your grandmother's been through a lot. Be respectful of her needs."

I check my face in the black mirror of the uncharged phone. Not a single scratch or bruise betrays what I just went through. But the back of my neck throbs. I flip down the sun visor to check my skin more closely, and a folded piece of yellow paper falls from the visor into my lap. Nanima swipes it. "Hey, that's mine. I think."

"No, no, I put it there," she says.

"What is it? A pamphlet? Let me see." I reach into Nanima's lap, but she grabs the pamphlet before I can reach it. She shoves it under her butt and wriggles in her seat.

"Erm, okay, then." I wipe the mirror with my cuff and fluff my eyebrows back into position with my nail. I spot boxes stacked behind me.

"Why are there so many of these on the backseat? Why don't you put them in the trunk?"

"Let's play some music." Nanima blares a song from the soundtrack of our favorite movie, *Pakeezah*, and sings along.

"I said, why don't you just put the boxes in the trunk?"

"It's full." She turns the volume higher.

"Full with what?"

We trundle over a pothole, and the boxes jostle and threaten to tip off the seat, as if agreeing with me. "They should go in the trunk. You know it's actually really dangerous to crash with loose items rolling around in the backseat. Those things pick up speed and they can hurt you more than the car in front."

Nanima grabs my hand and laces her fingers through mine. She waves our hands in the air. I bash my knuckles against the rearview mirror. "Sing, lalee! We love this one! Chalteeee chalteeeee."

I yell over the music. "I said, what's all in the trunk?!" Nanima sings at the top of her lungs and waves our hands until we pull into the parking lot of a strip mall. She takes me by the hand and practically dances into the famed spice shop.

STEP 7

BEWARE WHITE SAVIORS

NOOR

WE'VE BEEN WORKING on the Guide separately, checking in and asking questions through comment bubbles and footnotes for the past day. Laylah writes then deletes **Have you told S?** in section 7A of the Guide beneath a list of roving clinics we still haven't finished fact-checking. **Haven't told S**, I write back, next to a number for a food truck called the Dairy Godmother.

Don't. She types and then highlights the word in pink. *Delete.* I call her so I can explain that Sara is cool, but it goes straight to voicemail. She must be working in the library.

I switch out my silver septum piercing for a rose-gold hoop, to glam it up a little. *Sara will love this style,* I think, turning the delicate metal in my palm. I hope she'll love the book of Sappho's poems, the ones I'll read aloud when she's in a food coma after the best phở in Dallas. I saw how poetry sent Laylah loopy for JJ.

Laylah, of all people! Poetry must be useful for something.

I pin up one side of my hair with a bobby pin, slip the thin book into the inside pocket of my jacket, and shout to whoever is in the house that I'm headed to Laylah's for the night.

Sara is early. She arrived minutes before the restaurant opened at five. I wanted to get here before her so I could hide the book beneath her napkin and watch her face flush pink with surprise when she found it. Instead, I hug her and tell her I have a gift. But she'll have to wait till later to find out what it is. Her eyes sparkle at the suspense.

"So, tell me everything! Tell me what happened at your stakeout!"

I gulp a sip of tea, expecting it to be cold and sweet. Instead, it's bitter and boiling hot. I almost burn the roof of my mouth. "Oh. Right." I cough. I forgot I texted Sara that I was reporting an important story and that's why I had to cancel our lunch date earlier. It's hard not to share details with her when I'm caught up in the excitement of an investigation, but I don't remember calling it a stakeout.

"It's an investigation. It went okay. I got some intel."

"Ooh, intel. Sounds so important. So, like, what were you doing? Spying on people? What did they say? Tell me everrrrry-thing." She sucks a chunk of ice out of her water cup and swirls it around her mouth.

"Well, I can't say too much. I've got a lot of loose ends I need to tie up before I can tell . . . before I can write this story."

"But you can tell me about today, can't you? Who were the two people you said you were watching?"

Laylah's voice rings in my head. "Don't tell your silly little crush! She's a loudmouth! Think with your head, Noor! Not with what's between your legs!" I squeeze my thighs.

"I shouldn't really say. Not yet. But maybe I can tell you later?"

"Later when we're watching movies at my house?" Sara runs her fingers through the end of her long ponytail.

We had gone back and forth about going to the movies, but Sara's dad insisted he could download the old indie film I wanted to watch onto their home system. "And they won't mind me staying over?" I had texted.

"Why would they mind you staying over?" Sara had texted back.

She sticks out her tongue and goes cross-eyed looking at the tiny nub of a cube melting on the tip. She swallows it. My phone vibrates with messages from Latif. I take a quick look, in case it's something urgent, but he's taken to forwarding me screenshots of every text HH sends. Pointless nonsense that makes no sense without context and only implicates me in this whole illegal phone-hacking scandal.

"You're so exotic and mysterious." Sara swoons as I tuck my phone between my thigh and the seat cushion. "Intel!" A waiter walks over and hovers over Sara's shoulder. I order the vegetarian phở and Sara orders the pork. She spoons another ice cube into her mouth.

Sara's dad texts to confirm that he has downloaded the film, *Korean Superstar*, about a queer girl in Seoul who discovers her true self by entering a televised talent contest. But when we collapse onto the sofa, our bellies sloshing with broth and green tea and ice cream, we discover the subtitles didn't download with the file. Sara texts a long complaint to her dad, who is heading out the front door. "Sorry, honey. That's the only version I could find!" He closes the door behind him.

We pop popcorn and try to watch the film in Korean, debating if the older characters are aunts or mothers or cousins and if the smiling girls are actually happy or secretly depressed. Sara lays her head on the armrest and stretches her long legs across the sofa. Her feet settle in my lap. "Are you getting this?"

"I guess those girls in that group are giving her some information? Like a secret code? To help her win on the TV show. I'm not sure."

"No, those girls are jealous because she's pretty and younger. They're throwing her off. That's why she keeps losing."

"Those video messages they send her are helping her, aren't they? I think she's going to win the contest. Do you think that word the presenter keeps shouting means 'superstar'?"

Sara wiggles her feet as if to say yes, and her toes rub the soft space beneath my belly button. I try to stay dead still so that she won't move. I want us to stay like this forever. But the fluttery wings inside my stomach make me slide down in the sofa a little. I feel like I'm floating.

"You comfy?" Sara's head pops up off the armrest. The room darkens when the girl on the screen enters a studio and all the lights go out.

I nod my head and lift my hands to cover my face. I watch the screen through my fingers. "Run! It's so dark!" Sara scooches over to me and pushes her shoulder into mine. "You a bit scared?" she whispers into my ear. My lobe tingles.

"Terrified," I whisper back.

We've kissed before. But never in the dark. Never in a house. Never truly alone. "Won't your parents . . . ?" I lift my body away from the sofa so she can pull the T-shirt over my head. "It's Wednesday. They won't be home till later." She nuzzles my neck and presses the softest lips in the world against my collarbone. "Much, much later."

My first instinct is to text Laylah. Not even words, maybe just a fireworks GIF. But she won't be happy for me. Just concerned that I'll have spilled the tea to S in the heat of the moment, even though I would never lose my cool like that. I haven't said a word. Even though I know now that I can truly trust S. I feel closer to her than I have ever felt to another soul.

She rests her hand on my stomach and plays with my navel piercing. "Do you believe in love at first sight, Noor?" I mumble a yes, amazed that she can read my mind. "Is it too soon?" She looks up at me with those blue-green eyes, and I feel my energy connect with hers. She kisses my stomach. "I feel like I can tell you everything." And then she does. We talk for hours, stopping only to hydrate and pee and to pop more popcorn. In the kitchen, I make a caramel syrup to coat the kernels and S tells me about her father, who left when she was a baby, her stepfather who is more of a father than her biological dad could ever be, and how her mother's side of the family became distant after the divorce. As if her mom was the one in the wrong. "They thought her new husband was bad because he didn't have a fancy job like my bio dad. He was a lawyer. Barry's a building manager for the health department, but Mom doesn't care what anyone thinks. She says love is all that matters."

I throw a syrupy kernel at her mouth but miss. It disappears down her tank top, leaving a trail of sticky amber on her chin. I lick it off and scoop the kernel from her cleavage with my tongue. When I place it between her lips, she chews and asks me to tell her my biggest secret.

"Biggest? I don't really have anything big."

"Okay, then, tell me something you haven't told anyone else."

"Laylah knows pretty much everything."

"Well, tell me something only she knows, then."

I cradle the bowl of popcorn against my chest and we walk back to the living room. "It would be really bad if you told this to anyone."

"Then I won't. You know you can trust me."

And I know I can. We sit cross-legged on the couch, shoving scoops of sticky popcorn into each other's mouths. When her mouth is full, I tell her my biggest goal in life is to help people.

"That's what I love about you," she says. My heart stops. "I love that you're caring and that you want to make the world better."

I pretend she didn't just say that word and try to gather my thoughts. "With everything going on in the world. In Texas." I look around for my water cup and take a sip. "I just knew I had to do something to help people in need." That's when I tell her. About the Guide. S looks at me wide-eyed and still. She stops chewing and playing with her hair. Eventually, she lies back on the couch and puts a hand on her stomach. "That's super scary." She looks away from me at the TV. "And brave."

When she goes to shower, I know I have to tell Laylah. It's the right thing to do. But Laylah doesn't answer. I message her in the Guide and she texts back a number.

"Did you get a new phone or something?"

"Just now," she says, the sound of a mixer or some kind of machine in the background. "Mine stopped working so Nanima gave me her old phone. I'm at her house now."

"What's that pinging sound?"

"It's so annoying. This phone keeps getting all these random texts. I should block the spam. But I'm getting a new phone delivered in the morning. She ordered it for me." The mixing sounds combine with the sound of Indian music.

"Hey, Laylah?"

"Yeah?"

"If my parents get in touch, I'm staying with you. Tonight."

"Oh. Okay. Where are you?"

"Sara's."

"Oh. Well, they wouldn't be able to get through to me anyway. Not with my phone lost."

"I thought it was broken?"

"Yeah. How's Sara?"

"She's cool."

"So you're staying the night."

It's not a question. I flop backwards onto the sofa. "I gotta tell you something, Lay."

"You told her, didn't you." Another not-question.

"It's going to help us, Lay. You'll see. Look how behind we are and it's already Wednesday. Where did this week go? And we *have* to go live on Saturday. People really need all this info." I clamp my palm over my damp forehead and imagine Laylah is doing the same, even if her hand is covered in flour or sugar or butter. "It's not fair to the people who need us for us to be this slow." I hear the shower turn off and soft footsteps pad across the ceiling.

"She's agreed to help?"

"She will."

"So you didn't ask her to help? You just told her for the sake of telling her?"

I hear disgust in her voice. I can see her nose crinkling in disapproval.

"You know it's not like that. Of course she'll help us." I hear Laylah take a breath through the phone. Her grandmother sings in the background. "I gotta go, girl. Just make sure she zips it."

When S walks back into the living room, she's wearing a peachy robe. She takes me by the hand and leads me up the stairs. "You would never tell anyone, would you?" She turns to look at me from the step above, closes an imaginary zipper across her lips, and flings away the key, almost as if she'd heard Laylah say "zip it." Maybe my soulmate is psychic after all. I squeeze S from behind and we shuffle up the stairs in sync, as if we are one.

LAYLAH

I KNEAD THE dough to make mithi roti, the sweet round flat-bread that Nanima will fill with a cinnamon-laced lentil mixture and serve with piping-hot masala chai. *Plop.* The warm lump lands on the flour-dusted wooden board. I sink my knuckles into the mound until my fingers are swallowed by the dough. I imagine my arms sinking into the softness until my shoulders and torso disappear and I dive headfirst into the mound and fade into darkness. *Thwack.* I pummel the fatness until it flattens, scoop the edges back into the middle to reform the ball, and sink my knuckles into the mound again. I imagine Sara's face when Noor spilled our secret.

"If you punch any harder, I fear it might punch you back."

"Hmm?"

"The *atta.* I said to knead it gently, not assault it. Did it offend you?"

Nanima turns from the old-fashioned radio, whose volume knob she is constantly adjusting, to face me. The tip of her nose is dusted with flour. I beckon for her to come closer so I can blow on her face.

"Ayeee!" She squeals, rubbing her nose. "It's fine, it's fine. Think of this like face powder for me and"—she points at the pummeled dough—"therapy for you. See, baking is good for everybody."

She juts out her hip and scoots me away from the countertop where I've been assaulting the bread, allegedly. "Gentle, gentle, lalee." She rolls up her sleeves to show me how it is done. Gold bangles clink around her wrists. I see a flash of the silvery pink sliver of a scar that runs up her left arm from the wrist to the elbow. I trace the line with my finger. Nanima shivers at my touch.

"Tell me how you—"

"Like this. See? Gentle, gentle."

"The scar. Tell me the story. You always say you'll tell me but then you change the subject, and when I ask Mom, she says—"

"Many moons ago, lalee. Many, many moons."

"You always say that, but I want to know!"

"What do you want to know? You were there, weren't you?"

"Where?"

"You were with me."

She's so cryptic, my grandmother. I think back to a time when she was hurt while she was with me. There are none. Nanima clears her throat. "Did you know that when I was pregnant with your mother, when she had been in my womb for only a few short weeks, before *I* even knew that I was pregnant, even then, inside of her tiny ovaries lived the very egg that would become you?"

I cock my head. Was this true or some woo-woo, desperately-needs-to-be-debunked pseudoscience. "Nanima. Have you been watching Dr. Mo on TikTok again? I told you that man spews so much garbage."

"Areh, betah. This is true. Just because you haven't learned it yet doesn't make it untrue. It's a scientific fact that when I was pregnant with your mom, you and I were also one. You were a part of me then and you're a part of me now." Her eyes sparkle as if she is tearing up, but it might be the fumes from the dried red chilis sautéing in a skillet.

Nanima isn't emotional in the have-a-big-cry-and-get-it-off-your-chest kind of way. She doesn't tear up often. Mom tells me that's typical of people from that older generation. "They went through a lot. Back in India," Mom likes to say, cryptically. She's so annoying when she leaves out all the details and makes things sound like a confusing poem. "It's only now that it's trendy to talk about trauma all the time and to write poems about intergenerational trauma. Your grandmother's generation isn't really into parsing the past over and over or writing poems about things like that."

Nanima doesn't dwell on the past. She's more of a roll-up-your-sleeves-and-let's-find-a-solution kind of woman. When I was ten, Nanima started to pick me up from school so we could spend more time together. One day she found me clutching the school gate with my coat strangely placed over my head. I was trying my best to hide while out in the open. When Nanima peeled back the coat, I let loose a bucketload of tears because Naomi Chastin had called my dad a pirate on account of his limp. My chubby cheeks were quivering, apparently.

"Areh! What on earth has happened?"

"She said he walks with a peg leg. She . . . said . . . he's a pirate," I whimpered.

"She said *what*?" Nanima's eyebrows were knitted together. She crouched and angled her ear toward my face.

"A pirate! She"—I pointed to Naomi across the playground— "she said . . . *sob* . . . my dad . . . *sob* . . . walks like a . . . a . . . pirate!" I let out a giant wail as I repeated the slur. The fountain of tears I had been holding back was unleashed. Meanwhile, Nanima stood and hopped around me in her sari and cardigan as if her feet were on fire. She laughed so loud that the entire playground fell quiet and stared at us. Or at least, that's how it felt.

She cackled and hollered and eventually bent over at the waist and put her hands on her knees so she could catch her breath. "Oh, mara Allah!" she yelled, loud enough to make me squirm. (I was still in my internalized Islamophobe/desperate-to-fit-in stage.) "Oh, mara Allah, I needed that laugh. I loooove it when an insult is so creative!" Nanima hopped on one leg again. "Pirate, you said? Ohh, kids these days! The next time Yusuf picks you up, I must tell him to wear a parrot on his shoulder and a hook on his arm." She laughed till tears poured down her face. I stared at her with my stinging eyes and wet cheeks. Nanima took deep breaths and let out a long sigh. She saw my still-quivering cheeks, crouched, and put her hand on my shoulder. "It's okay to cry. It really is.

It's okay to let it out. But after all of this"—she wiped her palms across my face and dabbed at my cheeks roughly with the pallu of her pink sari for good measure—"after all of this we absolutely must find a solution. There's always a solution."

I had no idea what "solution" meant, but Nanima did. She marched us to Naomi's mom, who was holding Naomi by the hand, and gave Mrs. Chastin an earful about section 3 of the 1990 Americans with Disabilities Act. "Do you live under a rock, or are you going to teach this child not to bully people who were disabled by life-threatening infections? Or should my son-in-law have died from polio? Is that what you would teach your child? That it is better to be gone than to be disabled? Huh? What is this nonsense? It was your own president who signed the law into action! A goddamned Texan!" Mrs. Chastin, who was usually an orangey shade of brown on account of a permanent fake tan, turned pale and shook her head at the old Indian lady in a sari as pink as a strawberry milkshake. She mumbled an apology and chastised Naomi in front of the whole school. "You've been very naughty, Naomi!" It was the turn of my archnemesis to sob in the playground.

My grandmother has been my hero ever since. It's too bad that our culture is hell-bent on keeping sex a secret and that I can't tell her about what went down between me and JJ. We come from the most populated country on the planet but love to pretend that we reproduce like flowers, our pollen scattering across the skies to create babies.

The oven beeps. Nanima bends down to pull out a tray of

nankutai. Fragrant clouds of cardamon-scented steam drift across the kitchen. In a different world, a world where adults weren't so uptight, where sex education wasn't banned, where we were allowed to say the word "gay" in school, where books about relationships weren't burned in piles every Sunday, where my own culture insisted that sex was something only a cis man and a cis woman could do behind closed doors once they were married, I might grip on to Nanima's kitchen countertop as if it were the school gate, hold back a bucketload of tears, and tell her once more about how I had been wronged. How the stupid judges and the broken system and the messed-up pill ban led to this, to my whole world falling apart. To the LLP being ripped to shreds and the shreds scattered in a ferocious wind.

Nanima squats to lift a can of sunflower oil as big as her head from underneath the sink. She places it on the counter with a thud and pops open the strange plastic opening. I'm sure oil cans this size are meant for use in hotel kitchens and restaurants, not in old ladies' homes. She pours the golden liquid into a black metal wok and roots through a drawer for the flat silver strainer studded with holes. This means we'll be frying jalebi tonight. It must be a special occasion.

As she pops the lid shut, I imagine how her brows would lift and drop as I tell her my bad news. I imagine my cheeks would quiver again, but that unlike that day in the playground all those years ago, she wouldn't fall over laughing, or march to Pastor Jackson's megachurch to point a finger in his face, or cause any kind of scene. I imagine that even though she could never understand what it's like to have other people control what's happening inside your body, she would still try to help. In this other world, Nanima would roll up her sleeves, say, "Okay, lalee. Get it all out. Have a good cry. Now. We absolutely must find a solution." And even though my grandmother doesn't know the first thing about abortions, I imagine she would listen and make more tea and fill me with sweet, crumbly things to take the edge off the pain. And, oh, what a relief it would be to share this news with someone. If only the world were different. If only the sharam wouldn't drown me immediately.

The doorbell rings. "So early?" I head toward the hallway to let in the eager grandmother who has come for Nanima's Wednesday-night session a whole forty-five minutes early. Nanima tugs at my apron strings from behind. "You stay. Watch the oil, and can you move the chilis around so they don't burn? And go to the garden shed and look for the attachment for my blender that makes the extra-fine powder. In fact, go to the shed first."

"But we use the grinder for making the spice powder. Don't we?" The doorbell rings again. Nanima pushes past me.

"Shed! Please!"

I hate the shed. It's stuffy and musty. I slip my feet into the plastic slippers that live by the back door and shuffle up the garden path. But when I reach the shed, the door is locked and the key that usually sits in the padlock is missing. I head back to the house to find the key. Instead, I find Nanima hauling a dolly stacked with three boxes into the living room.

"More boxes?!"

She stands up straight and turns around. "Baking supplies! Did you look in the shed?"

"Baking for what? *The Great British Baking Show*? Seriously. Are you planning on feeding the whole of North Texas? And why is this freaking phone pinging nonstop?"

I take the phone out of my pocket to silence the pings, but Nanima grabs it from my hand before I can even look at the new messages. "Spam!" she declares.

"Yeah, I thought so," I say, loosening my hijaab. "But one of them mentions your name, and another has your . . . Here, let me show you." I reach over to scroll through the messages, but Nanima points the screen at me with a big smile. "All deleted!" she says happily. "You won't get any more messages. Now, back to these supplies. You can never have too many supplies, lalee. Never know when you might need them. Is that the chilis burning? Quickly, turn off the pan!"

"Fine." I slink back to the kitchen. "Couldn't find the key for the shed by the way!"

"Oh, I forgot that I took it out this morning. But it's okay. We don't need that blender attachment anyway. We'll use the grinder." She shuts the living room door with a sharp click and walks past me to the kitchen table. She raises her glasses, moves her phone an inch away from her face, and reads off the screen intently.

"Is that another phone? Wait, do you have two phones now?"

"Oh, this? I need to get rid of it. Too old." She seems to be firing off a whole heap of texts while also keeping tabs on the baking. "Check the oil. Too hot and the jalebi will scorch to death. Too cold and they'll turn out soggy." She senses me watching her as she scrolls and texts. "Don't you need to get in touch with Noor?"

"Noor? Why?"

"What time is she coming to pick you up? You told her exactly six fifty-five p.m., yes?"

"She's got her hands full." I stir the oil.

"Ah, okay. So you'll call an Uber at six forty-five to arrive before six fifty-five then? No problem. The gang will get here at seven, which is exactly thirty minutes away." She puts down one of her phones and walks to the fridge to pull out a large white jug. "Now, do you remember how to squirt the jalebi mix from the squeezy bottle into the hot oil?" She pours the yellow mixture from the jug into a red plastic bottle that was probably made for squirting ketchup, not sweet batter.

Jalebi have been my favorite thing to make for as long as Wednesday nights have been our baking time, which is as long as I can remember. Maybe it's because Nanima makes the jalebi batter by mixing corn flour, baking soda, all-purpose flour, ghee, turmeric, and food coloring on Tuesday night, and all that's left for me to do is "create chaos in the pan." That's how she would describe it when I was old enough to stand on a stool over the hot pan and squeeze swirly shapes into the oil. She always guarded me closely, making sure I was standing still and that the oil wouldn't splash my skin.

"You want me to leave before they get here? But Banu Aunty wanted me to look at something for her granddaughter's college application. I promised her I would."

"That Banu. Always wanting favors. I'll scan the thing and email it to you."

"Don't you think it's child labor if all you're calling me here for is to help with the baking but I don't get to eat any of the goodies or hang out with the aunties?"

"What do you mean?!" She puts down the squeezy bottle and flings both her hands against her chest as if my words have triggered a heart attack. "I would never! Look." She walks over to a round cake tin, pops it open, and lifts a piece of baking paper. The tin is half filled with the nankutai we made earlier. "And tomorrow I will drop off the mithi roti for you, Mom, and Adam to enjoy. Child labor?!" She giggles and hands me the bottle, but she doesn't stay to supervise the chaos in a pan like she once did. She heads back to her phone, lifts her glasses off her face once again, and squints at the screen.

I stand alone over the pan, squeeze a single drop of batter to check the temperature of the oil, and watch the blob sink and rise again. A circle of bubbles gathers around the blob as if the bubbles are helping it stay afloat. Nanima's phone pings and vibrates. She stares at the screen while I squeeze squiggly shapes and loops of yellow batter into the oil and watch them sink, rise, and harden in the heat.

By the time the jalebi are stacked high on a plate lined with kitchen paper, an alarm rings. It's Nanima's phone. "I called the Uber for you! She's heeeere!" Nanima ushers me into the hallway, transfers a stack of cake tins from her arms into mine, and practically shoves me out her front door.

NOOR

SARA'S PARENTS ARE the best. They even left out breakfast for us before they went to work. I lift the cover off the tray. Two croissants sit next to a bowl of cubed, pale melon. My stomach growls. I can hear Mom's voice. "What is this dry bread? Where is the fresh manakish? Where is the shakshuka? There must be eggs or how can you call this breakfast?!"

I take a bite of dry croissant and scroll through all twenty-six pages of the Guide at the kitchen counter without worrying about who might be looking over my shoulder. Laylah's newest edits are rows of question marks in the spreadsheet in section 4B: Underground Clinics.

Sara pops a cube of watery melon into her mouth and presses her still shower-damp body into the back of mine. "Shall we skip school?"

"Today?"

"No, next week. Of course today. My parents won't be back till six or later. We can watch movies and order takeout." I turn to face her, but she's seen my screen. "Is that . . . ?"

I scroll to the top. "Ignore all the comments and stuff. We'll delete them before it goes live."

"Will it say Noor Awad like that?"

"'Course not." I delete both names from the title page. "We go live on Saturday, which means we still have a lot to do. I think a lot of the meat is here, but we have to go through section by section to fact-check before it can go online. Do you know how to do that?" I feel her head shake behind me. Fat beads of water drip from her blond hair onto my shoulder. "You have to highlight everything that's a fact and then you find three corroborating sources for each fact to make sure it's watertight. It's pretty straightforward. But it takes time."

I wait for Sara to speak, but she chews the melon slowly. I lean my head backwards and pout. Sara tippy-toes and plants a kiss on my mouth. "If I gave you one section and showed you how to do it, would you fact-check with us?"

"Laylah's working on it, right?"

"Yeah, but we're so behind. This investigation I'm working on. And she seems distracted. I don't know. We've just fallen behind schedule, and we have to get this out there because so many desperate people need this info." I turn and kiss Sara hard. Her mouth tastes like flowers.

My laptop pings, and an iMessage flashes onto the screen. Exclamation mark emojis from Latif fill the page. They met this morning after Fajr. Look! A screenshot of a text message. HH thanking Asma for an early-morning chat.

How TF did we miss an actual meeting?

Another ping. I haven't hacked everything!

"Who's that and what's hacked?"

I slam the laptop shut. Sara jumps back an inch. "Sorry, I just . . . I thought you were going to tell me everything."

"It's no one. Latif. From the news team. About the investigation."

"Oh. You're doing it with him? He's a hacker?"

"No. Yes. It's not like that. It's hard to explain." Sara's eyes widen. She points her chin down and looks up at me. "Is it another secret?"

"No, habibti!" I grab the belt of her robe and pull her toward me. "It's not really hacking. It's just looking. To see what's going on with some people who might be shady. It's . . . kinda confusing. I'm not being clear because I'm not really sure of all they're up to. Might not be important."

She reaches behind me and nudges my laptop open. It pings six times. "Sounds important." I don't want her to see the screen, but I need to see the texts. It's a series of screenshots from Latif. Messages from HH to someone or some people. CPC? What does that mean? he asks.

"No, they fucking didn't!" I slam the screen shut again, this time nearly catching the tip of Sara's finger. "My phone! Where's my phone?!" I run upstairs and fling pillows off the bed. It's Sara who finds it beneath a pile of sheets. Two missed calls from Latif. He answers on the first ring.

"Bro!"

"Bro! We missed the meeting!"

"Fuck the meeting. Do you not know what a CPC is?"

Sara sits cross-legged on the bed and fixes her eyes on me. I put Latif on speakerphone. "CPCs are the most messed-up thing on the planet." *Do* you *know what they are?* I mouth to Sara. She shakes her head.

"I'm just googling it now," Latif mumbles. "Crisis pregnancy center. A clinic, basically."

"No, not a clinic! Very, very not a clinic! CPCs are the most evil thing ever."

"Hold on. I'm still googling. It says here they offer care to—"

"They're not clinics. They don't care!"

"They're for a crisis, it says here. I don't get why you're freaking out. Isn't every pregnancy a crisis these days?"

I slam my phone onto the bed. "You're not listening. CPCs are fake fucking clinics. They pretend to be legit to lure you in, but once you're in, they grab on to your fear and take all your details and pass them on to the feds and show you photos of bleeding women who died having an abortion." The blood drains from Sara's face. I flop onto the bed and bury my head in her lap. "They literally keep tabs on pregnant people."

"You're mumbling."

Sara puts the phone next to my head. I turn my face to speak into the phone. "I said, they keep tabs on people. Read me the rest of that text. Is she texting Asma about a CPC?"

"Not sure who. She wrote, 'At the CPC.'"

"That's it?"

"That's it. I can't see what's incoming, remember? Or who she's texting."

"So she's responding to someone. And she's involved in a CPC. That's what this means. She's involved. I bet she's texting her new BFF."

"Is *that* where the donations are going?"

I bolt upright. "OMG, yes. HH is only *pretending* to be Asma's friend to get money and really she's on the same page as Norm Miller, and Asma's only *pretending* to be a feminist but really she's antiabortion like the rest of those fake hypocrite Haram Police and she knows exactly where the money is going. I knew it!" I throw my head back into Sara's lap. She stays completely still.

"She's texting about another meeting!" Latif hollers.

"Should we turn the volume down?" Sara whispers.

"Why? Is someone home?" I turn onto my back and look up at Sara's face. It's three shades lighter than usual.

"Another meeting! Look at the screenshot!" Latif yells.

10. At yours.

"Jeez, that could be anyone and anywhere, Latif. These one-way messages are not great."

"At yours means at Asma's place, which means RICC. Obviously. We have to get to the mosque, now."

"For what? To get caught?"

"To listen in on their meeting."

Sara's eyes grow as wide as dinner plates.

HH's car is nowhere to be seen. Not in the RICC parking lot. Not on the street. Asma's car is parked next to the imam's. Latif yanks a crinkled brown hoodie out of his backpack and shoves it at me. "Pretend you're a boy." The hoodie smells like fries. I walk behind him toward the main entryway, where we take off our sneakers and shove them into his bag. I tighten the cord of the hood as we creep through the main prayer hall, where two older men are sitting in prayer. The space looks even bigger now that it's mostly empty. A few hundred people will squeeze into it for Jummah prayers tomorrow.

The mosque cat prances around the perimeter of the space, ignoring us. I breathe in a deep inhale of woody incense. Memories come flooding back. Once upon a time this was my happy place. Now I'm a literal intruder.

Latif hurries toward a set of double doors, closing them quietly behind us. We turn left toward the corridor that leads up to the second-floor women's prayer room and Asma's office. But as soon as he turns, Latif steps back around the corner and reaches an arm back to stop me. It's Asma. I can hear her voice. And her footsteps. My heart pounds. She must be on the phone because there is no other voice. Her footsteps grow quieter. Latif pokes his head around the corner. "She's headed to the door. To the basement," he whispers. "Fuck, that was close." He looks up at the ceiling. We hear the door click shut and wait a few seconds.

"Why would she leave HH alone in the office, and why would she be going into the basement? What's in there?"

"Nothing. It's always locked."

"Something. Why else would she go down?"

Sixty seconds feels like three years. My scalp sweats beneath the hoodie, but I pull the cord even tighter to hide my face. We stand there, in silence, planning our next move. Asma's voice emerges from behind the door. She treads softly back up the stairs toward her office.

"We need to get into the basement."

"It's permanently locked. No one goes down there."

"Well, she does!"

I run to the door and turn the handle, but Asma made sure to lock it behind her. Latif gasps when I pull the thin, black pin out of my hair and poke it into the lock. Must I always be surrounded by drama queens? "Oh my God, oh my God. That only works in movies! I'm going to find the key before you . . ." His voice trails off. Before I can stop him, Latif has disappeared halfway up the stairs. I wiggle the pin in and out until something gives. *Click. Click.* I turn the handle. "Bingo."

It feels the same as it did on Saturday mornings all those years ago. Musty, warm, strangely comforting. I remember walking along this hallway with an ice-cold coffee milkshake in my hand and a metal-clad smile across my face. Only the scent of lip gloss and Victoria's Secret body spray is missing. I push open the first door. Empty. Second door. Empty. The third room still has the low tables that we read Qur'an from while we sat on the floor, except they're stacked against the walls. I walk in to inspect them. Maybe they're the same ones. I trace my finger along the edge of the smooth wood and peek underneath to see where we etched our names. SR LOVES

YA. MLH LOVES MG. I don't see my name, but I know who these initials belong to. Saidiya had the prettiest mouth of any girl I'd ever seen. And Malaika. The Angel. She could talk for Texas.

A door clicks shut. Footsteps. It's too late to close this door. I leave it ajar and hide behind it. Someone is mumbling. It sounds like an old man. The sound of jingling keys gets louder and louder. My heart races. I'll say I got lost! I'll say I was taking a trip down memory lane! I'll say . . .

Latif pops his head around the corner. "Look what I found!" He jingles three keys dangling next to a Porsche-shaped key fob. I slide down the wall and grasp my knees.

"Jesus!"

"I can't believe you broke in!"

"I can't believe you stole her fucking *car* keys!"

"You can't swear in here! Say astaghfirullah! And forget the keys. Wait till I tell you what I just heard!" He shuts the door and sits cross-legged opposite me. "Noor. It's all starting to make sense. All of this shit. Argh." He taps his cheeks with his fingertips and mouths astaghfirullah and tobah tobah.

"Spit it out!"

"That stuff about IVF. You know? What you heard? It's because *she's* the one doing it! She's trying the IVF thing!"

"Who?"

"Asma. She's in her office right now. . . ."

"With HH?"

"What? No. With the imam. She's saying how there's no point in him giving her injections in her stomach because they can't do

IVF or they'll both go to jail. She was crying a bunch, and he was saying he paid some guy in an alley nine hundred bucks for the injections and why did he bother."

The lipstick and the Scotch bottle. Where does poor Asma fit into that messy equation? Maybe she sees herself and the imam as the couple needing IVF to start a family, even if, in HH's example to Norm, that couple was a "Good Christian Family." Maybe Asma and Imam Khoury were the exact couple HH was talking about? Maybe she made them Christian in her conversation with Norm?

Latif holds the keys an inch from his face and turns the fob every which way. I snatch the keys from him. "Latif! They're both up there now? And you took her *car* keys? What if she needs to go somewhere?"

"They were just sitting there on a table in the ladies' lounge."

"And you didn't think to take the basement key off the loop and leave the rest behind?" He shrugs. I wonder if we should bail and come back when Asma isn't already in the building. Or do we stay, now that we're here? I wish Laylah were here. She would know the smart thing to do. I don't want to leave without looking at the fourth classroom, the last one along the hallway. It's the one I used to take classes in. The room filled with secrets. "Come. I want to show you something."

Latif pops his head out the door. "Coast is clear, Agent N."

"This isn't a joke."

The room is emptier than the last. Except for a bookcase with half a dozen leather-bound books scattered across its dusty shelves.

I close my eyes, inhale a deep breath, and push back the memories. Then I go to the bookcase and push its right side. It slides across the carpet, and Latif's mouth opens wide.

The hidden door is still there, still painted the same shade of pale pistachio as the rest of the wall. The handle is an old-school wooden knob. I give it a tug and the door opens. Latif shines his flashlight over my shoulder.

A padded examination bed is stacked with piles of yellow paper. A white coat hangs from a hook. There are no windows, but there is still an annex around one corner. It is crammed with brown boxes stacked almost to the slanted ceiling. We used to store books in here so we had an excuse to say we needed to go in pairs to fetch them.

Latif hits the light switch. I pull open drawers and cabinets. A blood-pressure cuff, two stethoscopes, a cupboard filled with dark blue scrubs, and another packed with boxes of latex gloves. Not a medication packet in sight. Maybe they're in the brown boxes. But when I crack a box open, it's filled with condoms. I pocket some for Laylah.

"Since when is there a clinic in our mosque?" Latif squints at a metal device as big as his palm. He snaps it open and shut and peers into the mysterious tube from all angles.

"That goes inside the vagina. To look at the cervix." The metal clangs to the floor. "Stop. Making. Noise. Look around for evidence!" I speak through gritted teeth. This kid is getting on my last nerve. Not only did he steal Asma's car keys, which means he has to figure out a way to return them before she comes looking, but now he's busying himself with a speculum.

"I can't believe we discovered a hidden clinic."

"This ain't no damn clinic." I turn to find Latif has put on the white coat, its sleeves barely reaching past his elbows.

"What do you mean? This is definitely a clinic."

"Then where are the medications?"

Latif flaps the stirrups on the exam table up and down.

"This is the CPC. How evil can these people be?" My voice cracks. My throat feels scratchy. Maybe it's the dust. Maybe it's the fact that a place of worship has yet again been turned into a place of betrayal. I imagine all the frightened people who lie down on this examination table only to be lied to. Lied to and chastised by the very people they respected.

"Asma's not a nurse. She can't be doing anything bad here."

I peel back the brown tape on a box, hoping to find hormone tablets or syringes or even pamphlets. Something with accurate information and actual help for those in need. Latif is quiet. "Help me look through these boxes. Peel the tape off carefully so we can put it back on."

We rummage through a dozen boxes. More blank yellow paper. Yellow pamphlets with diagrams of a developing fetus and WHAT TO EXPECT! printed across them. More gloves. Condoms. I sit against a stack of unopened boxes and put my head between my knees.

"Don't be depressed, Noor. Can we assume it's a bad clinic just because we can't find any medications? All that stuff's illegal. How would they even get it?"

"You don't understand. The people that want to help, they get their hands on that stuff and they put their lives on the line and they help people, okay?"

"Okay," he mutters.

I stand up and root through another box. It's filled with nothing but packing peanuts. "This is bullshit!" I fling the box against the wall. "Missing money, secret meetups between Asma and HH. HH hanging out with the biggest misogynist in the world, then sending texts about a meeting with Asma and a CPC. And now this." I pick packing peanuts off the floor and toss them back into the box. "These people are beyond wicked. The worst kind. Pretend to be do-gooders so they can win our votes and our trust and be our role models."

I stand and walk toward the door. But while Latif schleps his big feet across the floor, a woman's voice echoes somewhere outside the secret room.

"Wait a second. The door is open and the light's on so I *think* she is here," the voice says. I grab Latif and hurl him toward the boxes in the annex. "Hide behind! Behind!" He scoots through the narrow opening between a stack of boxes and the wall. I follow and stick my back to the wall.

"But I'm looking inside and I don't see her. Don't you think that's sloppy, though? To leave the door open like this and the light on? Mmm. Okay, maybe. I don't know. Let me try to get ahold of her and I'll call you right back. If you talk to her first, tell her to be more careful. Okay, bye."

The light turns off and on again. "Helloooo? You hiding? The place is empty. No need to hide today."

My phone buzzes in the pocket of my jeans. Latif grabs my entire thigh to stop the vibrations. I clasp my hand over his and stifle a yelp. That fucking hurt.

"Hello?" The voice grumbles something, and then the person turns off the light and shuts the door.

I push Latif's hand away and rub my thigh. "You grabbed the wrong pocket and that really fucking hurt!"

"That was Asma! Who was she looking for? Someone else knows about this place? Who did she think was hiding?" He shuffles out from behind the boxes, his lanky frame jostling them. I yank him back. "Just wait a minute until she's gone upstairs." I rub my thigh and check my phone. It was Laylah. It buzzes again. I send her to voicemail.

"Are we trapped? Do you think she moved the bookcase back?" Latif uses his phone's flashlight to avoid bumping into more boxes. But when we turn the doorknob, the door opens slightly into the empty room. I tell Latif to reach his long arms around the door and push the bookcase hard so we can open the door wider. We leave the secret room and then peek out of the classroom into the empty hallway.

"You need to find a way to put back those keys without being seen. It's more believable that you would be here, if you get caught, I mean. Meet at the car?" Latif jogs ahead of me, jumping two steps at a time. I pull my hood down and fan my sweaty scalp. I look around the classroom of memories and hear the giggling and whispering. Then I hear the bellowing thunder of the angry imam. I shudder and pull the hoodie tighter over my head.

There are footsteps in the light-filled hallway that runs along the back of the prayer hall, so I wait before pushing open the door from the basement. The sound of footsteps is gone, but when I peek my head around the door to check if the coast is clear, I see a flash of pink, maybe the trail of a long dress or an abaya, disappear around the far corner.

LAYLAH

I WAKE BEFORE sunrise to say the Fajr prayer. The house is dead quiet. Not even the odd creak of the wooden staircase or the occasional rumble of the ice maker interrupts the silence. Only my body disturbs the peace. Anxiety bubbles like an angry green fountain deep inside my stomach. I'm sure the gastric growls are loud enough to wake Adam in the room next door. I roll onto my side and curl into a tight ball.

"Try us again on Wednesday. I can't guarantee we'll be in North Texas, but I promise we'll try to help." Dr. Hogarth's words play over and over in my mind. "Promise we'll try to help. Promise we'll try to help."

No one is here to help. I called and texted Tito's Tacos at least fifteen times yesterday, but there was no answer. Sometimes it didn't even ring, as if the number was completely out of service.

I slip a hand beneath my pillow and silence the alarm ringing on Nanima's brick of a cell phone. I don't understand why she needs this many phones, but I'm glad she was so quick to offer me one.

I imagine that Noor is waking next to Sara. She doesn't know that I caught the two of them giggling and acting silly when I walked past them in the hallway the other day. Noor was so absorbed in her crush-of-the-month that she didn't even look up. Normally, in week two of a crush, she would have flooded my phone with texts and demanded at least three sleepovers so she could drown me in questions. *Am I catching feelings too soon?* (Yes.) *Am I playing it too cool?* (Definitely not.) *Should I ask her out officially on Monday or should I wait till Tuesday?* (Umm, what's the difference?)

She rarely takes my advice and answers all her own questions. My job as her best friend is to be a sounding board. A nonjudgmental, mildly sarcastic sounding board that can instantly transform into a shoulder to cry on when shit goes left (which is usually at the end of week three). If I say anything about how quickly her relationships stop and start, she says I'm judging her. I still have the text that says, Habibti, as a str8 you just don't understand. You should read a book that came out back in the day, *This Bridge Called My Back.* It explains everything. Basically, queer romances, especially between two femmes, work on a different timeline to y'all's. Cuz we're unique. Which I get, and that's fine, usually. But nothing is usual right now. We're supposed to publish the Guide in two days, and we are so far behind. Avoiding each other because of 1) a secret that's too shameful to share and hopefully

will go away any day now and 2) a hypnotizing crush is not helping us meet our deadline.

I stick a hand out from under the covers and reach for the
bullet journal at the edge of my desk. I crack it open to a page
filled with notes for a college admission essay. It's the wrong journal. The last thing I need right now is to be reminded of how far
behind I am with this month's to-do list for the LLP. My other
bullet journal, the one for the Guide, is inside the white tote I was
carrying on Monday. It's stashed somewhere beneath my desk. I
roll out of bed and dig for it, turning the pages till I reach the
latest to-do list: Section 3B needs to be fact-checked. Section 5
needs to be fleshed out some more. Section 7 has to be written.
Did Noor make a start on that section? When I swipe through the
Google Doc on my phone and see the title "Section 7" followed
by a series of yet-to-be-done items, my stomach churns at the sight
of unchecked boxes.

☐ Explain how the diff meds work
☐ Explain what to do if only one type of med is
  available
☐ Explain what to do when it gets too late to get a
  medical abortion (meaning an abortion you can
  get at up to at least 70 days using just pills).

My abdomen cramps. I slam shut the journal and fling it against
the bed. It bounces off the box frame, and something small and
white slips out from between its pages. The handwriting on the

card is a scrawl. "If you can't get us at the usual number by Weds, try 214-555-3797."

Was this from the nurse? I faintly recall her digging in her hair and pulling something out, but was it *this*? Is this her handwriting? Why didn't she just tell me there was another number to call? Was she hiding this from the doctor? Why didn't *she* text *me* when she had my number all along?

I think back to Nurse Ali's gawking face. The excitement in her voice when she was telling bullshit stories about Pakistani child brides. Should I call a number scribbled by a woman with a culturally appropriated hairstyle and terrible eyeshadow-blending skills? What if . . . oh my God, my worst nightmare . . . what if this is a trap? My stomach cramps like there are hands squeezing my organs from the inside. What if Tito's Tacos was a front and all of this is a ploy to get me back there? What if it was just a mobile version of those fake crisis pregnancy centers where they pretend to offer you an abortion but really they're just using the facade of a clinic to lure you in and manipulate you into keeping the pregnancy? But then why wouldn't they have responded to my calls and desperate, pleading, pathetic texts yesterday?

I don't know whom I can trust. I grab my LLP journal, turn to a fresh page, and make a list of pros and cons. "Text the new number. Pros: might have pills! Cons: might be a one-way ticket to jail."

I want to call Noor. I want to pluck this dilemma out of my overpacked brain and drop it into her problem-solving, analytical brain. Noor could solve this puzzle the same way she figures

shit out when she's investigating secret bank statements and texts
between shady politicians.

I could text Noor. But even if I brace for the tsunami of sharam that will engulf my whole body and probably trigger another
blackout, Noor likely won't see my text for an hour or two. I bet
she's dreaming about applying to the same colleges as Sara somewhere on the West Coast with absolutely no thoughts of me and
my East Coast plans.

I close the journal. *Fuck it, I'm screwed anyway. What else could
go wrong?* I text the new number and go to the bathroom to wash
so I can pray.

Wudhu is supposed to be a spiritual and physical cleanse. One
of my favorite rituals. I feel fresh and brand-new each time I wash
to pray. Not these days. These days I feel sluggish and heavy and
like no amount of water can rinse the lies off my skin. Still, I
stand over the basin, stare into the mirror, and make my intention.
"Bismillah. God, please purify my soul and my heart." I run water
over my right hand three times, then my left, looping my fingers
around my wrist each time. I fill my cupped palm with warm
water and pour it into my mouth. A soft voice interrupts the sound
of gargling.

"Can you turn that off, please, Laylah betah?" I have my
head tilted back, staring at the ceiling, when Mom speaks gently
through the bathroom door.

"*Grrrgggggggg?*" I spit out the water.

She pushes the door open and squints at my dripping chin
in the mirror. Her long black hair is falling out of its ponytail,

her velvet scrunchie hanging on for dear life.

"Sorry, sweetie, but the ringing is loud."

"What ringing?"

Mom steps into the bathroom and reaches past me to turn off the gushing water. "It's nice that you pray, but wasn't it you who said that if worshipping Allah in the early hours disturbs those you live with, then God would actually prefer it if you were considerate about their sleep and maybe skipped a prayer or two? Something about how being mindful of your family is a type of worship? Go and turn it off. I don't want to rummage around in your room." She ruffles my hair.

"I don't hear any ringing, Mom!"

She tilts her head. The scrunchie slides from her hair onto the floor. She stoops to pick it up, still listening. "Hmm. It's stopped now. Just maybe turn it down a little. For next time." She plants a kiss on my cheek and shuts the door behind her.

Maybe I hit the snooze button. I turn to face the mirror and that's when I hear it. *PEOWWWWWW!* It's not the alarm. It's the obnoxious siren of a ringtone I set yesterday so that I wouldn't miss any (non-JJ) calls or texts. But who is calling before sunrise?

I walk quickly to my room. Four new messages flash in the Signal app.

> Yes, this number is working.
>
> Who is this?
>
> How did you get this number?
>
> Can't say anything till you explain.

My wet thumb hovers over the screen. Don't do anything silly, Laylah. Think carefully about everyone's safety. Think carefully about what you say next. I wipe my hand on my T-shirt, swipe to my phone settings, and turn off location services. A lump the size of Texas sits in my throat.

> I was given this number
> by a trusted source.

Who?

> I can't say.

Why?

> To protect their identity.

When did they give it to you?

> Monday.

What time on Monday?

> I think 8 am. Ish.

Before 8:30 or after 8:30?

> Before . . . I think.

Oh, hey! It's you! Girl in the turban,
right? I knew you would call.

Turban? Did a Sikh person or another hijaabi go to Tito's Tacos straight after me, because I was definitely not wearing my hijaab in a turban style that day. And how did they know I would be in touch?

> Do you know who I am?

Yeah! Lila?

My heart pounds. I put the phone on my desk and dive beneath the covers. *What if the same vigilantes who went after Bella's Bundts yesterday are coming straight to my house? What if I'm about to be trapped!* A car stalls and starts on the street below. My heart pounds in time to the stuttering engine. I smoosh my half-wet face into the pillow. The phone beeps loudly and I grab it to turn down the notifications sound.

> Did you find any meds?
> Do you have them?

Not really. Something else . . . Go to 2626
S Pearl Expwy in two hours. Gray door
with a vet sign. Press the buzzer and say
my name and you'll get in. I'll probably
see you there in a few. Be safe. Bye.

> What meds do they have
> there? This is Ali, right?

The Uber drops me at the far end of the farmers market. I enter through a side entrance as if I'm going to get a latte at the Italian café, but I march straight past the glass display of cannoli and out the other side of the building. My phone is already on airplane mode. I use a screenshot from the navigation app to make sure I turn in the right direction to walk the three blocks to South Pearl Expressway. I turn left and then right and see the industrial zone where the building must be located. It's a block away, but the sidewalk abruptly ends, forcing me into the middle of what looks like a highway. I pray that no cars suddenly come speeding by.

A tall metal fence opens into what looks like a graveyard for cars. Rusting trucks, stacks of giant tires, and heaps of exhaust pipes are packed throughout the open space. I squeeze between an old blue car and what used to be a motorbike to reach what must be the building. There is no number on the door. VET CLINIC. APPTS NECESSARY is spray-painted onto the gray paint. I press the buzzer and listen for the crackle of white noise as someone pushes a button on the other side.

"Yes?"

"Nurse Ali sent me."

The door buzzes open.

The thing about cats is they pee when they freak out. I know this because when Adam begged Mom for a kitten all throughout the pandemic, Mom's main argument, the one that she kept explaining to him over and over again, was that the smell of cat pee soaking into the carpet every time the cat was anxious would make her feel sick and the smell would make Adam cry, since any kind of odor upsets him.

But who can blame these poor kittens for peeing everywhere? At least two dozen metal crates line the far wall of this open room. A small brown receptionist's desk is straight ahead of me. Behind it sits an older White woman. She taps away at the keys of her laptop as if I haven't just walked into the cold, gray room that is empty except for me, her, and a lot of cats.

A distressed ginger paws at its cage. "It's the hormones," says the receptionist, pushing her glasses up her nose and not looking up from her screen.

"Whose hormones?"

She hands me a white pamphlet and looks me up and down. Fronds of silvery hair frame her face; the rest is tied in a neat bun. The metal door bangs shut behind me. The receptionist leans her head to the side to look around me at the tall figure in a black baseball cap and dark blue overalls. The strange man has wheeled a dolly loaded with boxes into the room.

"Over there." She points to the spot where four empty metal chairs are pushed against the wall, facing the cats on the opposite side. I can't tell if she's telling me where to sit or telling him where to dump the boxes. I pray there are bottles of mifepristone and misoprostol inside those boxes.

"Lila, is it? She said you'd be here about now. Take a seat."

"Is she here?"

"Who?"

"Ali. She said she'd be here."

"Not yet. Take a seat."

"I just need to . . . Do you . . . ?" I bend over the desk a little. "Do you have the medications here?" The door slams shut.

She nods and taps away at the keyboard.

"You do have the meds? It's just that she said it's something . . ."

The door buzzes, opens, and clangs shut. A White woman who looks to be in her early twenties, although she's dressed like a tween, stands in the doorway, as if she can't take another step. Her bell-bottom jeans graze the streaked floor. A pale pink T-shirt with dark pink writing says GIRL POWER. She turns her head left to right, from the cats to the receptionist to me.

The row of metal chairs is not far from the desk, and even

though I slink away from the desk and pick the chair closest to the receptionist, I can't hear a word they are saying. Between the sound of the cats meowing and the receptionist and the new woman whispering, all I can make out are mumbles.

The room is small but has high ceilings, which are lined with massive silver pipes. It's cold. The walls are painted dark gray like the front door. The floor, which was probably shiny and white once upon a time, is streaked with some kind of light gray liquid, as if a dirty mop has been dragged across it too many times. And the whole place smells like cat pee. The new woman walks past me, the scent of her flowery perfume mingling with the smell of urine. She sits as far away from me as she can, leaving two empty chairs between us, and reads something on her phone. It rings. She quickly silences the call and looks up in a panic. *I get it,* I want to say. *I really, really get the whole avoiding phone calls thing.* But her face is pinched and mean-looking, so I turn away and look at the cat rattling its metal cage. It has ginger fur and a narrow face, which I think makes it a female. I wonder who the ginger cat has seen walk in and out of this cold building. Who sat in this chair before me and what became of her life? The cat paws at her crate, then turns, lifts her tail, and arches her back.

"What you need to know about spaying and neutering your cat," reads the pamphlet. I look up at the receptionist, ready to tell her she gave me the wrong paperwork, but she is staring at the other girl, gesturing to her. "Along that corridor," she says, pointing behind her. She seems to have forgotten that I was here first, that I had an appointment. That I am desperate. *Hey! Hello! Hi?!* I want to say. But of course I say nothing, coward that I've become. If Noor were here, she'd be saying, *Oh, so blondie gets to go in before us even though we got here first?!* And the receptionist would have blushed and said she'd made a big mistake and of course we should go back to see the doctor before anyone else.

Noor would have investigated this place from top to bottom before we even sat down. She would have unpacked those boxes herself, told the receptionist to stop making a fuss, and then she would have taken me by the hand and said, *Laylah. This place looks shady as fuck. We have to bounce.* And she would have been right.

But I am alone. I trekked along a highway, squeezed past rusting cars, and got buzzed into a nasty clinic for stray cats because I have no options and no one. I lost my voice and my ability to stand up for myself somewhere between Poetry and the gutted cars outside.

I open the pamphlet to learn about the number of days it takes for a cat to heal after its balls have been snipped. They experience only minor discomfort, apparently. Pink T-shirt walks past the receptionist's desk and turns left down a corridor as if she knows exactly where she is headed. When she walks back to her seat a few minutes later, the receptionist has disappeared into a back room and Pink T-shirt is rubbing her stomach. Her lips look shiny.

"They gave you the meds already?"

She wipes her mouth with the back of her hand and burps.

"Here, you want this?" I reach for a pack of tissues in the bottom of my bag. She takes it and mumbles something through closed lips.

"Sorry?"

She looks at me with pink eyes and dabs her mouth.

"What did the doctor do?" I whisper. The receptionist emerges out of the back room with a white bowl. "Next." She points down the corridor, and I want so badly to hold the silent, mean girl's hand and take her with me. *Will you stay while they do whatever they do back there?* I want to say. Instead, I leave her with her white bowl, walk slowly past the cats and down the long hallway alone.

They say that all of us store racism in our bones. That self-hatred of our Brownness, our Muslimness, our queerness, our desires, of our immigrant parents and our sari-wearing grandmothers is woven into the DNA of each and every cell—a side effect of growing up in America. That's not true of me anymore. Last year Noor and I did this journaling project with fifty-two exercises, one for each week, that help you process that shit and clear internalized racism out of your system. Noor called it a cleanse. I called it common sense. The woman who wrote the guided journal with its "exorcisms for internalized racism and misogynoir" said the reason that Black and Brown women (Noor said she should have written "femmes") have the highest rates of autoimmune disease is because our bodies are filled with so much self-loathing that our immune systems turn against us and attack our own organs. It makes sense. None of my MCAT questions says it, but it's true. Diseases like lupus are literally caused by the part of your body that's supposed to defend you against intruders going haywire. Instead of being on high alert to fight viruses and bacteria, our immune systems go into overdrive and attack our own skin, kidneys, and brain.

I told Noor that lupus causes a butterfly rash across the face and that's when she went into overdrive with the self-love affirmations, adding on extras even though the journal was filled with them. "I don't want a facial rash!" she said, scribbling new affirmations into both our books. We paced my living room in circles with our hands on our hearts repeating the affirmations on the pink pages of the guided journal: "I am enough! My body is my friend! I love all of me!" Adam joined in, dragging a blanket in one hand and a toy truck in the other. "I love my toys! I love my aloos!"

"I don't want my body attacking me!" Noor said, taking a breather between the chanting. She pressed a fist against her chest as she spoke.

"I think you're supposed to be gentle on yourself." I had lifted her hand off her chest and rubbed her rib cage.

"Come on, Lay! Say it with me: I am more powerful and more magnificent than the lie of White supremacy and I love my body! I adore it! I honor it!"

So tell me, after all that guided journaling and chanting, after almost a year (we didn't completely finish the journal project) of exorcising our internalized racism, why am I gawking at the educated baddie standing in front of me? I pick my jaw off the floor. I must look as foolish as Nurse Ali, who wouldn't stop staring at my hijaab on Monday.

The doctor stands in the middle of the tiny examination room pouring purple liquid from a brown bottle into a clear plastic cup. "Here." She thrusts the cup at me. "Come inside. Close the door."

I step forward as if I'm sleepwalking in a half dream, half nightmare in which my body has betrayed me but someone who looks like the future me is about to be my savior. The doctor has skin the color of hot chocolate (I know we're not supposed to compare our skin to edible things, but it's true) and long black hair that falls in waves down her chest. A white coat hangs loosely over her dark orange V-neck shirt. She looks young and wise. Her brown eyes are lined with black, just the way Mom does it, and I imagine that she closed her eyelids over a brass stick of surma, in the traditional style, rubbing back and forth this morning until the black powder coated her top and bottom waterlines. I read her nose, lips, and chin and try to calculate which stretch of India, Pakistan, Bangladesh, Sri Lanka, or even Afghanistan she comes from. I want to say, "So . . . where are you from?" but I can't inflict that wretched question on another Brown woman.

"Take it." She raises her brows. Her perfectly arched, possibly ombre microbladed—but in a very subtle way—brows. She looks annoyed, as if I'm wasting her time and she'd rather play with the cats.

I stick my hand out like a robot. She watches me watching her and flicks her hair over her shoulder. For a moment the dark blue lettering on the front of her white coat is revealed: K. M. KAPOOR. Her hair settles back over her chest, concealing the all-important letters that follow. The letters she earned through years of preparation, hard work, and sticking to a plan—not falling victim to a Rumi poem and a field full of flowers.

She raises her eyebrows again.

"Kapoor? Like Kareena?" I whisper.

"Yeah. My mom's a fan. You're gonna need to drink that quickly," she says, her voice lifting at the end of the sentence, as if she is speaking to a child.

She walks past me and reaches up to open a cupboard above my head. Her hair swishes aside. That's when I see it. K. M. KAPOOR, BS, MPH, DVM.

"Wait. What kind of . . . ?"

"Mostly livestock and large animal. But I volunteer here on Thursdays. For the cats."

My heart drops into my stomach.

"Please drink that now because we have to keep you for thirty minutes once you've taken it." She eyes the clock on the wall.

I sniff the cup and wretch.

"Don't smell it. Knock it back. No sipping."

"What is it?"

"Medicine." She opens a slim white box she took down from the cabinet. The pill inside is longer than my thumb.

"I'm not going to swallow *that*!" I don't mean to speak my thoughts out loud, but the monstrosity she is holding in her slender fingers looks like a horse tablet.

"It's not for swallowing. And it's not all for you." She snaps the pill into two jagged halves. "This bit's for you. This bit's for her."

"The other girl?"

"Ms. Mandy Lou," she says under her breath, dropping each fragment of the jagged pill into a plastic cup. She uncaps a black Sharpie with her mouth and writes *M* on one cup and *L* on the other.

Do vets have a different code of ethics? It might be okay to repeat one cat's name in front of another cat, or a cow's name in front of a horse, but it is never okay to say a human patient's name in front of another (human) patient. Dr. Kapoor seems to have caught her slipup.

"Hurry, please!"

I knock back the syrup and try not to spit the bitter stickiness back into the cup. Thick syrup coats the back of my tongue and throat with the taste of copper pennies. I ask for water, but she ushers me out of the room. "Best you don't drink anything now. Miss April will give you a bowl. I'll call you back in thirty minutes." She walks out of the room behind me but turns left and disappears farther down the long corridor.

Mandy Lou is sitting in my seat hunched over a white bowl. Another bowl sits on her old seat. I suppose it's for me. The crying cats sound like a chorus of human babies. Miss April is nowhere to be seen.

"Did it clear you out?" I say gently, picking up the bowl.

She heaves and holds her stomach. "There's nothing left." She sits up straight and rubs her palm in circles over her chest. Strands of blond hair stick to her wet cheeks. I can't tell if she's sweating or crying. I want to give her more tissues, but suddenly my stomach lurches as if the entire organ is trying to escape out of my mouth.

"Oh my God," I mumble, dropping to my knees. "What did she give us? What was that syrup?"

"It makes it go away." She spits into the bowl and wipes her mouth with her fingers. "It makes it go."

My entire life pours out of my mouth and into the bowl before I can ask for help. The metallic bitterness of the syrup mixes with the sourness of my stomach's contents. Mandy Lou sobs between heaves. "It hurts so bad," she says, squeezing her legs together.

The cats cry louder and bash at their metal cages. Mandy Lou stretches out her arm toward me, but it blurs into a long streak of yellow and pink. A deep ache in my pelvis drags me to the ground. "This isn't right. Something's not right. They shouldn't have left us like this." Mandy Lou cries louder.

I feel a dampness between my legs. The room spins. *Is this happening now? Here?* Miscarrying is a punishable offense. I need to get home. I reach for Mandy Lou's hand, but the distance between us stretches. The room expands like the walls are made of elastic.

"My phone. Has anyone seen my grandma's phone? I mean my phone. Where is it?" A cat brushes past me and jumps onto my chair. It sits with its paws on either side of my phone. I grab it, turn it on, and do the first smart thing of the day. I call my best friend and tell her to save my life.

UNBECOMING!
THE BOLLYWOOD MUSICAL

FEATURING: Laylah Khan as *Priya the Panda*! And
Joshua Jackson as *Sam the Seahorse*!

FADE IN:

EXT. FIELD OF ROLLING HILLS AND BLUEBONNETS - DAY

Priya the Panda rolls over from a nap and stares
at her reflection in the lake. The reflection
ripples as a seahorse swims to the surface and
pops its snout out of the water. Priya touches her
face to the seahorse.

                    PRIYA
          Oh, Sam! Ain't I lucky? I'm a panda!

Priya rolls onto her back and talks toward the
armadillo-shaped clouds.

                    PRIYA
          It's better to be a panda than a girl
          if you're in Texas. Pandas ovulate only
          once a year. Less chance of getting

pregnant. And if they do get pregnant,
the fertilized egg floats around the
uterus for months before attaching to
the uterine wall. It's almost as good
as being an armadillo. Armadillos can
pause their pregnancies for months.

Priya flops onto her belly and looks back into the
water.

PRIYA
To be a pregnant panda is to be in
control. I could just put this pregnancy
on pause and give birth when I'm ready.
Or even better, Sam, you could get
pregnant, since you're a male seahorse.

Sam floats out of the water and the two dance
together and disappear into the hills.

FADE TO BLACK.

STEP 8

KNOW WHO TO TRUST

 Anonymous Armadillo
at 22:09

Shouldn't this say "Don't Trust Anybody?"

 Anonymous Seahorse
at 23:17

But then how would anyone get help?

NOOR

LAYLAH SHRIEKS AND mumbles and makes no sense at all.
I pace alongside Latif's car, waiting for him to get back. All the
while I eye the trash can on the corner and wonder if I should
ball up this smelly hoodie and throw it away. "You're breaking up.
Hang up and call back."

"Ma . . . marriage." She slurs her words as if she's knocked back
five Red Bull vodkas. Except Laylah Khan doesn't drink. And
she sure as hell doesn't cry. At least not in front of other humans.
"Marriage is illegal."

"What?"

"Miscarriage. Illeeeegal."

"Yes, miscarriage is illegal. I know. Are you working on the
Guide? Section 4? Why does it sound like you're crying?"

"I'm not crrryyyying. I'm . . ."

"Shut her up!" a voice snaps through the phone.

"Laylah? Laylah! Who's that? Laylah, where are you?"

Latif jogs over.

"The cat . . ."

"What cat? Laylah? What cat?"

"The cat doctor. Cat doctor! I'm telling her, Noor. They don't believe me. I'm haaaving . . ."

"You're having . . . ? What?"

"Miscarriage."

"But how . . . ?" My legs turn to stone. The engine starts, but I can't move my body. "Where are you? I'm coming right now!" I hear sobbing. Then a woman's voice pleading with Laylah. "Please hang up now. That's enough. Turn it off. The location. Please."

Then another woman's voice. "Just take it!"

"No!" I scream, loud enough for Latif to get out of the car. "Laylah! Hayati! Where. Are. You?"

"Farmers. Market. Not inside. Gray. Door," she mumbles. The line goes dead.

Latif drives like he's a getaway driver and I've emptied a vault of diamonds into his trunk. He takes a sharp left away from the mosque before I can even fasten my seat belt. My body is hurled against his shoulder.

"The farmers market? A cat doctor? She said that?"

"Yes! I don't know what it means either. A vet?" I fumble for my seat belt with fingers made of sausages. Someone must have snatched her phone and turned it off. My app shows her last locations from her old phone a day ago, somewhere far east of Dallas. It must be a mistake. I search for vet clinics near the farmers market, trying not to get carsick as Latif speeds down

Central Expressway. The closest vet clinic I can find is in Deep Ellum.

We circle whole blocks over and over, passing the farmers market what feels like a million times. Suddenly every door in the neighborhood is a shade of gray. There are no vet signs, no one walking along the streets that we can ask for directions. Typical Dallas. Latif flashes his lights at a man driving slowly out of an auto shop behind the farmers market, but the man assumes Latif is asking about the Veterans Affairs hospital. "No, *vet*. Like for hamsters," Latif says again and again. That's when I spot the car depot with its row of gray metal doors. Latif drops me at the metal gate, and I run into what looks like a wasteland. The gray doors line one side of the space, all of them unmarked except for one. VET CLINIC. APPTS NECESSARY.

Cat doctor. I hammer the door with my fists and pound the small white buzzer. Nothing. "I'm calling the cops if you don't open this door!" I pound harder. "I AM the cops!" I hear a buzz, yank the heavy door open, and walk into the foulest-smelling room on the planet. Vomit and cat pee mixed with bleach so thick, it's risen from the sopping ground to choke the air. A woman in a white coat and long hair is crouched over Laylah, who is splayed out on the floor with two cats at her feet. The woman looks at me with big brown eyes. "It doesn't usually cause such severe emesis. I think they gave me a bad batch."

"Of what? What did you give her?" I push the woman away from Laylah. "Laylah! Lay!" I grab Laylah's chin and shake her face. "Laylah! Wake up!"

She mumbles, her eyes still closed. "Blood."

"Oh my God! Where?" I look her body up and down and pat her legs with my hands. Her clothes are soaking wet, but there's no blood on my hands.

"It's not blood! I keep telling her!" The doctor gets to her feet and stands over us. "She vomited in her lap before she blacked out. It's not blood on her legs. She's just been sick, but she won't listen."

"Blacked out! Because you've poisoned her! Laylah! You've been sick. Wake up!" I pull Laylah into a sitting position and drag a chair closer to her back. She flops against it.

"I'm in so much shit," she says, still slurring. I wipe her face with the sleeve of my hoodie.

I stand eye to eye with the doctor. "Yo! What the fuck did you give her! Tell me or I'm calling the abortion offender hotline and telling them everything!" I pull out my phone and snap a photo of her miserable face.

"It doesn't usually do this!" She grabs fistfuls of her hair and tries to cover her face. I can still see her bottom lip quivering. She darts toward the door, pulling her white coat off and flinging it onto the floor. I grab Laylah's bag and empty it over her, searching for her phone.

"Here." My heart stops. An old White woman appears out of nowhere, standing over my shoulder with a large Android in her hand. "You can have it if you leave now. We had to take it from her. She could get us all found out."

"Yeah, you and this stinky fucking clinic *need* to get found out. And that's not her phone." Laylah whimpers, and I remember that she's using her nanima's spare Android. The woman curls her upper lip and backs away. That's when I see her. Another girl, or is she a woman? She sits quietly behind a desk as if she came into work on a sick day. She's thin and White with stringy blond hair. She rests her elbows on the desk and grabs the sides of her head with her hands. There's a white bowl in front of her. She's being sick, too, just not as violently as Laylah.

The girl-woman spits into the bowl and looks up for a second. That's all I need to recognize her. "Mandy Lou?" I whisper her name, but she hears. She goes to say something but vomits a mouthful of green slime before she can utter a word.

I reach for my phone. "Latif. Come back to exactly where you dropped me. But get out and help me carry her." I pocket Laylah's huge phone and slide my arm around her neck. "We're gonna get up on three. One . . ."

"You can't tell anyone about this operation," the older woman sniffs.

"Two."

"We'll be long gone by this afternoon."

"Three." Laylah presses the side of her body against mine and hobbles to the door. "Mandy Lou," Laylah calls out, trying to turn back.

"You know her?"

"Please help her. We're dying."

"You're not dying, habibti. I've got you."

"How do you know? You're not a doctor!"

"Neither was that woman you paid to make you sick!" I shove the door open, but Laylah stands her ground in the doorway.

"We can't leave her!"

"Lay, you're delirious. She could get us in some serious shit."

By the time we reach Sara's house, Latif's car smells of vomit, even though he drove with all the windows down and made me spray half a bottle of cheap body spray that he pulled out of his glove compartment. I wedged myself in the backseat between Laylah and Mandy Lou, paranoid that their heads might loll back and they'd inhale their vomit. I jostle both of them awake as we pull into Sara's driveway.

"And you're sure she's cool with this?" Latif turns the engine off and looks at me in the rearview mirror.

"Of course. I texted her."

Sara opens the door. Laylah shivers by my side. Mandy Lou and Latif sway behind us. Sara looks paler and sicker than Laylah. "You okay, Sara?" She closes the door a little and speaks through a narrow gap.

"Sara, open the door!"

"You can come in, but they have to stay out," she whispers.

"Sara! What the hell? I explained everything in the text. I know you read it."

I help Laylah steady herself against the doorframe and look back at Latif. His eyes narrow. I push open the door and find Sara crouched on the floor clutching her phone to her chest. "Why didn't you text back?"

"I had to delete the texts."

"Why?"

"I can't do this. I can't. I'm so sorry, I just. I'm not strong like you." She stands and paces up and down the entryway next to the same steps we climbed while we cuddled together last night.

"Sara!" I grab both her arms. "Get it together. This is an emergency. We need to get them hydrated and rested and we can't have anyone find out."

"But my dad! He works for the government! We could all wind up in prison!" Fat tears roll down her cheeks.

"Sara. Your dad works as a facilities manager for the Department of Health."

"That's like the same as the police these days, and I can't put him in jail." She fixes me with pink eyes and wipes a snot bubble from her nose. "My mom. I can't. . . ."

I back up toward the door, my hands shaking in some combination of anger and pain. "I can't believe you're not helping me."

"It's not you. It's all those people."

"They're girls. Like us, Sara. What would you do if you were in their shoes?"

She looks away from me and up the stairs. "Well, I'm not and I'm sorry, okay. I'm really, really sorry." She whimpers and slowly collapses onto the bottom step. My heart aches beneath my ribs.

"Ally is a verb, not a noun!" I hiss, charging out the front door and slamming it shut behind me. "Right! Change of plan!" I smile at the gang as if they didn't just hear our fight.

Aunty Fatimah opens the door with a pencil tucked behind her ear and a mouth slack with worry. "Noor, you're such a good friend, betah. Here, I've set up the living room for them both. Lucky you didn't eat the tuna salad in the cafeteria, hey?" Adam races to the door in a red cape with a pink stethoscope around his neck and a bottle of blue Gatorade in his hands. Aunty Fatimah unloops Laylah's arm from around my neck and leads her toward the room as I explain that Latif works with me at the school newspaper.

"Aunty. Laylah said she wants to shower and sleep in her bed. Would you mind taking her up and I'll help our new friend get settled? Poor thing. She only just joined our school this week and the food's already making her sick!" Aunty Fatimah nods and leads Laylah out of the room.

Mandy Lou sinks into the sofa and lets Adam press the stethoscope into the tops of her feet. "Need a change of clothes?" She looks down at her chest and lap and shakes her head. "I'm okay. I wasn't as sick as your friend." It's the first time I've heard her speak a full sentence.

"Your car . . ." Latif plonks himself next to Mandy Lou and doesn't see me shaking my head. I put a hand on his leg. "Not now. Not here." I nod my head toward the open door and to Mandy Lou, who looks like she needs to shower and sleep some more. Not to mention that Adam is stuck to our new friend like glue. Latif doesn't know we used to call Adam "The Parrot" on account of his repeating everything we said, word for word, back to his mom.

Mandy Lou reaches inside her pocket. "Can I charge this?"

"They didn't try to confiscate yours, huh?"

"I just need to arrange a ride and call work. I have a shift tonight."

I put a finger to my mouth. "Don't let Aunty hear you say that. We need her to think you go to school with us."

Latif inches closer to Mandy Lou. "I can take you home. If you want me to?" All the while he reads my face.

I nod. Maybe Mandy Lou will open up to him. Besides, I desperately need to talk to Laylah.

Laylah sits in bed, the ends of her long hair wrapped in a white towel, her face pale. She runs her finger along the outline of a sealed iPhone box. I put two mugs of tea on the side table and sit on the edge of the bed. Laylah closes her eyes as she speaks. "It's a long, long story, Noor. I just wanted it to go away."

I nudge her arm so that she'll open her eyes and sip some tea. "I understand," I say, lying. How does anything like this "go away" without help from your best friend?

"I'm sorry I put a rift between you and Sara."

"Fuck Sara."

She puts the mug back on the table and slides down the bed. "Don't say that. You have to keep her close. She knows. Everyone knows. Mandy Lou. Even that boy. Why was he here?"

"We were working on a project this morning when you called. He doesn't know what's going on. I haven't explained anything."

"Yeah, well, Sara knows because you texted her and she's got a big mouth so I'm double extra screwed."

"She's scared. She won't . . ."

"You don't know that. Did you know she'd kick us out of her house like that? You didn't. You don't know what she might do."

I take the box from her hands and peel back the plastic.

"Scared people do dumb shit, Noor. Look at me."

I unbox the phone and press it into Laylah's hand. I lie next to her and look up at the ceiling. "How long have you known?"

"Friday."

"How far along?"

"Too far."

I turn to face her. She turns her head away. "Lay. We can fix this. *We* can. *Us*. Look at us, we're the writers of the Guide. We've got so much info at our fingertips. We just need to find one person in the whole of Texas who has the pills. It's not too far for the pills, is it?"

"Almost."

"Almost is good, Laylah. Almost doesn't mean too late." My fingers search for her empty hand. I squeeze it tight.

"Can you believe this shit?" she says, her head still turned away from me. I think I hear her sob. Just once. Laylah turns to look me in the eye, her eyes shining. "How could this happen to *me*?"

I press my forehead into hers and close my eyes. "It could happen to anybody."

"I thought third time lucky." She laughs a kind of sighing laugh.

My eyes open wide. "You went to that vet *three* times?"

"Three different places."

I sit up. She's still looking away.

"Three different places before you could tell me?"

"I just thought I could make it go away."

"At a vet?"

"Probably wasn't even a vet."

"What did she give you?"

"I don't know. Cat medicine? Or cow. *Mooooo*." She laughs.

She'll make a perfect doctor. Only a doctor could crack jokes at a time like this. I flop back onto the bed. My heart aches and my head hurts. I want to take a shower, change clothes, and sleep until this has all gone away. But there's a secret crisis pregnancy center in the basement of the mosque and my best friend is actually in crisis and I have to make it all stop.

"Noor?"

"Laylah?"

"Can you do me a favor?"

"Anything."

"Take my nanima's phone to her house for me? She keeps asking for it back, and I don't want her to drive over here and see me sick and make a fuss. It seems she really needs that phone."

I root through Laylah's bag for the brick. She dangles her hand off the bed. "And set this one up for me before you go. So you've got the number and everything. And let's make a promise, Noor."

"Anything."

"No more secrets."

"No more secrets."

The drive to Nanima's house feels longer on account of all the pinging sounds the old phone makes. Latif begs me to silence it, but when I go to change the notifications, I find myself scrolling through the texts. "Bro, these are not spam messages."

"Are you reading someone else's texts?" He raises his eyebrows and sticks his tongue out.

"Only cuz I thought they were spam!" I smack his arm, and he pretends to lose control of the steering wheel. "Drive straight, drive straight! Matter of fact, turn . . . right. Here. It's some kind of group chat. Weird as shit. Why would Nanima . . . ?" I read Latif the directions to an address that popped up in the second from last text. It's for a place that's a short detour from where we are. "It's near your uncle's shop, kinda. On the east side," I explain.

Latif is annoyed that I won't explain where Laylah was or why Mandy Lou was with her. He gathered no intel because Mandy Lou offered up zero information on the ride from Laylah's and had him drop her off at a friend's house so he can't even say he knows where she lives. "All this random driving is taking away from the bigger picture. The donations? Remember? You've forgotten about all of that."

"Right here. And no, I haven't." We park opposite a strip mall with a few shops and not much foot traffic. Comics. Skates. Spice Emporium. Empty storefront. Pawnshop. Pupusas. Guitar repair. A beige car pulls into the parking lot and stops outside the comic book store. The trunk pops open and a small figure gets out of the driver's seat. I zoom in with my camera. "That's just some old lady. Why are you watching her?" Latif looks away to rummage through the center console. He pulls out binoculars and a packet of gum.

"What in the . . . ?"

"I got these on Amazon after the stakeout. I figured we might need them sometime. Although, I don't think this is it." He unwraps a piece of gum. I grab the binoculars.

The old lady is dressed in a kurta the same beige as her car. She disappears behind the opened trunk and scuttles back to the driver's side too quickly for me to see her face. A taller, olive-skinned woman exits the empty storefront and closes the trunk. She looks about fifty. Or sixty. She looks down at the ground, and it's only when the beige car pulls away that I can see what she's observing. There are four, maybe five, brown boxes sitting on the curb. She stacks the boxes on a dolly and pulls them into the spice shop next door. She walks back out, looks around, and walks into the empty, nameless store.

A message pings. **Complete**. I take the piece of gum Latif is holding out and chew aggressively. I rub my temples. "Nah, man." I shake my head. A brown Prius pulls into the same spot. The woman appears from inside the nameless store and plops a pile of duffel bags into the trunk and knocks twice on the rear window. The brown Prius pulls away.

"What is up with these spice deliveries? Can we go, please?" Then, just as quickly as he wanted to leave, Latif leans forward and lets out a long *oooh*. "Isn't that the car? I see it all the time at the mosque." He stares at a car pulling into the strip mall's parking lot. "Blue Prius. Looks like Laylah's car."

"How would Laylah's car be here when she's in bed?"

"I said *looks* like." He grabs the binoculars from my hands. "Nah. That's the same car. I've definitely seen it at the RICC. It's got that bumper sticker. 'Free Palestine.'"

Coincidence, I think. My stomach gurgles. "Is that Laylah's license plate? Is her car stolen?"

"I have no idea what her plate is." I yank the binoculars back. "And no, it's not stolen. Wasn't it in her driveway?" The woman walks out of the nameless store with an empty dolly, pops open the trunk of the blue Prius, and takes out six or seven boxes. She looks around, slams shut the trunk, and knocks on the hood of the car as she passes. The driver of the blue Prius lowers the driver's-side window and passes a small brown bag to the woman. I see a flash of gold on the wrist. A long, flared sleeve dangles. The window goes up, and the car drives out of the lot.

A baby-blue Beetle pulls up next to where the Prius had parked. The woman is still inside the spice shop. The car doors stay shut, but someone moves inside the car. Maybe two people. A door opens, a box, or maybe two small boxes, land on the ground, and the door slams shut. The Beetle quickly pulls back out of the parking spot and disappears around the back of the strip mall. "Looooot of activity for a spice shop. I had no idea this many people were buying spices." Latif smacks his gum.

"Why are they *dropping off* boxes if they're *buying* spices?"

I drop the binoculars in my lap, snap a photo, and enlarge the image. The Beetle looks familiar.

"I thought you said one of them was putting duffel bags in the car."

"But the rest of them were dropping off big boxes."

"Only one way to find out."

Without warning, Latif pulls off and drives into the parking lot. I duck, as if anyone can see through the illegal tint in his windows. He drives to the spot where the boxes were dropped, opens his door, and grabs the top package. He throws it into my lap and drives out of the mall and toward the main road.

I breathe so fast, I almost hyperventilate. "What the fuck was that?"

"You wanted to see what was inside them, didn't you?"

"You gotta warn me before you pull a stunt like that, Latif!" I eye the package in my lap as if there might be an explosive inside. *Old ladies. Spices. How bad can it be?* I slide a key along the length of the box and freeze. But my second brain is already letting me know what this is.

Beneath a stack of blank yellow paper is a stash of small plastic packets of turmeric powder no bigger than a smallish Post-it note. I squish a packet between my fingers, moving the bright orange powder around between the layers of plastic until I feel it. It's hard and thin. I tear open the package with my teeth sending a plume of orange onto the black roof of Latif's car and across my face. I pull down the mirror, leaving orange prints on the flap. I look like I'm at a Holi celebration. "OYYYY!" Latif yells. "That stuff will survive an atomic bomb! Haldi never comes out of anything! You're gonna die with that stain on your face. And my car?! Oh my God. My car!!! You've got it everywhere!" My mouth is frozen open. My eyes cannot move from my lap. In the middle of a pile of turmeric heaped in the crease between my thighs is a glimmer of hope in the shade of copper. *Genius. They hid the copper IUDs in orange powder.*

LAYLAH

NOOR BARGES INTO my room, her face streaked in orange. "I'm sorry. I'm sorry. I'm sorry. I should have told you earlier. I just needed to know more stuff and now I know more stuff and I can tell you everything but I couldn't tell you everything earlier because it wouldn't have made sense. To you."

She jumps onto my bed and pins me down so that I'm looking up at her painted face. "Why do you smell like curry, and what did you do to your skin? Haldi mask?"

"I told your mom it was a cooking experiment gone wrong, but, Laylah, you have to know the truth and you have to listen and you have to believe me, but most of all you have to understand. Okay? Promise me you'll understand why I had to keep this a secret?"

She doesn't breathe between words and I can't catch my breath.

She speaks so fast and the smell of spices makes me hungry and then nauseous, as if my stomach remembers I poured poison into it only hours earlier. I wriggle beneath Noor until she jumps off the bed. I hand her an individually wrapped makeup remover wipe from the top drawer, fully aware that the haldi on her face is going nowhere.

"It started with Asma and Operation X but then it became about HH and then it was this clinic we discovered only just this morning but now it's about your grandma." She rubs her face furiously. I can't get a word in although I'm not sure what I would say.

"Grandma."

"Yes! *Your* grandma! I'm not saying that *it's* your grandma, obviously, but yeah, your grandma is involved with *it*. We think."

I sit back on the bed and reach for the mug of tea. It's cold. A thin brown skin shimmers across the top.

"Nanima's okay, yeah? She's been texting me to get her old phone back. She seems okay."

"More than okay. She's amaaaazing! Those text messages! Not spam!" She points the brick in my face. The brick I had asked her to give to Nanima so that Nanima wouldn't be so pressed about me dropping it off today. Clearly, it's an important phone.

Noor flings the still-white makeup remover wipe onto my desk. "You won't believe it. The texts. Shady fucking shit but gooooood shit. Oh my God. Laylah!"

"Noor?"

"I might become religious, Lay! How can all of this happen in one day? One day and it all makes sense!" Noor drops to her knees and raises her hands to the ceiling. "We needed a solution and we got it. Just like that! Is that how the prayer thing works these days? Instant?"

I'm beginning to worry that some of the poison I drank passed on to Noor through osmosis. "And Asma?" Noor's face drops. She flings her arms to her sides and puts her forehead to the ground as if she's in sijdah. Maybe she is becoming religious.

"She's been stealing money." Noor speaks into the ground with all the tact of a doctor who skipped the class on how to break bad news.

My stomach sinks into my pelvis. "What did you say?"

"Asma is stealing mosque money, donations, and using them to build a CPC in the mosque basement. It's a secret, but HH knows. That's the congresswoman, Humairah Hilal, who happens to be in bed—not literally—with Norm Miller, remember him? Which means the money goes from your mosque via Asma's hands to HH to Norm and they're all in on a secret disinformation campaign to hurt Muslim women and make sure no one ever gets accurate information about abortion; meanwhile, Norm is the one who got Mandy Lou pregnant. But your grandma, she's the opposite. Absolute fucking hero." Noor grins. She sounds like an absolute fucking conspiracy theorist.

"You've got it all wrong."

Noor crawls toward me. "Your grandmother is a drug smuggler. Well, she smuggles these for sure. Probably drugs, too." She pulls a piece of yellow paper slowly from her pocket and carefully unfolds it. She leans toward me, her eyes wide.

Sitting in the middle of the sheet of paper is a copper IUD.

I blink. I hear angels sing. I hear a sitar play the beginning notes of "Aap Ki Nazron Ne Samjha." I blink fast and snatch the IUD from Noor before I black out. I twirl it inches from my eyes. I press it into my cheek. It's real. "Where did you get this? And why does it smell like curry?"

"That's what I'm trying to tell you. I got it from Nanima." I make a fist around the metal and cradle it against my aching stomach.

"My grandmother? Gave you this? At her house?"

"She didn't give it. We stole it. From the parking lot."

"We?"

"Latif stole it. I dug through all the stuff to actually find it."

I clutch the hot metal harder and squeeze my eyes shut. If this is a dream, I really fucked up, because if I had learned how to lucid dream, I could rewind this dream and put the IUD inside my uterus before the damned school trip. Then this wouldn't be a nightmare. A ping interrupts my fantasy.

"These messages, Lay!" Noor scrolls through the texts, reading them one by one. They sound like jumbled codes with addresses and dates and times. She goes on and on about a plot to hurt Muslim women by making us believe a secret clinic was a real clinic when it was, in fact, one of those god-awful crisis pregnancy centers. She makes no sense. Why would a fake clinic be hidden in the mosque? Asma would never allow it.

"You've misunderstood." Noor finally stops talking. "I don't know where you got all this weird information, but Asma would never. Whatever you might think of her . . ." I take a deep breath. "Whatever you *might* think, she's actually pro-abortion, and I can prove it."

"So prove it."

"Well, first, you're not thinking about the fact that she can't say, 'Yay! Abortion!' in public. If she ever does that, the mosque will get shut down. But there's an even deeper reason. Don't tell anyone." I watch Noor's face. She pouts and leans in toward me. "Asma's doing IVF."

"I know."

"How would you know what Asma's doing?"

Noor's eye twitches. She looks off to the side and sits cross-legged. She tells me it was Latif. He overheard something the imam said about black market injections. She goes quiet. "There's something else. We hacked a phone."

I feel my cheeks burn.

"Not Asma's phone. The congresswoman's."

I stand from the bed and sit back down. Noor sits next to me. "I know it sounds really bad, but they're hurting people."

"You have no clue about that. You sound jumbled and confused right now."

"I know it, Lay! They say they care about women, but really they hate women. They must hate themselves."

"And you're saying that to justify spying on Muslim leaders? You know Muslims are the most spied-on group in America? We're constantly under surveillance." I take a breath and whisper, "Even from our own."

"That's not what this is!" Noor jumps up. "How can they be real Muslims if they're hurting others?"

"Oh, so now *you* get to decide who's a real Muslim? What does 'real Muslim' even mean to you?"

"Asma is stealing money and she's giving it to HH. They're in this together." The more she speaks, the more confused she sounds. Her reasoning becomes grayer and muddier. Noor is starting to sound like those YouTube influencers who start off interested in organic farming but end up sixteen videos in telling you how pure soil is connected to pure blood and that we should never mix races.

I twirl the IUD. "How is this connected to Nanima? You saw her with this?"

"No, but . . ."

"So you didn't see her with this?"

"No, but she can help us!"

"How?"

Noor jumps up and down and waves the phone around. The texts. The old ladies. The baking. The spices. She explains over and over again a sequence of events that makes no sense. Of course Nanima's friends aren't smuggling IUDs into Texas. They get together to drink tea and talk about movies and grandchildren. "Noor. You found this in a box. I get that. But you didn't even see if the box this came from belonged to Nanima!"

"I saw your car and she was in your car and someone else was driving her car and they were all in sync with these text messages and it was old ladies and I didn't see your grandma but she must have been in your car! Who else could it be?" She grabs my fist and shakes it wildly. "If she can get her hands on these, imagine what's in the other boxes. Pills, Laylah! Pills!"

I yank my fist from her grip. "Drop it. You've got it twisted. All of it. Asma. Nanima. I don't see what that congresswoman has to do with this either."

"Huh? You're not thinking straight."

"Neither are you."

"*She* can sort this, Lay. She can probably even get you on birth control so this never happens again!"

I shake my head.

"Lay. I can tell her it's for *me*. She never has to know it's for you."

"Don't you dare tell her a thing. Not the truth. Not a lie. Not any of this."

"Laylah?"

"She's my *grandmother*. She can't suspect a thing. It's bad enough that you and Latif and Sara and Bella and Carly and Ali and Dr. Hogarth and Dr. Kapoor, they all know." I stand and lean against the desk. "Promise me that you won't tell her a thing."

"Laylah. We need her."

"I don't need her! I'll figure this out!"

"Like you nearly figured out getting poisoned in a vet clinic this morning?" Noor lowers her head. She speaks softly. "How you gonna figure this out, huh, Lay?" She reaches for my arm. I move away. "Look! I get it! You made a mistake! Ms. Perfect, *Dr. Perfect*, made a mistake! Big fucking deal. Shit happens. But now you need help."

"I don't need . . ."

"YES! YOU! DO!"

I shuffle papers on my desk and crack open a journal. Great time to make a to-do list. *Item number one: make sure best friend doesn't tell my grandmother—who she thinks is a drug smuggler— that I am pregnant.*

"We're wasting time and she's probably out there right now dropping off six boxes and two bags of the exact medications you need! You're being hardheaded."

"And you've fallen down a rabbit hole. Do you really hate the mosque that much?"

Noor flinches. "It's not like that." She skulks toward the door.

"If you tell her, we are over, Noor. How could our friend-ship mean anything after that?" Noor sniffs and closes the door behind her.

STEP 9

DO THE RIGHT THING

NOOR

I WRITE AND delete texts.

Hi, it's me! Wondering if there's any way you could help me out?
You see . . . I was confused one day and I thought I liked boys
again. I know! They're so gross! But sexuality is fluid, after all.
Anyway, I got carried away and accidentally got pregnant. Crazy,
right? In this political climate! Oops! I know what you're thinking.
Laylah told me you know about me. But I've been trying to be open
minded and look where that's gotten me! Anyway, I've actually
been identifying as pansexual for the last year so this could happen to anyone really. . . .

Delete.

All night. Draft and delete. Now I'm here. The smell of freshly baked nankutai hits me before the front door opens. "Noor." Nanima cracks open the door. "I was expecting you."

The round yellow cookie she passes to me on a flowery plate sticks in my throat. I cough and splutter at the kitchen table. Nanima hurries to get me a tall glass of water and rubs my back.

"Is it betrayal . . . ," I say, between coughs. A clump of sweetness jams in my throat.

"'Betrayal'?" Nanima looks down at me. "There, there. Don't try to talk," she says. So I cry instead.

"Is it betrayal . . . *sob* . . . if it's saving . . . *sob* . . . her future?"

"Betah, I don't know what you're saying." She wipes my face with her hand and then with her sari, tugging the pink fabric free of a pleat and loosening it over her shoulder. "Have a good cry. Let it all out. But then we drink tea and we find a solution. We fix this, whatever this is." The kettle boils. She steps away to fill the teapot.

"Is it Laylah?" She hands me a pink teacup, her gazillion gold bangles clanging against the saucer. A cloud of cinnamon wafts over my face. Tears fall from my cheeks. "Here, you're making the tea salty." She takes the teacup and places it on a crocheted place mat, pulls a tissue out of her sari blouse, and wipes my nose.

"It's without her consent." I sniff.

Nanima freezes with the tissue on my nose. "Someone did something to Laylah without her consent?"

I shake my head. "No. No one did. I'm about to. How did you know I was coming today? Laylah told you about me dropping off the phone?"

Nanima sits back in her chair and watches me cry. She shakes her head. The table wobbles in time with my breath. I release the shame as I prepare to do what no best friend should ever have to do. Maybe what a real best friend would refuse to do.

"She said she's never going to talk to me ever again if I do this. If I tell her secret. But I know *your* secret so I know you will keep hers." I look up at Nanima. She sips. "I know what you do. You have to help her! She's only got two days left."

Clink. Nanima sets the teacup in the saucer and picks up a pendah. "Secrets are like baked treats." She holds the yellow disc up to the light. "They begin life as raw dough, a little bit of this, a sprinkle of that, and then oops! You've made a mistake. You think you can bury that secret, that mistake, in the dough." She splits the yellow disc in two and passes me one half. "Eat, betah. Maybe the mistake was too much bicarb, maybe. Maybe not enough jeera powder. Maybe you fall into trouble and think you will fix it all by yourself." She shrugs. "So you mix and you add and you tinker and you mix some more, hoping you can disguise the mistake. Cover it up with more sugar, more furious mixing. But the secret always comes out in the bake. No amount of mixing can hide it. In fact, the more you mix, the more you toughen the dough so the cookie just splits more easily, showing the world that something is wrong deep inside its structure." She dusts a crumb from her chin.

"But that's what she's been doing. Mixing. Hiding. And it's making it worse. But she'll never forgive me if I tell you. But if you help her, if you can get her the meds. You can get her the meds, right? Then she'll talk to me again. One day. Maybe."

"Meds?"

My jaw clenches. I can smell the stench of cat pee in the clinic from hell, the odors mingling in Latif's car. I push my chair back from the table and dangle my head between my knees. Nanima walks over and rubs my back.

"Is Laylah pregnant?"

"How did you know?"

"Come. It's okay." She pulls me into a hug that smells like vanilla. She doesn't stop rubbing my back. But the words that come next knock the wind out of my chest. She might as well have punched me in the back.

"Betah, no one has the medications right now. We had one packet delivered this week. Just one. That was it. And we handed that over to someone in a drop-off this morning. Very tricky situation. Awful. Poor girl." She clucks her tongue.

I don't move. She keeps talking. "The more stringent laws from last month, they led to even the bravest of pharmacists shutting down their kitchen compounding labs."

"But the spices? Those boxes?" I pull myself out of her embrace.

"Ahh, you know about the deliveries. Clever girl." She sits back in her chair and swirls a teaspoon around her cup. "The ones today? Mostly IUDs and gloves. Basic supplies to keep some clinics going, so they can do exams and things." She drops the spoon in the saucer.

I can't believe what I'm hearing. This was the conversation, the spilling of tea conversation that could end my friendship—but it was supposed to be worth it. There were supposed to be pills—and tears—yes. But pills. Nanima was supposed to turn Laylah's fate around. Instead, I've spilled Laylah's secret, destroyed our friendship, and for what? Nothing. There are no pills. The last one was given away. I stand and push the chair back. "We have to help Laylah! We have to."

"And we will," Nanima says, taking a sip. "I'll make some calls right now. But first I have to send an email." She pulls a phone out of her sari blouse and lays it next to the two phones on the table. She squints at the screen, scrolls, and texts.

"She won't come here, you know. She won't talk to me once she knows I've told you. And she won't want to talk to you. She's so embarrassed by everything. It was just a mistake! It could happen to anyone!"

Nanima nods. "If she won't come to us, we'll go to her." She pushes the third phone away and walks to the sink.

"But if we go to her, it will feel like an ambush. She'll run and hide. That's what she does when things don't go to plan. She hides."

"Yes. Even from herself."

"She'll hide from me! She's going to hate me forever. She's going to ruin her life and not let anyone help her because she thinks she can handle this all by herself, but she's not strong enough. No one is."

"She's stronger than you think." Nanima rinses a pan, her back to me. She turns off the faucet and leans over the sink. "I tried to tell her. This intergenerational trauma they talk about these days. It's true. It is passed down in our DNA. But so is intergenerational strength. We've been through some things, our people."

I've read about this. How my grandparents surviving the nakba could make me anxious and depressed, although it hasn't. It's just made me angry and committed to becoming a journalist, like Shireen Abu Akleh, so that I can report the truth. But that's not what I'm thinking about now. I'm thinking about how my best friend is going to hate me when she finds out that I've betrayed her trust.

The oven beeps. A blue light flashes. "Those are for tonight's fundraising gala." Nanima eyes the clock. "I have about three hours to make and cool two more batches of these and two lots of jalebi." She walks to the oven, slides out a tray of pale brown circles, and places them on top of the stove. She sprinkles each with a pinch of crushed pistachios. "I heard you like these. Nankutai. Why don't you help me bake? It will calm you and give you perspective. We can drop them off together. And talk to Laylah."

I roll up my sleeves and listen to Nanima make a dozen calls to a dozen other nanimas on speakerphone, zigzagging between two phones and the phone she had given to Laylah. All the while she pours orange liquid into a bottle and screws on a nozzle. She heats oil and teaches me how to knead dough made from milk powder and nutmeg. She gives me a pen and has me write down the instructions delivered by each nanima. Town names. Times. Street addresses. License plate numbers.

By the time we lift the orange squiggles out of the oil and stack yellow circles in cake tins lined with crinkly paper, it's six o'clock. Time to head to the gala.

LAYLAH

AN EMAIL LANDS in my inbox with an attachment from pkthebaker@sarinotsari.com. And this is how I know the longest friendship of my life is over.

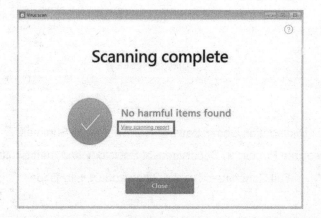

"OUR BODIES ARE NOT OUR OWN"

WOMEN-LED ACTIVIST MOVEMENTS DURING
INDIA'S EMERGENCY PERIOD, 1975–1977

A dissertation
submitted in partial fulfillment
of the requirements for the degree of
Doctor of Philosophy
at George Mason University

by

Sumaiyya Aguilar

Dissertation Committee Director: Dr. Abigail Summers,
Associate Professor, Department of Sociology and Anthropology
Full Committee: Dr. Mel Singh and Dr. Lilly Chen

First they came for our men. Women are safe, or so they said. But how could we feel safe when our husbands were being snatched off the streets by men with guns? I was twenty-one. I couldn't understand all of what was going on. By the time they declared that men would be forcibly sterilized to curb the population of our growing nation, the newspapers were under government control and nobody could tell what was rumor or reality. Which men? What age? Would newlyweds be spared? What about my Hamza? Nobody would say. My country had become my enemy. Overnight. Neighbors turned against neighbors. Everyone turned into a government spy, desperate to snitch on the next person for a minor rule violation, just to save their own skin.

The nightmare began on June 25, 1975. At the stroke of midnight. Prime Minister Indira Gandhi came on the radio to make an announcement. Me and Hamza and Ammu and Abbu, we huddled around the transistor to hear what she had to say. For days we had listened to the whispers. In the market, in the masjid. Change is coming . . . the army will take over . . . all these kinds of things. Hamza turned up the volume as the prime minister began to speak in that bumptious tone of hers. "The president has proclaimed an emergency. This is nothing to panic about." She spat those words in crisp English, the language of the oppressor. Of course, when someone says not to panic . . .

They canceled the elections. They censored the newspapers. They locked up the journalists. Anyone who dared
to speak the truth was tortured. Paychecks were suddenly
halved, or they didn't come at all. Abbu had to close his
jewelry shop. Armed guards patrolled the streets to keep
us in our place. We were no longer free in our own homes.

Who did the government blame for this horror? Us, of
course. They blamed "internal turmoil." They blamed the
ordinary people of India. They said we were causing "dis-
turbances." That we didn't work hard enough and that's
why the economy was failing. They said it was because
of us that they were forced to declare the Emergency, an
endless period of martial law and dictatorship where even
our own bodies were not under our control. It was all a lie.

When they came for the men, I didn't understand what
was happening. Why were men being forced to have surgery? Sterilized against their will? Why? But then it all
started to make sense. I began to understand how power
really works.

How you police lovers is how you control the future.
Want to control a nation? Start with policing what happens
in the nation's bedrooms. The personal is always political. Do you understand that? That's why governments
are obsessed with making laws about marriage, about
sex, about contraception, about pleasure, because they
want to have power over us in our most intimate spaces. If
they can do that, if they can control our love, our desires,

well then, they have control over every part of us. You've heard of the nuclear family, the so-called typical family with one man and one woman and 2.4 children, yes? That number is not an accident. Who came up with 2.4? It is all someone's design. When you control how big or small a family is, you dictate what kind of support networks exist, what their community looks like, what *society* looks like.

Of course I didn't understand all of this at the *beginning*. I was barely twenty-one! It was later, after I stared death in the eye inside one of those hellish, bloody camps, that I began to understand the larger forces at play. This was about *my* body and *my* India, yes, but it was also about the United States. It was about Russia. I mean, the Soviet Union. Men in suits ruling over superpowers were also ruling over my uterus and my fallopian tubes.

But before we get into all of that, let me tell you about my Hamza, my jaan. Hamza was tall and slim with eyes the color of chestnuts and a goatee that he trimmed and oiled religiously. He was a writer. A writer of short stories and poems. And a teacher. Hamza would brilliantly deconstruct a sentence and discover hundreds of hidden meanings in a single line of a sonnet and leave his students staring at the poem thinking, *But how come I didn't see all of that?* That's how I met him. In a senior writing class in college. All the girls swooned and acted silly when he walked out of the classroom. We adored him because he was as kind as he was dashing.

Hamza and I were married the September before the Emergency. He was twenty-three and I was twenty. We were still childless when the announcement was made, but we planned to have children that very year. I desperately prayed that I would be pregnant already, but every month, the blood dotted my underwear. Like clockwork.

Hamza's parents were good to me, even if they were disappointed that no baby had arrived. When the official declaration was made that men must report to the camps or be jailed, we thought we would be fine. Hamza was young and childless, after all. Why would they come after him? But that wretched police captain in our town, Leery Lakhshman, we called him, the one who used to make eyes at me when I walked home from school, he stretched the already dastardly rules to exact petty revenge. He never liked Hamza. Hamza, who was highly educated and handsome. Hamza, who was adored by all.

One morning, when the official sent his cronies to come look for Hamza, we hid my sweetheart in the outhouse and said he was at the masjid. That's when we knew: nobody is safe! We would have to send Hamza away! I tried to be strong. I didn't want him to see me cry. I wept to Ammu instead. "Why are they punishing us like this? What are we supposed to do?" She wept with me. My father-in-law was no better. He stomped around the house as if that would fix things. A former jewelry maker, his business had been shuttered since July.

We sent Hamza to Rangoon. Even though our people had been kicked out of that country a decade earlier, Abbu said he had a friend who would hide Hamza. One frosty morning before the Fajr adhan, my darling left with a kiss and a poem that I tucked into my sari blouse. *I'll see you soon, jaan.* His final words to me. This was in November of 1975, five months after the Emergency began. I still couldn't believe what had happened. Even after months of this never-ending terror, I was in shock. I woke every morning to what felt like a nightmare. I pinched myself. Am I still sleeping? Please, Allah, let me be sleeping. But when I searched the bed for my love, his place was empty. I stopped praying soon after that. My heart was broken. I had lost my faith. What was there left to believe in?

Sending Hamza away didn't make us feel any safer, at least not for the two and a half weeks it took for him to reach the border. Every morning I would wake with red eyes and dark circles beneath my eyes. My jaw was clenched. Abbu said I was aging one whole year every day. I would grind my teeth all night. I dreamed of them cutting him open on a wooden table. Ammu said I was starting to look like a widow. I wore only white.

Hamza did reach Burma safely, where he was far away from this despotic government but under the rule of another. At night, my hips ached for him. I would read his poems before I slept. His words became my prayers, my incantations. I moved through each day in a dream state, biding my time.

So, when they came for me, I was wholly unprepared. There had been rumors for weeks that they would come for the women next. Pulling out our tubes so we could never have children, even those of us who were childless. How cruel! But there was so much, what do you call it now? Misinformation. So much gup shup, so many rumors about who was who and what was what. I thought, it will be okay. Hamza is far away. One day he will come back, or maybe I will escape this hell and we will run away and have our family.

You know, I used to oil and comb Aunty Sunnu's hair every night. That was our elderly neighbor. But she had started asking lots of questions. "Oh, but where did that handsome husband of yours go? Did he have to work somewhere? I thought they said no traveling allowed? How did he manage to get on the train? Did he depart from Surat train station or from Ahmedabad?"

Do you understand what that feels like? For every question to hang over you like a future prison sentence? To be robbed of your voice, your anger, your words? It's like having your tongue ripped out of your mouth. You're a researcher. This is an anthropology project for you. But this was our lives.

They came for me early in the morning. I was washing my hair when I heard the screaming. Somebody was pounding on the door. *Dhoom, dhoom, dhoom!* Somebody was trying to break down the door. Loud voices boomed through the house. It was Captain Lakhshman himself. He was vexed, of course. Hamza had escaped so now he was coming for me. I ran out of the bathroom with just a thin cloth wrapped around me, dripping water across the floor, acting shameless in front of my father-in-law. But Abbu didn't see me. He was frozen before five armed guards, transfixed like a statue. The men barked orders: "She must come now! Now! Now!"

Five of them! To take away one skinny twenty-one-year-old! That piece of shit Lakhshman leaned against the doorframe with his greasy hair and his yellow teeth and smiled. Ammu clutched her chest and cried and cried. She told a lie; the first lie I ever heard come out of her mouth. She said, "Ye mere larkee heh, woh pregnant heh!" But I wasn't pregnant. My stomach was flat as a pancake. Ammu threw herself onto the floor and pounded and kicked the ground. Her hair came loose from its long braid. I threw myself on top of her, afraid that she would hurt herself. She had grown so weak since Hamza left. Lakhshman sent his men rushing in with their batons. They beat my back and my thighs. They pulled me off Ammu so they could beat her, too. An old lady! For all this talk of modesty and honoring women, I was half naked when they dragged me out of that house. All the neighbors saw, including Aunty Sunnu. I felt so utterly ashamed. My izzat dragged through the dirt. When they threw me into an army truck, I was met with the stares of a dozen other women, some young, some old. Some half clothed, like me. Ammu ran behind the truck, her face filling with dust. The last I saw, she stumbled and fell to the ground.

The sterilization camp was inside a school they had turned into a hospital. If you can call it a hospital. Rows and rows of wooden desks where children once laid their pencils and opened their books were now being used to lay out women, to open our pelvises. On every desk a body. Each body trembling beneath the pain of the scalpel. I sat on the floor against the wall, waiting my turn. It stank like an abattoir. There was blood on the floor. And shit. Sneering surgeons looked more like butchers. Their white coats stained with the insides of innocent women.

Sitting in front of me was a woman who sobbed and wailed. Oh hoh, she made such a terrible noise. I told her, "Be quiet or they will beat us!" She said, "I have three children at home. The youngest is still drinking from my breast. They made me leave my babies behind." And even though we were near the back of the line, they picked her out and cut her open. Just like that. Right in front of us. To shut her up. To shut us all up. They cut into her belly button with no anesthetic. No iodine. No antiseptic. Nothing to clean her soft, brown skin. Her body was still healing from childbirth. I could see. They didn't even wash their filthy hands. They treated our flesh like the carcasses of cows they were preparing for a feast.

That's when I knew this was not just an effort to control us. They were trying to break our will. And as I watched that woman drip blood onto the floor, something big and hot and powerful grew inside my belly. My rage took on the shape of a bird, a mighty bird with huge wings and a giant beak. This feeling was bigger than me. It was bigger than all of us. I started to feel that I had been possessed by a djinn; that's how brave and powerful I felt.

The woman bled and bled until she convulsed like an epileptic. I threw myself on top of her but an officer picked me off and flung me against the wall like a rag doll. They wanted us to watch her die. They wanted us to know we had no control. Oh, but they didn't know! Show a woman her bloody future and she will rise up and fight for freedom. As I slid down the wall and crouched on the floor, I realized that I was wearing more than a cotton cloth. I fingered the ring on my middle toe. A thick gold band that was part of my dowry. I slid it off my foot and closed my right palm tightly around it. I thumbed the wedding band on my left hand and slowly wiggled that off. I was wearing small golden hoops in my ears. I slipped those off along with my thick bangle and the ring in my nose. I weighed all the gold in my palm. *I must be holding at least two tola of solid, eighteen-karat gold in my hand*, I thought, remembering how Abbu weighed gold nuggets first in his hands and then on his scale.

I made a fist and waited for a guard to walk past me. I needed a scrappy, young-looking one, not a fat, older one. I spotted him. When the young lad walked past, I opened my fist and flashed my gold. He stopped mid-stride. I closed my fist around the hot metal, terrified that he would take all that I had left and leave me. Instead, he grabbed me by my closed hand and threw me onto a table. My head smacked against the metal legs. He yelled at the surgeon, "Do her next!" I screamed and I cried. I lunged at the surgeon. All the while two guards were holding my arms. But I told you, I was a woman possessed. This new power was growing inside of me. I got free of the guards and lunged at that surgeon and got so close that he sliced my arm with his scalpel. I think the look in my eyes frightened them. They flung me onto the table and the surgeon stabbed me in my belly button with the dirty knife.

I blacked out there and then. When I woke, the surgeon was holding my gold, the greedy beggar, and he was yelling at the guard. I said to him, "You can have it! There's more gold! My father-in-law is Mr. Nadeem Khan! He will give you all his gold." But the surgeon kept yelling at the guard, and that's when I heard him say it. "Just take her! She's pregnant. I can't do this operation." I don't know if Ammu was psychic or what, but that's how I found out I was with child.

I didn't come to America for another two years, but

in the meantime, we moved to Ahmedabad, where I gave birth to Fatimah. The first time I laid eyes on her, she let out the most ferocious roar, her eyes squeezed into tight, angry lines. And that's when I knew what had saved me in the camp—it was her, my firstborn. *She* was the hot, rising power I had felt growing inside of me. Rising. Pouring its will to live into my veins. The next month I strapped my baby to my back and walked to a secret gathering place in the basement of an old mosque. It's where a women's rights organization that freed people—men and women—from the mass sterilization camps had its monthly meetings. By the time Hamza came home, Fatimah was two months old and I was fully radicalized. Me! The girl who thought activists were noisy complainers! Me, the girl who would have been content with a life of jotting down poems and reading Shakespeare to our children. But it was the women in that group, with their bright pink saris and their songs of freedom, who taught me that this was even bigger than us, that Indira Gandhi was not acting alone. Her orders came from America and the United Nations. It was the 1970s, you see. The Cold War between America and the Soviet Union was raging, and America was oh so frightened that we Indians, with our huge families and our love for community, our willingness to help raise one another's babies and look after our neighbors, might align with the Communists. Our way of living was less capitalist, after all, so we could easily become Soviet allies, they thought. And phew, scary for America. That would mean another six hundred million enemy Commies on the planet. Brown ones.

They used science to back up their plan. Five years before the Emergency, a scientist at Stanford University in California wrote a very popular book called *The Population Bomb*. He said humans were breeding too much, especially us Brown folk, and that soon the English would dic of famine—all of them!—and that two hundred million Americans would starve to death. All because Brown people were breeding and eating all the world's crops. So what did the Americans do? They said to Indira Gandhi, look, we know you need aid because the British colonized India and stole trillions of dollars from you, but we won't give you any money or any food or any help at all unless you do something to stop your people having babies. Unless you do something to make your society look more like ours. We want smaller, isolated families where no one knows their neighbors and they don't understand the meaning of *it takes a village to raise a child.* I'm not making this up. You can do research. It was President Lyndon B. Johnson who said something like this about India. He said, "I'm not going to piss away foreign aid in nations where they refuse to deal with their own population problems." As he dangled that threat, another American, Douglas Ensminger at the Ford Foundation, drew up a plan for India's mass sterilization program, the one that nearly killed me and my unborn baby, Fatimah. So you see, the blood of Indian men, women, and babies is on all their hands.

Indira Gandhi is still to blame. I will never forgive her. But let's not forget that it was American presidents, the United Nations, the Ford Foundation, the Rockefeller Foundation, and places like Stanford University who nudged India into the Emergency and turned me into a twenty-one-year-old activist. More than six million Indians were sterilized in one year of the Emergency alone. That's fifteen times more people than the Nazis sterilized.

I know I said yes to this interview, but I want you to understand something. Please don't write about my story as just another bloody chapter in human history. Yes, to you I am an old lady and this happened to me before you were born. But this has happened elsewhere. It isn't only history—it is happening right now. It happened in Puerto Rico. It happened here in our beloved America, in California. And when I say now, I mean now. In Raipur, India, in 2014, they dumped the dead bodies of women who were killed in a mass sterilization camp. 2014. The fight for our bodily rights is not over. Not in India, not in America. Not anywhere.

Oral testimony of Mrs. Parveen H. Khan, a key leader in the movement for Indian women's rights.

The scar. Her arm. The gold bangles that she refuses to take off even as they become splattered with cake batter and oil. The toe ring that flashes when she sits on a chair cross-legged, like a yoga teacher.

"Your grandmother's been through so much."

How could they keep this from me? Key leader? Nanima? You think you know someone your whole life, but all the time they've been hiding a secret as big as the world.

LAYLAH

I CAN SEE them whispering about me. Huddled together at the top of the stairs. They look down at me on the stage, standing beneath the banner; my lilac hijaab clashing with the neon-green bubble letters above my head that scream MOSQUE GALA!

My filthy secrets drip from Noor's tongue and into Nanima's ears. Her lips dance to the tune of betrayal. My wretched mistakes elevate Nanima's eyebrows, cause her lips to purse and her cheeks to hollow.

I am stuck. Stuck behind the podium. Stuck in their line of vision as they whisper and spill and ooh and ahh. Stuck in a sludge of sharam between the imam on my left, who is jittery off coffee milkshakes and possibly khat, and a flank of fidgety girls to my right, pages with typed-out speeches fluttering in their hands.

Noor clocks me watching and pulls Nanima back from the

edge of the top step. But Nanima stands solid. She stares straight at me, lifts a phone to her ear, and descends one step.

"And next up in our line of gala speakers! To give voice! To the needs! Of young Muslim women! Please join me in welcoming Laylah Khan!" The imam punctuates every few words with an exclamation and drags out my name like he is dragging it through the mud. "Laylaaaaaaah! Khaaaaan!" There is applause. "Go, girl!" Zeba hollers from the side. Amina pats me on both shoulders and pushes me forward. More applause. But my feet have grown roots and my tongue has grown heavy. I inch the tip of my tongue out from between my lips, but the whole thing slides out of my mouth and flops onto the stage with a thud. I cannot speak.

It feels different this time. Maybe ipecac still swirls in my stomach alongside whatever cocktail of cat medicines the vet fed me yesterday, but the room doesn't spin. I do. I spin and I spin until my back is on the stage and I am staring up at the banner. And here is Noor, floating down the stairs, a stack of cake tins bouncing in her arms. And here is Nanima, four cell phones waving in her hands as if she is a pink Ganesha running through the mosque. And here is Asma with winged eyeliner that would give Amy Winehouse a run for her money, except the eyeliner is fluttering on her face like little black butterflies. Asma steadies her turban with one hand and grips my wrist with the other. Next to her stands a boy whose face is rearranged in a scowl; tall and slim, he jostles with a White man in a black suit and tie.

"*You* don't touch her! *You* get your corrupt hands off her!" Noor is yanking Asma and someone is yanking me and a security guard who says he works for a congresswoman is asking everyone to please calm down or he will have to evacuate the building. The imam shouts down at an uncle from the edge of the stage, and that's when I smell it. Waves of sandalwood waft over me, and in the blur of bodies I think I see JJ's kind face getting closer and closer. Somewhere deep in the crowd I hear Adam wailing, "Laylah! Laylaaaah?"

The tall boy speaks. "We know what you're doing in the basement! You lying, thieving criminal. You took all the donations my dad fundraised and you built a fake clinic to lie to people about abortions and we have the proof and we should have gone on a trip." Someone is saying *shhhhhh* and the banner is flapping above the commotion like a warning flag. A jumble of voices: "Shhhh. Not here! Not where people can hear!" "But people need to hear!" "Hey, you! Badmaash, you've got it all wrong!" "It was for IVF! Who said it was for abortion?" Another voice: "Abortion is haram!" Then another voice, one of the mosque aunties perhaps: "Someone! Quick! Find the key to the basement."

Of course the room fades to black and sitar music trickles through the speakers. Of course bright lights flood the prayer hall and the mosque congregation appears dressed in red and green lehengas and sherwani. I spin and I spin and the mosque aunties link arms and break out into dance. They twirl in a circle near the edge of the stage. Through the rising music, I hear Mom soothing Adam. A deep, soft voice quietly calls out for Noor.

The music gets louder. The crowd rushes the stage. A congresswoman jumps on the back of her security guard, who dashes toward the front door with the imam at his heels. Asma takes command from the pulpit while her husband flees, the black butterflies dancing on her face elevating her slightly from the stage. "It's all a big, big misunderstanding," she pleads, pulling the black bulb of the microphone closer to her dark red lips. "We have esteemed guests with us tonight. If everyone can please settle down and listen, I will explain everything." A thunderous bhangra beat plays on an invisible dhol drum and drowns out her words.

But there is no time for Bollywood drama. No time for bhangra music and explanations. No time at all. The banner comes loose and tumbles to the stage. The flimsy plastic envelopes me like a shroud, rendering me invisible for one sweet second. Nanima lunges in my direction and Noor unwraps me from the neon-green tangle. "Someone has what we need, but they are exactly twelve hundred twenty-two miles away. In Las Vegas." Nanima clasps my face with both hands and whispers inches from my nose. Her eyes move right to left in case anyone is close enough to hear but there are five separate tussles onstage and Asma and the sour-faced boy, who I now recognize to be Latif, are fighting over the microphone. "Donations!" he keeps shouting. "Costa Rica!"

"We must get to a halfway point exactly six hundred and nine miles away in . . ." Nanima glances at one of her phones. "In nine hours and thirty-five minutes. Or else we'll miss the connection." Noor balls up the banner, tosses it over her shoulder, grabs my hands, and lifts me up. I shake my hands free from her grip. Nanima frowns, disappears three cell phones into her sari blouse, and marches us both out of the mosque, her balled-up hands digging into the smalls of our backs. It must look like a perp walk.

The green and red FREE PALESTINE! sticker has been peeled off the back of my car and replaced with a jaunty HUMAIRAH HILAL FOR THE 32ND DISTRICT! decal. The boxes have disappeared from the backseat. In their place sit Mom and a wet-faced Adam.

I freeze. I heave. I take two steps back, crouch behind the car and spit bile onto the parking-lot asphalt. I hold my head between my hands to stop my brain from spinning. *What. Does. She. Know. What. Does. She. Know. What. What. What.*

"I only told Nanima. I swear."

Only.

Noor speaks to my back because she doesn't deserve to speak to my face. I hear her pacing behind me. I swirl my furry tongue around my mouth and spit. "Yeah, well, she told Mom, so this is your doing."

"She said she—"

"What? She said she *what*? That she wouldn't tell anyone? Same way you said a million times you'll take my secrets to the grave?"

"She said she can *help*. She can get us the pills. She's done it before. This is what she does."

"I know this and I said NO. I am finding the pills MYSELF. But we always have to do things your way, and now everyone—"

"Laylah?"

The world stops spinning. Or my head stops. Either way, everything becomes dark and still. The voice as deep and thick as honey floats through the air above my head.

"Laylah?" JJ says. "What pills?"

NOOR

WHITE SETTLEMENT. BROCK Junction. Desdemona. Rising Star. Four towns, four car changes. In each back road, cemetery, or derelict gas station, another nanima switches keys with Laylah's nanima, presses a cake tin into Laylah's hands, and offers a hug and words of reassurance—or caution—about our journey west. "The road ahead is lined with our people. You'll be safe." Or, "The next two exits have cops or vigilantes, can't tell which. Be extra careful, okay?"

We swap the Prius for a Range Rover for a Cadillac for a Jeep. Still, we are less than halfway through the nine-hour road trip and Laylah hasn't uttered a word. She sits in the front silently following Nanima's orders. "Switch this chip out of that phone and put it into this phone. Throw that phone out the window. Text 29-99-09 to this number. Delete every text from that other phone."

Adam sits wedged between me and a silent JJ. He snores into my armpit. His small fist is clenched tightly around my sleeve as if holding me back from reaching forward and shaking sense into his sister. "Everyone in this car is on your side, you hardheaded perfectionist!" I want to scream. But instead I make small talk with Aunty Fatimah and JJ, which leads to an epic conversation about a poem that only the two of them have read.

I scroll through the Guide on my phone, accept Laylah's most recent edits and clean up section 3B. I type a new section heading: The Controller and Her Network. Laylah's phone pings as I hit enter and save changes. She glances at the notification but tucks her phone beneath her leg. Maybe we'll never publish the Guide. Maybe this road trip will be the last thing we do together.

JJ and Aunty Fatimah laugh nervously at something nobody else understands. "See, it's good he came, betah. At least . . . you know . . . makes this look like a family vacation," Nanima says to Laylah, who turns to look out the window.

Whose story is this to tell? Sure, I was the first snitch, but now Nanima has dragged JJ and Aunty Fatimah into the car without so much as a word of explanation. Only: "We are driving to a national park called White Sands in New Mexico. We will arrive shortly after five in the morning. My friends are meeting us there." The car slows to take a turn. A cake tin slides from beneath Laylah's seat and hits JJ's sneakers. He opens the tin, roots around for a cookie, takes a bite, and yelps. "I think I busted a tooth."

"Arehhhhh." Nanima shakes her head. "Betah, we bake the IUDs into the cookies for transporting across state lines. You can do that with the copper ones. Here, eat from this Tupperware."

This is Laylah's story to tell. But Laylah misunderstands. She thinks a big announcement must be made. A declaration issued. A statement of facts about Her Mistake, The Consequences, The Situation Now. Does she not realize that everyone who loves her already knows? Even Adam. Especially Adam. Adam who was distressed by the onstage commotion but insisted, before he drifted into a deep sleep, on placing both his special blanket and toy truck on Laylah's legs. "So she would sleep good too."

My Laylay. Hell-bent on following some Post-it note–labeled, bullet-journaled, calendar-scheduled, regimented order despite us existing in this fucked-up, disordered, makes-no-sense world. I remember in middle school when some mutant yellow jacket bit her on the ass at a pool party so that a boil the size of a golf ball swelled beneath her panties. Laylay refused to let me look, not even to see if it was infected, believing instead that if she didn't show her ass to anyone, that if she hid the ugliness from even her best friend, the wound would vanish. Of course it grew and grew and burst and scabbed and made her walk funny so that the whole world knew she'd been bitten on the ass. I thought she would have learned then that there is no shame in sharing trauma. Doesn't she know? God made best friends so we each have someone to show our ugliest wounds.

LAYLAH

THEY WILL NOT see me sob. They will not see me black out. They will not hear me whisper my truths in my sleep. They will not. They will not. We reach White Sands National Park at 5:35 a.m. with at least these personal goals achieved.

We have amassed twenty-six tins of baked goods at our various stop-offs; some of them concealing contraceptives, some of them simply a foil. Nanima turns off the lights as we approach the fence and the car trundles over the sand and around the perimeter of White Sands. She parks at a stretch of wire fencing emblazoned with a DO NOT CROSS sign. A small pink dupatta tied next to the sign flaps in the wind.

Nanima straps a headlamp around her head, hoists her sari up to her knees, and trudges up a sand dune. The beam of her lamp bounces a bright white light off the sand. I balance a dozen cake tins in my hands. Noor follows, lugging a duffel bag filled with the rest. We plod up the dune, my feet sinking into the softest, whitest sand on earth. It seems there is nothing ahead of us except for more bright white sand. But when Nanima disappears over the top of the dune, I hear a clink and a voice. There is a silver trailer. A nanima wearing a white kurta and a kind smile stands in the doorway and ushers the three of us inside. It smells of incense and vanilla, not chimichurri, carne asada, or cat pee.

White-kurta nanima tells me to sit, asks me if I want to go ahead with this and hands me a pill. I put the pill on my tongue, and she places a mug of hot chocolate as big as a bowl into my hands. I trace the faint scar across her right jawline with my eyes and swallow. She places a small blister packet onto my thigh. "In a day or two, you put these pills between your gum and cheek. Take a pain medication thirty minutes before that. Parveen will bring you to one of us for a checkup in one week." She pulls me into a tight hug. And just like that, the nightmare is half over.

NOOR

I DON'T SEE her at first. But my first thought when I hear her cough and look around to catch a glimpse of her straggly blond hair peeking out from behind a half-drawn pink curtain, is *How the fuck did she get here before us?* Private plane and car, it turns out. She says as much, admitting it boldly, as if it's entirely normal to be flown from one state to another to appease one of the richest men in Texas. But when she speaks again, my heart sinks. A little flame of empathy flickers. Maybe her life is wrecked too.

"I wanted this baby." Mandy Lou cries into a mug of hot chocolate. She sits toward the front of the trailer, half hidden behind the curtain so that Laylah doesn't spot her until I pull back the curtain to crouch next to her. The same tote bag she carried at the vet clinic on Thursday is nestled between her feet. She nudges the bag with her foot. "I wanted the baby. That's why my body keeps rejecting these medicines."

"Then you don't *have* to take the medicines!" I half whisper through gritted teeth. "If you want to keep the baby, just don't take the medicine!" But what I really want to say, what I want to scream is: *Other people actually* want *this medicine! They* need *it! You shouldn't be using up these precious resources!* But I keep my mouth shut.

"It's too late." A fat tear rolls down her pale cheek and drips into the mug.

Mandy Lou was given the last mifepristone in Texas yesterday morning. Maybe that's who Nanima was talking about while we drank tea and talked about Laylah in her kitchen. "Very tricky situation. Poor girl." She didn't know then, as she gave away the most precious pill in Texas, that her granddaughter was in an even worse state, that although Mandy Lou looked like the priority, being the girlfriend of the poster boy for the Texas Ministry of Family Preservation and all, she didn't want this.

"Did you take it?" I whisper. "Just now?" She nods. The older woman in a white tunic gave her the medicine minutes before we turned up with Laylah. Things are starting to make sense. Sort of. I look behind me and see Nanima watching us from the far end of the trailer.

Mandy Lou takes a sip of hot chocolate and coughs. "My stomach's still messed up. That's probably why I threw up that pill from yesterday. I vomited in that basement *before* they gave it to me, but I thought I was going to be good after that."

"Basement?"

She nods. "But then I was sick again. In that car. On the way home. My body doesn't want it."

"Which basement?"

"Chalo, chalo! No time for journalist interviews. We have ten hours to talk and clear everything up," Nanima yells while heading toward the door. Laylah and I groan in sync imagining the ride home. The awkward silences. JJ and Aunty Fatimah talking about poetry and every subject under the sun except for why we are crammed in a car on the world's most conversation-less road trip. Nanima cycling through burner phones like a drug kingpin and Laylah staring out the window refusing to say a word.

Nanima opens the trailer door and points out into the twilight. "We need to move. Now. My friend here has to get back to Vegas."

"What about . . . ?" I point my chin toward Mandy Lou. Laylah glances at her and quickly looks away.

"Someone is coming to get her."

"Who?"

"Chalo, chalo!"

Cool air drifts into the toasty warmth of the trailer. I swear I hear a helicopter in the distance. Nanima and her friend hear it too. They glance upwards and then at each other. The lady in the white tunic hugs Nanima and kisses her on both cheeks. "You made this happen, Parveen. Like always. Been a minute since we did a chain-gang road expedition, hehnah? Reminds me of that time back in—"

Nanima pulls her comrade into another hug. "It was less my doing and more that big guy this time. He made it happen, bhen. What a world."

The lady hands Nanima a silver thermos. "Yes, by any means necessary. But none of this happens without you. Even he wouldn't have been able to help . . ." The two women glance over at Mandy Lou.

"Chalo, kul. We'll talk. Love you, bye!" Nanima turns and flaps her hand in a casual wave above her head, as if she's waving goodbye after visiting a friend for a cup of coffee and a morning bagel, not headed on another nine-hour epic road trip after a life-changing expedition across state lines that's rewritten the course of history, changed the futures of two women, and transformed the lives of the people who love them.

"What did she mean, it's been a minute since you—" I slide halfway down the dune, past a silent Nanima, and land on my ass. Laylah is walking more carefully behind us but this is no time to tread slowly. I have questions that need answering immediately. Nanima doesn't speak even when we're back in the car. She tucks the pink scarf that was tied to the fence deep within some sari fold. Only when we switch to a Tesla on the outskirts of a tiny airport in Alamogordo, ten minutes later, and only after she's toggled through all the available temperature settings for her seat, does she start to tell the truth.

Truths. So many of them. The kinds of truths that make me feel as queasy as Mandy Lou looked in the trailer—and her face was practically green. Truths that make me think I should seriously reconsider a career as an investigative journalist, the only thing I've wanted to be since I discovered the reporting of Shireen Abu Akleh when I was eleven.

You were wrong. You were wrong, You were wrong wrong wrong. You were so wrong that you couldn't possibly have been wronger! You were so wrong that if you had been any wronger, you would have ended up being right! Nanima doesn't say this because she doesn't need to. She just drops the truths casually, the way old people do, speaking flippantly about topics as heavy and crushing as boulders because they've heard and seen everything before. At this point, nothing can faze them. So no, Asma isn't a fake feminist; she's well-meaning but flawed like the rest of us. And no, the basement clinic most definitely isn't a CPC. "Ha ha, could you imagine?! And yes, of course I've been helping Asma get hormones, including IVF meds, into the basement clinic; why wouldn't I aid someone involved with the resistance?"

"The resistance? Asma? She's involved with that sellout who supports Norm Miller *and* she steals money! Donations!"

"Without that money and without that man none of this would have been possible." Nanima reaches across the center console and rests her hand on Laylah's leg. Laylah looks out the window as if she could possibly turn her head any farther to the right.

"Excuse me, but that doesn't make sense."

"Perfect sense."

"No! It doesn't!"

Nanima eyes me in the rearview mirror. Everyone is silent. Aunty Fatimah reaches across Adam, whose foot is tucked beneath my leg, his arm looped around Aunty's wrist, and puts her hand on my leg. "Let her explain, Noor. It's complicated."

"Do *you* know about all this stuff?"

"No, not the details. I mean, I had no idea just how involved my mom was. No idea about this whole Nanima Network. But I've heard things. People trying to do the best they can by—"

"By stealing money and paying off an evil man who's a hypocrite?"

"I didn't say we paid him! Why would we pay that salah haramzada? No, we used the money for the clinic. The supplies. Medicine."

"That *he* got for you!"

"No, no, betah. It doesn't work like that. Back in 2022, when the Supreme Court first overruled *Roe v. Wade* and nearly every state followed the ruling by banning abortion, back then it *did* work like that. The only way we could get Aunty Nasreen's daughter's cancer medicine was by paying off one city councilmember after another." She shakes her head. "But when the death penalty started being discussed, even those folks were spooked. Couldn't get anything for months. Hey, Fati? Did I ever tell you that's how that poor boy died? What's his name? You know, Saima, from the spice bazaar? Her daughter's eldest brother-in-law. With the cancer. Down below. The hormones were just being banned and so the doctors were confused about what was allowed and what wasn't allowed and we couldn't pay off anyone for anything. Not a single packet. Not even for hormone medicines for his cancer. Inna lillah."

The words make me shiver. Baba says inna illah and Allah yarhama whenever he hears someone has died. And right here, in the Middle of Nowhere, New Mexico, I feel my will to live die a little.

I had let Latif yell at Asma on the stage. I had let him shout into the microphone accusations about the basement that we couldn't yet prove. Accusations that were wrong. Sort of. Asma did steal the money. But she was trying to help people. And me . . . What chaos did I leave behind at the mosque? What will the police do to the RICC?

"Will they arrest Asma?" I say it softly, as if that will reduce the likelihood of Laylah hearing me. But her head flips so sharply to the left that I fear she'll get whiplash. Nanima takes her eyes off the road to look at Laylah.

"I don't know."

"No. They won't. At least, they haven't." We all turn to look at JJ. He turns his phone so we can see the screen. A series of texts. "From that kid, Latif. The one who was yelling onstage. I calmed him down and got his number when you guys disappeared. I thought I'd lost you all. He's been texting me. . . ."

"And you didn't think to share the updates?" I want to shake sense into this guy as hard as I want to shake sense into Laylah.

JJ lowers his head. "There was other stuff. More important stuff. We needed to support Laylah and not worry about . . ." His voice trails off as Aunty Fatimah smooshes the side of her head into his.

"Hopefully the masjid community realized that if they did report the clinic, the whole place would be shut down and then the police would raid all the mosques in all of Texas to look for more secret clinics, and then they'd do financial audits of Muslim leaders, et cetera, et cetera." Nanima makes a tutting sound.

"But Asma stole money."

"Did she? Is it stealing? I think Mr. Sharif and his network of Pakistani business owners knew exactly what they were fundraising for."

"The uncles? Supporting abortion access? No effing way."

Silence again. My mind a whirl of faces. Aunties and uncles, shop owners and tea makers and spice sellers. A trail of pink abayas disappearing around corners. Asma crying because she was breaking the law trying to get pregnant. I was so carried away seeing everyone the way I thought they were that I missed the fact that my best friend was in danger. I missed the truth. I missed the biggest universal truth: People are complicated. People are not who they seem.

LAYLAH

WHITE SANDS TURN to a gray road that stretches ahead of us forever. Murky. Muddy. Messy. Nothing is black and white, and people are not who they appear to be. The goondas are the heroes, and the heroes, well, they're a bundle of good intentions and messiness, as are best friends—including me. These are the gems Nanima and Mom impart on the drive back east.

I wonder if they are directing these pearls of wisdom at me or Noor. Noor, who got the facts mixed up with the truth. Noor, who loves me despite my bullshit. Noor, whom I can't blame for keeping a secret, because I was holding a secret that was even bigger. The car is quiet, everyone is breathing deeply in the back, their heads lolling against the headrests. Nanima hums a Bollywood song, and I scroll through the Guide as the sun appears on the horizon.

"Step 10," Noor has written, next to a bunch of sentences she has bolded and struck out. The checklist at the end of the document shows that three and a half sections remain to be fact-checked. That's two days' work. A day if we split it. Less than a day if we cocoon ourselves in her house, stock up on all the snacks, and blitz through the document while amped up on Topo Chico and Blue Bell. That would put us only one day behind schedule. That would mean we could put this lifesaving information out there this weekend.

My stomach growls. Nanima reaches her hand across and gently pats my belly. "Bhook laghee?" She raises her eyebrows and drops her jaw as if she has diagnosed the worst ailment in the world: hunger.

Before Nanima can root around beneath her car seat or in the pocket behind mine, a hand stretches out from the back with an opened cake tin. Golden-brown balls of syrupy goodness dusted with crushed pistachios and arranged in layers between parchment paper practically smile at me. I devour a gulab jamun in two bites. Then another. I lick the trace of cardamon from my lips and take a swig from the silver thermos Nanima hands me. Piping-hot masala chai soothes me from the inside. When I reach behind for another morsel of sweetness, my sticky fingers land in Noor's palm. She quickly grabs my hand in an awkward embrace.

I close my eyes, one hand in my lap, the other in her hand. The golden orb rising from the road turns the inside of my eyelids red. I build a bonfire in my mind. I pile on the planners, the sched-ules, the calendars, the journals, the expectations, the secrets, the sharam. I stand at the edge of the pit with a white coat on my back and a black stethoscope around my neck. The kerosene I pour is Single-Mindedness. The match I drop onto the pile is Believing Things Will Always Go as I Plan. I burn effigies of those I thought I knew inside and out: Asma, Nanima, Mom, Noor, JJ, me. No one is what they seem, and everyone is so much more than they appear to be. Orange flames dance and reach upwards toward the sky. I dance around this bonfire of my old dreams as we drive east into the sun.

STEP 10

LEAN ON EACH OTHER

GRATITUDE

MY WARMEST THANKS to:

My mother, for everything. Truly. (But especially the inherited bibliophilism.)

Bollywood, for legitimizing my high drama and for enabling an outlet for Laylah's surrealist fantasies.

Parminder Sekhon, for *Madhuri, I Love You*. Your storytelling and voice have shaped me since 1990-something.

Shawn Wong, for telling the Third Dessert your story about selling a novel on pages. You helped me to believe.

Tania James and Padma Viswanathan, for planting that dangerous seed of literary ambition at Kundiman: "I think this short story wants to be a novel. . . ."—Padma V.

Ginu Kamani, for the utterly Gujarati gift that is *Junglee Girl*; and my mother, who gifted me *Junglee Girl* when I was too young, but oh so ready, to read it.

Lilly joon, agent extraordinaire! Thank you for being the baddest, most unrelenting boss in all of Literary Land. I am the luckiest author on the planet. I love you! And that is not a Freudian text-slip.

Justin Chanda, you make this journey so much fun. Let's do it again!

To everyone at Simon & Schuster who makes *this* possible. Thank you, thank you, thank you!

Dr. Jennifer McQuiston, for embodying and exemplifying the epidemiologist-novelist life. You are a multihyphenate legend. Thank you for teaching me how to hunt disease-laden ticks, embrace infested stray dogs, and for dropping gems about writing novels at 5:00 a.m. with all the brilliance and nonchalance that made me fall in love with the idea.

Dr. Emma Tarlo, for one of the few ethnographic studies of the Emergency, *Unsettling Memories: Narratives of the Emergency in Delhi* (University of California Press). Vishwajyoti Ghosh for *Delhi Calm* (HarperCollins India). Leaping Windows, the magical comic book café in Andheri West, where I discovered Ghosh's gem of a graphic novel.

Rana Tahir, for a multitude of blessings: being my (half?) djinniyah muse, the plot whisperer, teaching me how to use Scrivener, making endings seem possible, and for pep talks during the early and late days of the novel. You are بركة personified. Thank Allah for you.

Yalini Dream, for that magical Bed-Stuy evening in which you may or may not have worn your wings while reading aloud while we ambled. I watched your words come to life in the night sky and my skin tingled. You are a light.

Arlo, for the sweet cuddles, encouragement, and bodyguard duties. You are the best neighbor and friend a novelist could ask for. The other two are awesome, too.

Jehanne Dubrow, for teaching me radical enjambments, which I misheard as "radical enchantments" for the longest time.

Hedgebrook and Kundiman and the Millay Colony for the Arts; all the spaces that nurture creativity and art.

Seema and Amanda, for being there when it was done. I love you both.

Serena W. Lin, this is all your fault.

INFORMATION

FOR LINKS TO resources about reproductive health, please visit
texasteensguide.com.

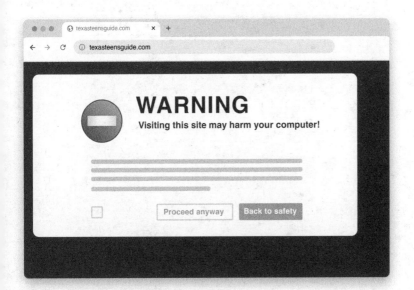

ABOUT THE
AUTHOR

SEEMA YASMIN IS an Emmy Award–winning journalist who was a finalist for the Pulitzer Prize. A public health physician, poet, professor, and author of eight books, she studied medicine at the University of Cambridge before joining the U.S. government's Epidemic Intelligence Service as a disease detective. Seema is director of the Stanford Health Communication Initiative and a visiting assistant professor at UCLA. She is working on her second novel, which is about a Cambridge medical student turned spy. Visit seemayasmin.com for more details.

ALSO BY
SEEMA YASMIN

*The Impatient Dr. Lange: One Man's Fight to
End the Global HIV Epidemic*

*Muslim Women Are Everything: Stereotype-Shattering
Stories of Courage, Inspiration, and Adventure*

Viral BS: Medical Myths and Why We Fall for Them

If God Is a Virus: Poems

What the Fact?! Finding the Truth in All the Noise

The ABCs of Queer History

*Djinnology: An Illuminated Compendium of
Spirits and Stories from the Muslim World*